RESHONDA TATE BILLINGSLEY

Her bestselling novels of family and faith have been hailed as:

"Emotionally charged . . . not easily forgotten."

—*Romantic Times*

"Steamy, sassy, sexy."

—*Ebony*

"Compelling, heartfelt."

—*Booklist*

"Full of palpable joy, grief, and soulful characters."

—*The Jacksonville Free Press*

"Poignant and captivating, humorous and heart-wrenching."

—*The Mississippi Link*

DON'T MISS THESE WONDERFUL NOVELS:

The Secret She Kept

"Entertaining and riveting. . . . A heartfelt and realistic look at the damaging effects of mental illness on those who suffer from it and the ones who bear the burden along with them. . . . Jaw-dropping, a drama-filled story. . . . Definitely a must-read."

—AAM Book Club

Say Amen, Again

Winner of the NAACP Image Award for Outstanding Literary Work

"Heartfelt. . . . A fast-paced story filled with vivid characters."

—*Publishers Weekly*

Everybody Say Amen

A *USA Today* Top Ten Summer Sizzler!

"A fun, redemptive book, packed with colorful characters, drama, and scandal."

—*RT Book Reviews*

A BET ORIGINAL MOVIE!

Let the Church Say Amen

#1 *Essence* magazine bestseller
One of *Library Journal*'s Best Christian Books

"Billingsley infuses her text with just the right dose of humor to balance the novel's serious events."

—*Library Journal* (starred review)

"Amen to *Let the Church Say Amen*. . . . [A] well-written novel."

—*Indianapolis Recorder*

"Her community of very human saints will win readers over with their humor and verve."

—*Booklist*

A Good Man Is Hard to Find

"Billingsley's engaging voice will keep readers turning the pages and savoring each scandalous revelation."

—*Publishers Weekly* (starred review)

Holy Rollers

"Sensational. . . . [Billingsley] makes you fall in love with these characters."

—*RT Book Reviews*

The Devil Is a Lie

"An entertaining dramedy."

—*Ebony*

"A romantic page-turner dipped in heavenly goodness."

—*Romantic Times* (4 ½ stars)

"Fast moving and hilarious."

—*Publishers Weekly*

Can I Get a Witness?

A USA *Today* 2007 Summer Sizzler

"An emotional ride."

—*Ebony*

"Billingsley serves up a humdinger of a plot."

—*Essence*

The Pastor's Wife

"Billingsley has done it again. . . . A true page turner."

—*Urban Reviews*

I Know I've Been Changed

#1 *Dallas Morning News* bestseller

"Grabs you from the first page and never lets go. . . . Bravo!"

—Victoria Christopher Murray

"An excellent novel with a moral lesson to boot."

—Zane, *New York Times* bestselling author

ALSO BY RESHONDA TATE BILLINGSLEY

Fortune & Fame (with Victoria Christopher Murray)
A Family Affair
Friends & Foes (with Victoria Christopher Murray)
Sinners & Saints (with Victoria Christopher Murray)
The Secret She Kept
Say Amen, Again
A Good Man Is Hard to Find
Holy Rollers
The Devil Is a Lie
Can I Get A Witness
The Pastor's Wife
Everybody Say Amen
I Know I've Been Changed
Let the Church Say Amen
My Brother's Keeper
Have A Little Faith (with Jacquelin Thomas, J. D. Mason, and Sandra Kitt)
The Motherhood Diaries
Help! I've Turned Into My Mother

AND CHECK OUT RESHONDA'S YOUNG ADULT TITLES

Drama Queens
Caught Up in the Drama
Friends 'Til the End
Fair-Weather Friends
Getting Even
With Friends Like These
Blessings in Disguise
Nothing But Drama

ReShonda Tate
BILLINGSLEY

What's Done in the Dark

A Novel

GALLERY BOOKS
New York London Toronto Sydney New Delhi

Gallery Books
A Division of Simon & Schuster, Inc.
1230 Avenue of the Americas
New York, NY 10020

First Gallery Books trade paperback edition July 2014

Interior design by Leydiana Rodríguez-Ovalles
Cover design © Dave Stevenson/Retinal Graphics

Manufactured in the United States of America

10 9 8 7 6 5 4 3 2 1

Library of Congress Cataloging-in-Publication Data

Billingsley, ReShonda Tate.
What's done in the dark / ReShonda Tate Billingsley.
pages cm
1. Adultery—Fiction. 2. Betrayal—Fiction. 3. Guilt—Fiction. 4. Loss (Psychology)—Fiction. I. Title.
PS3602.I445W43 2014
813'.6—dc23 2014013159

ISBN 978-1-4767-1492-9
ISBN 978-1-4767-1502-5 (ebook)

What's Done in the Dark

1

Felise

"ANY MAN THAT CAN RESIST THIS MUST NOT BE A man!" I giggled as I wiggled my toned behind in the full-length mirror in my bedroom. I made sure my snow white lace thong was situated just right, then brushed down the candy-apple-red negligee. I'd never in my life spent two hundred dollars on lingerie, but I wanted tonight to be special. I *needed* tonight to be special.

My commitment to Shaun T's Rockin' Body workout DVD had paid off. Everything was tight in all the right places, and my body looked like it belonged to someone who was twenty-five—not the thirty-five-year-old mother that I am.

I fluffed my curls and gave one last smile to my reflection. Today was my fifteenth anniversary, and I was determined that a sex life that died fourteen years ago would be resurrected tonight.

I had taken all of my sister, Fran's advice. Even though she was single, she never had a shortage of men. She swore it was her ability to give good loving that kept her Rolodex on fire.

I pressed play on my iPod to start setting the mood with all of our favorite songs. I dimmed the lights as the sounds of Luther filled the room. I had left a trail of rose petals—from the garage, through the kitchen, up the stairs, into our bedroom, then finally all over the bed. I wanted Greg to experience the alluring ambience the moment he walked through the door.

I checked, then triple-checked that everything—the wine, the rose petals, the scented sheets—was just right. But my smile faded when I noticed the time. It was eight thirty. Two hours past the time my husband had said that he'd be home. I immediately felt myself getting frustrated. I had moved heaven and earth to get someone to cover my shift at the hospital so I'd be home in time. I had hoped my husband could do the same.

I took a deep breath. I was not going to stress about tonight. Greg was a borderline obsessive-compulsive workaholic who was dedicated to his job as a successful investment banker. For our anniversary, though, I hoped he would try his best to relax and just enjoy himself. And tonight I was going to help him make that happen. He would relax, and we would rekindle the spark that had long ago been extinguished.

I threw on my silk robe and busied myself with my iPhone messages until I finally heard the door chime, signaling Greg was home. I glanced at the digital clock on the nightstand: 8:52.

Okay, Greg was late but not that late, I told myself. We could still salvage this night. I removed my robe and eased into a sexy position on the bed. I plastered on a seductive smile and waited for the door to open.

A few minutes later, I glanced over at the clock again.

9:06.

"Okay, what is taking him so long to get upstairs?" I mumbled.

When the clock hit 9:18, I had had enough. I got up, grabbed my robe, and made my way downstairs. That had to have been Greg coming in because our daughter, Liz, was spending the night with a friend.

I peeked out the small bay window near the staircase. Greg's car was parked in the driveway, so he was home. What in the world was he doing? Surely he had seen the trail of rose petals.

I had just reached the middle of the stairs when I heard the vacuum cleaner. Not understanding, I descended a few more steps. Then my mouth fell open when I saw my husband vigorously vacuuming up the rose petals I had so meticulously laid out.

"What are you doing?" I screamed over the vacuum.

He glanced up. "Hey, babe, getting all this stuff up off the floor. Liz must've made a mess or something."

I stared at my husband in disbelief. "Are you serious?"

He didn't reply as he took the hose off the vacuum and began sucking up the petals off the stairs.

"Liz didn't do that! I did!" I yelled over the vacuum.

He didn't stop cleaning. "You did this? What did you spill?"

I picked up a few petals at my feet, then threw them at him. Of course, they didn't do anything but flutter back to the ground. "I didn't spill anything. I laid them out! It was a trail of rose petals."

He looked at me like that was the dumbest thing I'd ever done.

"Well, you know I like to come home to a clean house." He finally cut the vacuum off and started picking up the rose petals the machine hadn't nabbed. "Why do you have all of this stuff laid out like this anyway?"

Only then did he glance up at me and notice the negligee. "What are you wearing?"

I wanted to cry. I knew we hadn't been intimate in a long time, but this was ridiculous. "What does it look like I'm wearing, Greg?"

"Oooh," he said, as realization set in. "I've just been preoccupied." He took a step toward me. "I'm sorry, you know things have been crazy at work." He stopped talking to manically pick up some rose petals that he missed. "I'm sorry, you know clutter bugs me. But I appreciate the effort." He leaned in to kiss me.

I pushed him away, though not hard enough to send him down the stairs. "Are you serious?"

"No, it just caught me by surprise. Usually, you have on a head scarf and some sweats when I get in." I was the one surprised when he added, "What's the occasion anyway?"

I stood waiting for him to break out into laughter. Tell me I was being punk'd, anything. Finally I said, "Today, Greg. Fifteen years."

The truth finally dawned on him. "Oh, my God, babe. Our anniversary. I am so, so sorry. You know I've been swamped at work, and I just completely lost track of what day it was."

I shook my head in disbelief. The tears I had been holding back made their escape. I had no words as I spun around and marched back to our bedroom.

"Come on, don't be mad," he said, following me.

I don't know why I was even shocked. I decided to turn around and give him a piece of my mind. But before I could speak, I noticed him picking up rose petals in the hallway.

"Ughhh!" I screamed, slamming the bedroom door.

I wanted to leave. I didn't even feel like taking the negligee off. I just wanted to get away from this suffocating house and away from my inconsiderate and unaffectionate husband.

Our once-a-week sexual escapades had dwindled to twice a month, then to once every other month. It was unreal. I used to think he was seeing someone else. After all, he'd cheated on me shortly after we got married. We'd gone to counseling and, I thought, moved past it. But the past three years especially had been brutal. I felt completely neglected. I'd even hired a private investigator to have him followed. But three thousand dollars later, all I discovered was what I already knew: my husband was simply a severe workaholic.

But tonight was the last straw.

I snatched a maxi dress off the hanger in my walk-in closet, then slipped it over my head. I then snatched a change of clothes and stuffed them in my gym bag. I couldn't stand to be in the same house with him another minute.

I marched back downstairs. I found my husband actually taking out the garbage. "You can clean up the rose petals in the bedroom now," I said, whisking past him.

"Babe, come on, don't be mad at me. I was just taking the garbage out while I gave you a minute to cool down."

"Well, I'm cool. Cold as ice."

"Where are you going?"

I ignored him as he followed me out in the garage.

"Felise! I said I'm sorry."

I continued to ignore him as I got in the car and backed out. I didn't know where I was going, but at the moment, any place that was far away from Gregory Mavins was exactly where I wanted to be.

2

Paula

I CAN'T BELIEVE I PRAYED FOR THIS.

I mean, growing up, all I thought about was becoming a mother. I wanted to be a wife and have a house full of wonderful kids.

That was my dream. This was my nightmare.

"Stevie, if you don't get your butt down off of that sofa!" I screamed at my oldest son. "And now, look, the twins are up there, too. You know they're going to do whatever you do." I swatted at my ten-year-old and turned my attention back to the phone. I'd picked it up when it rang, but I hadn't even had a chance to speak when I noticed my kids acting plumb fools. Again.

"Hello?" I said, exasperated.

"Just one time, I'm going to call your house and have a civil conversation without you going off on your kids."

I tried to smile at the sound of my best friend's voice. But I wasn't in a smiling mood. These kids had worked my last nerve. Again.

Don't get me wrong, I love my kids. I really do. But my oldest, Tahiry, was fourteen and in that stage where I couldn't stand her. Then my ten-year-old son was ADD, ADHD, or one of those other acronyms to describe a child who couldn't keep his butt still. And then, just when I thought I was done having kids, I got a double surprise three years ago. Marcus and Mason. You know that 99.9 percent effective rate for birth control? My twins are that 0.01 percent because I took my pills faithfully. So imagine my surprise when my doctor informed me that my ulcer was actually babies (with an *s*).

So, with three rambunctious boys and a teen who was feeling herself, I wouldn't be experiencing any peaceful moments in my house any time soon.

"Stevie, watch your brothers. I'm going out here to have a smoke."

"You know cigarettes kill people," Tahiry said, not looking up from her spot on the recliner where she'd been texting God knows who for the past two hours.

"So does having kids," I mumbled.

Stevie stopped jumping long enough to say, "For real, Ma. They told us at school that cigarettes turn your lungs black and you get all crippled and stuff and can't breathe. I can't be having a jacked-up-looking mom, coughing and stuff."

"She's not going to be jacked up," Tahiry said. "She's gonna be dead."

"You're gonna die, Mommy?" Marcus asked in horror.

"Of course not, son."

"If she doesn't stop smoking, she will." Tahiry shrugged nonchalantly. Did I mention I couldn't stand my daughter?

"My dad quit smoking and got run over by a Mack truck,"

I said, grabbing my pack of Virginia Slims and making my way out onto our back deck.

"Why are you telling your kids that?" Felise said on the phone. "You know your dad died in a regular car accident."

I plopped down on a patio chair. "Regardless, he'd stopped smoking and he died anyway."

I didn't start smoking until I had kids. I knew it was a nasty habit, and my husband, Steven, hated it. But I needed something to take the edge off, and since I wasn't much of a drinker, I medicate with cigarettes.

"What's up? What are you doing?" Felise said. "I was hoping I could come scoop you up and we could go have a drink or something." She sounded distressed, but as much as I would've loved to have spent the evening catching up with her over drinks, that was no longer my reality.

"Girl, please. Steven is gone. As usual. So I'm stuck at home with the kids. Their behinds need to be in the bed, but I just don't have the strength to fight with them. I hate summers." I lit my cigarette and took a long inhale. The smoke immediately began relaxing my nerves.

"Isn't your mom there?"

I blew out a puff of smoke. "Yeah, but she's about to go play bingo. Besides, I wouldn't be good company. I'm in a foul mood."

"Which is exactly why you need to get out. I'm in a foul mood, too, and I need to vent."

"About what?" I didn't give her time to answer before adding, "Why are you going to have a drink anyway? Isn't today your anniversary?"

"That's what I need to talk about."

Suddenly, the patio door opened, and Tahiry stepped

out. "Mom, you might want to get in here. The boys are having a water gun fight in your living room."

"Are you freakin' kidding me?" I screamed. "Felise, I'm sorry, you'll have to tell me what's going on later. I have yet another catastrophe to go deal with. Call you later."

I hung up the phone. I couldn't even hold a freakin' conversation with my best friend. That's how messed up my life was.

I took a quick last puff of my cigarette, tossed it down, and hurried back inside. I immediately told myself to follow my therapist's advice and use my "calm" voice.

"Stevie, Marcus, and Mason," I began, "please don't jump on the sofa and shoot water guns in my house." They looked at me for barely a moment, and then Mason sprayed Marcus as they took off running.

See? I don't know what kind of school my therapist went to or what kind of kids she was used to dealing with, but that calm mess didn't work on my kids. I wanted to whip their behinds—like my mom used to do me—but Steven didn't believe in spankings. To me, that was part of the reason our kids were out of control.

"If y'all don't stop it right now!" I screamed. That got the reaction I had been looking for, and everyone came to a halt. "Go to bed! Don't play with any toys, just put on your pajamas and get in the bed!"

They sulked as they walked off. Tahiry, who was still texting away on her phone, didn't bother looking up as she said, "You should have stopped having kids at me."

I wanted to tell her I should've never started with her. But since that's not something I'd ever verbalize to my children, I kept quiet.

Things had so not turned out like I planned. By college I'd shed those domestic dreams of childhood. I was going to be a big-time actress. I'd even dropped out of Howard University my junior year to pursue my dream. But after a couple of commercials, that dream had died really quick, and before I knew it, I was working in retail. I still got bit parts here and there, but nothing to consider a real acting career. Then, Felise, who had been my best friend since ninth grade, had introduced me to Steven when he'd moved to DC to go to Georgetown Law. Before I knew it, we were in deep. Tahiry was conceived two months after we started dating. Steven did the honorable thing and married me, and the course of my life was rewritten.

While I wouldn't say Steven had pressured me into marriage, it's not something I just had to do. But heaven forbid the esteemed son of Texas judge Walter Wright have a child out of wedlock. Not to mention the pressure from my family. Everyone made me feel so guilty that I felt that I had no choice but to get married. And although I'd learned to love my life, I now felt trapped. And resentful. On top of that, Steven worked so much. He was one of the most sought-after criminal defense attorneys in Texas. I was a stay-at-home mom, and I didn't want to be. My passion was the theater. Just last month I'd been offered a role in a local stage play by an old director I used to work with. But they were planning to go on tour, and I couldn't very well abandon my kids and go traipsing around the country with some play.

Meanwhile, my husband got a reprieve every day at work and with his out-of-town trips. Me, I never got a reprieve and it was taking its toll.

I made my way into the back guest room that had become my mother's room. Her door was open, and she was on her knees, praying.

"Heavenly Father," she was saying, "I end this prayer asking that you bestow upon me bountiful blessings tonight at bingo. If I win, I promise I'll give the church ten percent. Amen."

I shook my head at my mom's bootleg prayer and made my way back to my room. Her next step would be more practical. She would ask me for money for bingo.

I wanted out of my life. And as soon as my husband got home, I was going to tell him. I simply couldn't do this anymore.

3

Felise

I NEVER KNEW JACK DANIEL'S COULD BE SO COMFORTING.

I'd been sitting here crying for the past thirty minutes, and since I knew I wasn't much of a drinker, I'd been taking it slow. But the whiskey had me realizing one thing for sure: I was sick and tired of my husband.

Fifteen years of begging for affection. Fifteen years of living with an obsessive workaholic. After fifteen years you'd think I'd be used to it, but I was exhausted. I'd begged Greg to make more time for me, to give as much to our marriage as he gave to his job. And he'd try, and succeed for a while, but then he would go back to normal.

I needed a new normal.

Don't get me wrong. I had no plans to divorce my husband. At least I didn't think I did. He'd been the one who had repaired my broken heart when my one true love chose another. It's why I'd hung in for so long. But I knew that if something didn't change, a change of address would be in my future.

"Felise?"

I turned around to the voice behind me. I immediately smiled at the sight of Steven, my dear friend and Paula's husband.

"Hey, pretty lady," he said, hugging me. "What are you doing here?"

I raised my drink. "Drinking," I replied with a giggle. I wasn't surprised that he was here. The Four Seasons bar had some of the best drink specials in town. "What are you doing here?"

"I had a meeting with one of my frat brothers. He's trying to get me on board with this business venture. It sounds promising, but it may take me away from the family more, and I'm just not sure that's something I want to do."

That made me smile. Greg wouldn't have even considered his family.

"Good ol' Steven," I said, raising my drink to him in a toast. With the stretching I almost slipped off the chair.

"Whoa," he said, catching me. I could see the wheels turning in his head as he assessed my condition. "Okay, what's really going on? What are you doing here?"

I released a strained laugh. "What does it look like?"

"It looks like you're drinking"—he cocked his head and studied my drink—"whiskey."

I saluted him. "You're good."

A light went on in his eyes, and his face changed. "Felise, what's going on? Isn't today your anniversary?"

I couldn't help but laugh. Steven remembered it was my anniversary, but my own husband didn't.

"Where's Greg?"

I immediately lost my smile. "He's at home, cleaning up."

"What?" Steven said, confused.

"He's vacuuming up the rose petals I had laid out for our romantic evening."

"What do you mean, vacuuming up?"

I took a deep breath and set my drink down. I needed to leave that bourbon alone. It was starting to make my head spin. "You know my husband," I said. "He's cleaning. On our fifteenth anniversary. I know it sounds unbelievable. But that's my husband, good ol' Greg."

"Hey, man, can I get you anything?" the bartender asked, approaching us.

"Bring me something a little lighter," I said. "Apple martini."

"Should you be mixing liquor?" Steven asked.

"Should you be all up in my business?"

Steven smiled at that. He knew he couldn't push me too far. He turned to the bartender and said, "You know what? Bring me a cranberry and vodka." He slid into the barstool next to me. "You don't mind me sitting here and having a drink with you, do you?"

I shrugged indifferently. What I was thinking, though, was that right about now I'd rather sit with him than just about anybody.

When the bartender placed the drinks in front of us, Steven said, "Okay, tell me what's going on. You and Greg have a fight?"

I took a deep breath, sipped my martini, then relayed the whole sad story.

"Wow," he said when I was finished.

"Yeah." I leaned in. "So tell me, Steven, if I recall, didn't you whisk your wife away for a weekend in Puerto Rico for your anniversary?"

Steven held up a finger to stop me. "Ah, not quite. That was the plan, but remember, Paula bailed on me."

I nodded. "Oh, yeah." I remembered thinking Paula was out of her mind that day. Steven had called and asked her to meet him at the airport. He'd planned a surprise weekend trip for their anniversary, arranged childcare and everything, and Paula wouldn't go because she said they "couldn't just drop everything and jet off somewhere like they were single." I'd felt like Paula and I needed to switch spouses.

It was a feeling I quickly brushed off, even though Steven had been mine before he was Paula's. But that was a long time ago. Back in college when he and I were best friends who crossed the line. And when he'd gone to DC for law school, I'd hooked him up with Paula, my best friend since high school, who had gone to Howard University and was making her home in DC. I'd just wanted her to show him around. I never expected them to fall in love.

But the one thing I knew about Steven was he was a hopeless romantic. He would make up for that fiasco. No way would he let his fifteenth anniversary go by without some grandiose celebration.

Steven took a sip of his drink, then sadly said, "I don't know if we'll even make it to fifteen."

"What?" I asked in shock. I knew Paula had been unhappy, but I had no idea Steven was feeling the same way.

"Sometimes I feel like marrying Paula was the biggest mistake I ever made," he candidly admitted.

Immediately, I started feeling butterflies in my stomach. I tried to tell myself it was the liquor, but my heart wanted to believe that maybe, just maybe, Steven was thinking about us. As horrible as it seems, at that very moment I hoped that he was. Then I would know I wasn't the only one who still had unresolved feelings.

4

Felise

IT'S TRUE THAT LIQUOR BRINGS OUT THE REAL YOU. Because I had just asked a question that, had I been in my right mind, I would've never dreamed of asking. But I repeated it anyway.

"You can be honest. It won't hurt my feelings," I said. "Do you ever think about us? That's a yes-or-no question."

I was on my third apple martini. Couple that with the bourbon I'd had earlier and I was feeling pretty courageous.

Steven was nursing his third drink—since joining me—so I could tell he had a little buzz, too. Still, he said, "Come on, Felise, we agreed that was a chapter that was closed."

I playfully stuck my bottom lip out. "I know we made the right decision. We're too much alike."

"Yeah, and don't forget, you fixed me up with Paula."

"Yeah, I did, and here we are." My heart ached as I thought of their beautiful wedding. I loved Greg. I really did. But he was frugal and had considered a big wedding a waste of money, so we'd been married in a simple ceremony at the justice of the peace. The bad part was Paula had simple tastes, too. She couldn't have cared less about a big wedding. But Steven was from a prominent family and his mother would've died if she'd been denied the opportunity to see her son married in a huge ceremony. And talk about huge! They'd had ten bridesmaids (including me), ten groomsmen, and two hundred and fifty guests watch them exchange vows in a historic Catholic cathedral, followed by a reception for four hundred at an elite country club. Yep, I'd gotten a dirty courtroom at the courthouse and Paula had gotten my dream wedding.

When the minister asked if anyone saw any reason why the two of them should not be married, the only thing that kept me from speaking up was the one-twentieth-of-a-carat ring on my finger. Of course, Steven had pulled out a four-carat diamond that had made everyone gasp.

"Hey, are you still with me?" Steven waved his hand in my face.

I tried to laugh, but a distorted cry came out instead. "Sorry." I covered my eyes with the palm of my hand.

"Hey, hey," Steven said, scooting closer.

I turned my head as I tried to ward off the tears. "Sorry. It's just that sometimes I wonder about my marriage."

He sighed like he could relate. "You're not the only one. It's like, I love Paula, I really do. But after she became a mother, she changed. I try to do my part to help. I tried to hire a nanny, but Paula refused. I did what I could to make life easier for her. But it's almost like she's happier wallowing in pity."

I knew all too well what Steven was talking about. I knew full well how miserable Paula was. I talked to her about her negative attitude on a regular basis.

Steven was about to say something else when his phone rang. He pulled it out of the holder on his hip, glanced at it, and said, "Speak of the devil. This is Paula." He pressed Talk. "Hello." He paused.

"Naw, I'm still here," he said into the phone. "I am not drunk . . . Yes, I had a few drinks." He rolled his eyes and pulled the phone away from his ear as Paula's loud voice broadcast from the phone. He put it back to his ear. "Look, don't start with me, Paula. I told you I was going to be out late . . . I asked you to come. You're the one who wanted to stay at home . . ." He gritted his teeth as he stood up. "Oh, don't give me that. Your mom was there. Why is she living there if you don't ever want to leave the kids with her?" He paused again, and I could tell Paula was going off. "You know what, I told you about calling me out of my name . . ." His brow was furrowing, and I could tell he was getting upset. "I don't think so! I pay the mortgage. I wish you would put my sh—" I put my hand on his arm to calm him down and remind him where he was. He took a deep breath and said, "Stop threatening me with divorce. If you're going to leave, then leave . . . I wish you would put my stuff on the lawn!"

More muffled roars came from Paula's end. Then finally he said, "You are deranged! I was meeting with Kevin, not another woman! Why would I invite you if I was planning on meeting another woman? . . . I didn't think you'd refuse. You know what? You're being ridiculous, as usual. Don't call me rushing me. I'll be home when I get home! You . . . Hello? Hello?"

He tossed the phone on the bar. "Uggh!" He flinched as, unexpectedly, he grabbed at his chest.

"Are you okay?" I asked. Paula had mentioned he'd been having some chest pains, but she had just chalked it up to stress from his demanding job.

Steven stood deathly still for a minute, then relaxed before saying, "Yeah. That woman gives me heartburn." He signaled for the bartender, and I relaxed. "Excuse me, can I get another drink? And make it a double!"

I knew Paula wasn't happy, but I'd had no idea their marriage had reached this extreme. "What was that all about?" I asked. I definitely noted that he hadn't told her that he was with me.

"I swear, that woman! I just don't know how much longer I can do this. She's always accusing me of cheating! Felise, as God as my witness, I've never cheated on her, but for as much as she accuses me, I might as well be."

"Don't say that," I replied as the bartender set a double shot glass in front of us. "Your wife loves you."

"I'm just tired." Steven took his drink and downed it in one extended gulp. "See, you're not the only one who's unhappy."

I hesitated as I saw the pain swirl in his eyes. "Can I ask you a question?" I finally said.

He managed a smile. "Ask away."

"Why didn't you tell her you were here with me?"

He shrugged, not looking guilty. "I don't know. She didn't give me a chance before she started going off. It's probably best anyway. With the rampage she's on, you don't need to be dragged into our drama."

I nodded, for the first time wondering if she ever brought up our past.

"Don't worry," he said, as if reading my mind. "It's not

you. She doesn't have an issue with you, with us. Her issue is with me. Me and her."

Our eyes met when he said that, and I didn't know if it was the liquor or what, but I found myself saying, "Do you ever find yourself wondering, 'What if?' You know, with us?"

He stared at me as he somberly said, "All the time." He sighed heavily and returned his gaze to his empty glass. "When I want to be spontaneous and go somewhere, I wonder about us. When I long to just kick back and have fun, I think about us."

"We did used to have some fun." I managed to laugh. "Remember that day you woke up and said, let's just drive to the Grand Canyon?"

"Oh, yeah, I forgot about that," he said, finally smiling. "What were we, like twenty? We just up and went. It took us two days, but we had so much fun."

"Oh, my God. You remember that honky-tonk club we went to and were teaching those people how to cabbage patch?"

"What about when you told those people at that restaurant that we were Whitney Houston and Bobby Brown?"

"I completely forgot about that." Our laughter finally died down, and I grew somber again. "I haven't felt that in a long time."

"Me either," Steven said softly. At that moment his hand brushed up against my thigh. His touch sent shivers up my spine, and I was shocked. I'll admit, I was hurt when I'd learned Steven and Paula were dating, but I blamed myself, so that forced me to bury those feelings. But if they were buried, why in the world were they being resurrected now?

"Why did you fix me up with Paula?" he asked me.

I wanted to tell him that was my biggest regret in life. But Paula was my best friend. I would never utter those words. "I . . . I had met Greg and, I don't know, I just thought you and Paula would get along. I mean, I didn't know you'd fall in love and get married and I'd have to see you forever." I managed a smile.

He didn't return my smile. "You told me you saw me as more of a brother. That you didn't want me."

My mind raced back to that day, the day before he was supposed to marry Paula. He'd come to me because he "needed to be sure" that he was doing the right thing. This man was about to marry my best friend. I was one of her bridesmaids. What was I supposed to say? "I thought I didn't want you. I convinced myself that I didn't want you," I said, my voice shaking.

"I knew you did." His voice was husky as he leaned in closer. "I know you *do*."

Now was the time for me to tell him that he was out of his mind. To reiterate that no matter what I *used* to feel, we'd chosen our paths in life. But my feelings swam around in my brain and no words would come out.

"Have you ever wanted something so bad, something that you'd denied yourself for years?" he stood over me and whispered in my ear. His hot breath tickled my neck.

I couldn't answer. I couldn't say a word because all kinds of conflicting emotions were running through my body. We sat in silence for a few moments. Finally he said, "You shouldn't drive tonight. Do you want me to call you a cab?"

"I'm not going home tonight," I found myself saying.

He waited, then said, "Me either."

I knew we were about to venture into dangerous territory,

but I couldn't help it as my hand covered his. His touch was electrifying, and I didn't know whether to run or collapse into his arms.

He pulled himself away and motioned to the bartender. "Can I close out my tab?"

We didn't say a word as the bartender rang him up. For a minute, I wondered if Steven was about to take off running as he nervously shifted from side to side.

After signing the credit card receipt and stuffing his copy in his wallet, Steven turned back to me.

"I'm going to get a room," he finally said. "Wait right here."

He didn't wait for me to reply as he hurried off toward the front desk. Everything inside of me was saying get up and go. Right now. Go home before it was too late. But go home to what? A husband who no longer knew how to make me feel like a woman? A husband who hadn't *seen* me in years. A husband who thought so little of our relationship that he would forget our wedding anniversary? No, I had nothing to go home to.

I don't know how long I sat there, but Steven came back, leaned over me, and whispered, "Room 527. I'll understand if you don't show." He eased a room key into my hand, and his touch sent more chills through my body. I took the key and didn't turn to watch him as he walked away.

5

Paula

PEACE. THAT WAS A WELCOME SOUND IN MY HOME, SO I leaned back in my chair, closed my eyes, and relished the quiet.

The kids were finally in bed, and my mom was still out. A part of me wanted to be mad that Steven wasn't home yet—it was after midnight—but our argument had been pretty ugly, and he probably was going to get drunk with Kevin and talk about what a horrible wife I was.

That actually made me sad because I really didn't want to be a horrible wife to Steven. I just had so much bitterness and resentment, and I didn't know how to work past it.

I took a long inhale on my cigarette and let the nicotine work its magic.

"Hey, what are you still doing up?" my mom asked, poking her head out on the deck.

I blew a puff of smoke. "Just enjoying the solitude."

She eyed my cigarette disapprovingly, and like a child, I mashed it out. "How was bingo?"

She shrugged as she sat down next to me. "I didn't win. Lost forty dollars. I don't know why the Lord won't answer my prayer to hit it big."

I couldn't help but laugh because she was dead serious. My mom had a warped view of religion. She was the only person I knew who would watch *The Passion of the Christ* on bootleg video while reading the Bible she took from a hotel.

"So, where's Steven?" she asked, looking around.

I shrugged. "Out with his friend."

"Hmph. Kinda late to be out, huh?"

I didn't want to get her started. I knew having my mom around didn't help my marriage. She was always adding her two cents. But my mom had been dependent on my dad, and when he died two years ago, she was beside herself. My sister, Charlene, lived in New York, so my mother was all alone. She had come here from my childhood home in DC and, well, just never left. I knew Steven hadn't really been feeling the idea, but he'd gone along with it for my sake.

"Are you guys okay?" my mom asked pointedly.

I don't know why, but that actually opened up the dam and I felt tears gushing out.

"Oh, no, baby," my mom said, coming to my side. "What's going on?" She rubbed my back. "Why are you crying? Did Steven do something to you?"

I shook my head as I tried to compose myself. "No. I'm . . . I'm just so miserable, and I told Steven tonight I want a divorce."

My mom leaned back like I'd just delivered the most awful news ever. "And why would you do a fool thing like that?"

"I'm just so unhappy," I confessed.

"Unhappy? That man gives you a good life."

"Yes, he provides this big ol' house for me," I said, motioning around our six-thousand-square-foot home, "but Steven and I act like bickering roommates. We have no passion. I want to feel some sparks."

My mother didn't bother to hide her disgust as she stood and went back to her seat. "Girl, this ain't some kind of romance novel. Love don't pay the bills."

I sighed. "You loved Daddy."

"Not at first," she admitted. "Shoot, I was trying to get out of Arkansas and your daddy offered me a ticket out. He had a good job with the railroad, and he loved me more than I loved him." She wagged a finger at me. "That's the key. You always got to find a man that loves you more. That's the man you need to be with."

I let out a long sigh as I wiped my tears. "It's not only that, Mama. This being nothing but a mother wasn't my dream. I love my kids, but there's more to me than this."

She continued shaking her head. "Hmph, well, you better take up knitting or find you some kind of hobby."

"What about my dreams? Do my dreams fall by the wayside because I have kids?" I snapped.

"Yes," she said matter-of-factly. "If you talking about that actress crap, you got to grow up. That ship has sailed. You got a family now. *That's* your priority. And you going and tellin' your man you want a divorce. How are you gonna take care of your kids?"

I hadn't thought about all of that. I was just mad and mouthing off because he was out kickin' it while I was stuck in the house—again. I guess I didn't really want a divorce. I just wanted something different. I wanted to be happy.

My mom patted my leg. "Maybe you need to start having some more Paula time. Go out with Felise. Shoot, go out with your husband. You're the one who thinks you have to be stuck in the house all the time. It's like you like wallowing in self-pity. I'm tellin' you, you'd better get it together before Jody's got your girl and gone."

"What?" I said, looking at her confused.

She continued wagging a finger in my direction. "While you saying, 'Scat, scat,' someone else is 'round the corner sayin', 'Here, kitty-kitty.'"

I couldn't help but smile at my mom's cornball country sayings. "I have no idea what that means."

She sighed like she had to break something down to me. "You're not going to know how good you got it till you ain't got it no more. You gonna look up and some other woman is gonna have your man."

I couldn't help but laugh at that. "Nah, I know Steven. He's a lot of things, but he wouldn't cheat on me."

My mother narrowed her eyes. "I told you. Never say what somebody wouldn't do."

"Well, I trust my husband," I said pointedly.

"Okay, but just know, you walk around here in a constant funk, mad at the world, taking it out on your kids and husband. Someone wants to deal with that for only so long. It's no wonder Steven is never here. I don't blame him. I wouldn't want to lay with you and your funky attitude either."

I was shocked. "Whose side are you on anyway?"

"I'm always on your side, but I'm on the side of righteousness first." She threw her hands up. "Hallelujah." I pointed to her bingo stamp on her hand. She licked her thumb, then wiped it off. "I'm just saying, Mama knows best. And you best get it together. Talk to your husband. Tell him your concerns. Maybe you guys can find something you enjoy—besides running all over the country starring in one of those chitlin circuit plays. But you need to find something outside of the home that brings you joy. I guarantee you that man will do whatever it takes to make you happy. And once you find that, give as much to your husband as you give to your kids. Everyday life is terrible for love. Love needs time, and time is the air love breathes, and people have no time."

I stared at my mother, impressed. "Wow, that was deep, Mom."

"I know a little sumthin', sumthin'." She stood and winked. "I hope you heed what I'm telling you. But now I'm going to look up some Bible verses on money. Maybe I'm not praying right."

I would've laughed at her, but her words were weighing heavily on me. Was I pushing my husband away? Was I blaming my family because I wanted to wallow in pity? Was I not giving my marriage the time we needed to grow our love? I sat in silence as my mother's words sank in. Something inside me said that she was right. Maybe I was the problem. Maybe I needed to make a change.

The more I sat thinking, the more I decided my mother was spot on. So tomorrow would be a new day. I didn't know how, but I was going to end this pity party and try to focus on making my husband—and me—happy.

6

Felise

MY BRAIN AND MY BODY WERE IN A TUG OF WAR. MY brain said to go left toward the exit, but my body went right toward the elevator. Before I knew it, I was standing outside room 527, tears streaming down my face.

I knew that I needed to take my butt home.

But I needed *this* more. I needed to feel Steven again. If only for one night. I needed to know what it felt like to be loved on every inch of my body. Three long years ago was the last time I'd been taken to the heights of pleasure. I'd tried everything to talk to Greg: therapy—which he refused to go to—talking, books, everything. And still he wouldn't listen. He couldn't accept that my needs weren't being met. And he was insulted that I would insinuate that he wasn't doing his manly duties. He kept asking me to cut him some slack because of how hard he was working for me and our daughter, Liz.

I needed love. I needed *loving*.

I took a deep breath, then told myself if Greg had loved me right, I wouldn't be here about to do wrong.

I was crossing into dangerous territory. But in my heart, I was looking forward to going inside, anticipating what the night held.

You loved him first.

The little voice that had been guiding me up the elevator spoke up, as if to give me that one last push before I changed my mind.

I dipped the key into the lock, then walked in to see Steven sitting nervously on the edge of the bed. He was still fully dressed and looked like he had completely sobered up. He stood up awkwardly as I came in.

"I–I wasn't sure if you were going to come," he said.

My gaze shifted downward. "Me either."

"Believe it or not, I really have been faithful."

"Me, too."

"But, I . . ." He stepped closer. "I've never felt so alone."

"Me either."

"Felise, I don't . . ."

I held up my hands to stop him. "I know," I whispered.

He stepped closer, until I could feel the heat from his body. His breathing was labored, and I could tell he was having an inner battle—just like me.

Steven gently ran a finger behind my ear, then down my neck and around to my chest.

He still remembered what turned me on.

I released a slow moan as I relished his touch. "This is so wrong," I said, my voice barely above a whisper.

"It is. But I want you, Felise. I *need* you."

We each waited on the other to move until finally unbridled passion made our decision for us.

He kissed me with a ferociousness I hadn't felt in years.

Everything inside me wanted to protest, stop him before we went too far, but when I opened my mouth, once again nothing came out. And the minute I felt his tongue, my body reacted. When our tongues did a slow dance, I shivered. When he kissed my neck, I needed more.

He slowly slid off my dress. "Oh, my God," he said when he noticed my negligee, which I'd forgotten I was still wearing. "You. Are. Stunning," he said, running his eyes up and down my body. It felt so good to be appreciated. To be wanted.

He didn't ask why I had the negligee on. He just planted sensual kisses all over my body. Steven took me the height of ecstasy right there against the wall of the hotel room. And before I could catch my breath, he was guiding me toward the bed, where he did it again and again.

Waves of euphoria filled my body until I collapsed in his arms. I realized that slow tears were sliding down my cheeks. I wanted to believe they were guilty tears, but I knew better. These were tears of pure bliss, peppered with thoughts of what could have been.

After we finished, we lay in silence. I snuggled close to him as his arms formed a protective barrier around me.

"I don't know the last time I felt like this," he said.

"Me either." We relapsed into silence—a blissful, comfortable silence—for a while. Then I sat up. "Why didn't we work?" I knew I didn't need to be going there. But as I'd watched his happy life with Paula over the years, I can't tell you the number of times I wondered why that couldn't have been me. I didn't realize how much I'd suppressed my feelings until this unexpected release.

He sat up with me. "We were young, stupid. We didn't realize we were best friends for a reason."

I sighed, remembering a relationship I had long ago blocked out. Steven was my friend before he was my lover. He was the first boy I met at the University of Texas at Austin. He was a year above me and took me under his wing. He had a girlfriend at the time and never made any inappropriate moves. We were merely good friends who evolved into best friends. Our relationship became a source of contention with his girlfriend, and when they broke up, we grew even closer.

We made the mistake of briefly taking our relationship to the next level my junior year. And it was wonderful—until he announced that he was heading to law school in DC. I had no desire for a long-distance relationship and decided that crossing the line of friendship had been a mistake. I don't know if I really felt like that or if I just couldn't bear the thought of my boyfriend being so far away. At the same time I'd met Greg—a first-year grad student—and he was constantly in my ear about the life that he could provide if only I gave him a chance.

I thought the grass would be greener. It was a decision I'd regretted ever since.

I wanted to ask Steven more questions, but I knew if we kept talking, Paula's name would come up. And I couldn't bear the thought of mentioning my best friend while I was lying here with her husband.

"Well, everything happens for a reason. We both have wonderful children," he said.

That we did. My daughter, Liz, was my heart and joy. And I loved his daughter, my goddaughter, Tahiry, just as much.

I lay back down on his chest.

"You ever wonder what our kid would've looked like?" he asked after a few beats of silence.

I inhaled sharply. We hadn't spoken about that since the day we left the women's clinic. No one—not Paula, Greg, or even my sisters, who I was close to—knew that weeks after Steven announced he was leaving for law school, I found out I was pregnant. We had gone back and forth over what to do. I couldn't bear the thought of Steven giving up his dream of law school to become a father. But before we could make a decision, I miscarried. The doctors couldn't tell me why, just that "it happens." I was heartbroken, especially after Steven said it "must've been God's will." We were never the same after that. That's why when he told me Paula was pregnant, it was the biggest blow ever.

When I didn't reply, Steven said, "You know, I'm sorry. Let's not go down memory lane. It is what it is. We are playing the hand we've been dealt. Tonight, I just want to enjoy you."

I inhaled his scent and snuggled closer. After a few minutes, I knew it was time to say what we'd been trying not to say all night. "You know this can never happen again," I said, watching his face for his reaction.

He nodded. "I know."

I didn't know why, but that actually stung. He must've realized it because he quickly added, "I mean, trust me, I wanted it to happen, but we both know it was wrong. We both were in need, and so we found comfort in one another's arms." He pushed a stray curl out of my eye. "Don't worry, there will be no secret rendezvous, no clandestine meetings. Tomorrow, we'll pretend this never happened. Tomorrow, we'll go back to our normal, boring, miserable lives. Tomorrow, it'll be different. But tonight, I want to make you feel like the beautiful woman that you are."

He leaned in and once again kissed me passionately. Within a few moments we fell back into what felt like the most natural of grooves.

7

Felise

THE SUNLIGHT PEEKED IN THE LARGE BAY WINDOW overlooking downtown Houston. The rays tickled me out of my sleep. I yawned, stretched, and remembered that my body felt like it hadn't felt in years. I hated that this euphoria had to end.

I glanced over at Steven, who was still soundly sleeping. That man had been better than he was in college, and I hadn't thought that was possible. He'd definitely gotten better with time. Our lovemaking had run the gamut, from slow and steady to raw, unadulterated passion. We'd finally collapsed, exhausted, around four a.m.

I eased out of bed and went to retrieve my purse, which was leaning on my pile of clothes on the floor, exactly where I'd left it when I entered the room last night. I dug my phone out and looked at it. Greg had called a dozen times, sent two dozen more apologetic texts. Seeing the texts made me feel incredibly guilty. The reality was, I'd cheated on my husband. Something I'd never done before. But making matters worse, I cheated with my best friend's husband.

Steven was right. This would never happen again.

I thought about waking him for one last romp, but when my cousin was going through detox, she'd told me that the best way to let go of something that wasn't good for you was cold turkey. Since Steven had been intoxicating last night, this morning needed to be the beginning of cold turkey.

I turned on the shower and closed my eyes as the pellets of water hit my face. My mind started churning. How many days would I spend reminiscing about Steven's touch? Would I ever be able to get over the way he made me feel? What would happen when Greg remembered to offer his lackluster lovemaking? Would I have to imagine Steven to get in the mood? How was I ever going to face Paula again? As I realized that Steven and I had opened another whole host of problems, I released a fresh stream of tears.

Fifteen minutes later, I was fresh, dressed, all cried out, and ready to face the one who got away.

"Hey, Steven," I whispered, easing onto the bed. "I need to get going." I ran my hands along the bottom of his feet. "You probably should, too." When he didn't stir, I pulled the covers back and ran my fingers down his naked back. That's when I felt how cold his body was.

"Steven?" I said, turning him over. "Steven?" His arm fell on the side of the bed, and his head flopped to the side. "Oh, my God! Steven?"

I felt for a pulse. Nothing. I leaned in to see if he was breathing. Still nothing.

"Oh, no," I cried, glancing wildly around the room. Maybe someone had come in while I was in the shower. But there were no signs of forced entry or foul play. He was dead! He was really dead!

Visions of him clutching his chest last night at the bar flashed through my head. *Oh, my God.* Did he have a heart attack?

I backed on unsteady feet into the bathroom, trying to calm myself while I figured out what to do. I was hyperventilating, and tears were streaming down my cheeks. How could this have happened? I noticed the phone in the bathroom and immediately reached for it to call 9-1-1. But I stopped just as I was about to pick up the phone. 9-1-1 would bring on questions, and I wasn't ready to give answers. There would be a death report. Because I was with him, an inquiry. They'd take my information, include it in the report.

"No, I can't get caught up in this," I mumbled. I tried to take slow, deep breaths as I figured out my next move. Fran! My sister. *She will know what to do.*

I snatched my purse off the bathroom counter, fumbled for my cell phone, and nearly dropped it. At last I managed to call the only other person I knew who could help me out of this mess. I numbly watched my fingers scroll through until I came to Fran's number.

"You'd better have a good reason for calling me this early," she answered.

"Oh, my God, Fran," I cried. "You've got to help me."

"Felise? What are you doing? Are you crying?"

I couldn't help it. The waterworks had begun again.

"Oh, my God. You *are* crying. Who do I need to come jack up? Did Greg do something to you?" she said.

Any other time I would've smiled. That was Fran, the ever-protective younger sister who was like a Chihuahua in size but a pit bull in spirit.

"I . . . I'm in a bad situation."

"What is going on?" she demanded to know.

"You're not going to believe this! I'm in a hotel—"

"A hotel? So that's where you went for your anniversary?"

"I'm not with Greg."

"Shut the front door! What? Is my sister getting her freak on with someone else—on her anniversary?"

"Fran, this is serious," I cried.

"Okay, okay. Calm down and tell me what is going on."

"I'm with someone."

"Who?"

I couldn't bring myself to utter the words, but if I was going to get my sister's help, I had to tell her everything. "I'm with Steven."

Silence filled the phone. "I hope you know another Steven, not Paula's Steven," she finally said, "because I know there's no way in hell that's who you're talking about."

My sob was her answer.

"Are you freakin' kidding me, Felise? Why are you in a hotel with your best friend's husband? No, don't answer that. Tell me instead, why does it have you all worked up like this?"

"Because . . . because . . . he's dead."

Another pause before she said, "Come again."

"You're not going to believe this."

"Try me," she said calmly. It was as if she was waiting on the punch line of a bad joke.

"He's dead. Steven is dead."

"What? Dead how? Did you kill him?"

"No!" I exclaimed, then lowered my voice. "At least I don't think so. We just . . . We just did it all night last night and this morning . . ." I slapped my forehead. "Oh, my God, I wasn't thinking. I'm a nurse. I should've known his chest . . . his heart . . . I can't believe this is happening."

"Okay, sis, calm down. What happened? Start from the beginning."

I took a deep breath and tried to calm myself down. I don't know how I made it through the story, but I did, and a few minutes later, my sister had learned the CliffsNotes version of what happened.

"So, let me get this straight," Fran slowly said. "You just woke up this morning and he was dead?"

Dead. That word had such finality. I swallowed the lump in my throat. Steven was really gone. "Yes," I managed to get out.

"Are you sure he's dead? Maybe he's just a deep sleeper."

"I'm a freakin' nurse!" I snapped. "I know when someone is dead and when they're asleep."

"Okay, calm down."

"I was about to call 9-1-1, but I just freaked and called you first."

Her next words had a harder edge. "Yeah, calling 9-1-1 is something you *won't* be doing."

"But it's the right thing to do," I sobbed.

"Oh, okay, then, should I meet you at your house to help you pack your bags so you can get out of town? Because if your husband doesn't kill you, your best friend will," she said, her voice full of sarcasm.

"Maybe they don't have to know," I whimpered.

She let out a long sigh like I wasn't thinking straight, which, of course, I wasn't. "If you're anywhere near the scene when someone dies, police are going to take your information."

I glanced into the other room as if, in some kind of way,

I was expecting to see Steven's body gone. I couldn't believe what was happening. *I'm sitting here talking police procedure, and my best friend's husband is dead in the other room.* "I can give them a fake name," I finally said.

"And do you have fake ID on you, too?"

I groaned as I slid to the floor. "What am I gonna do?"

"Okay, okay, let's figure this out," Fran said. She paused, and I knew her devious mind was plotting. "Whose name is the room in?" she finally asked.

"His?"

"That's good," she said, sounding relieved. "I don't have to come help you move the body." I knew my sister was dead serious. If that's what I had needed, she would've been right there with plastic gloves on.

"I'm not attached to the room at all." As I said that, a starker truth dawned on me. I was attached to Steven. And now I'd never talk to him again. I'd never see him smile at one of the remarks I made. I'd never feel his body casually flowing around mine, keeping our long-held secret. I felt a pang deep in my heart as I fought back a flurry of tears.

"Okay, that's good," Fran said, moving full speed ahead. "Since you were meeting your best friend's man, I'd like to think you were discreet in coming up to his room."

I nodded like she could actually see me. I really did feel like I was having an out-of-body experience.

"You were discreet, weren't you?"

"Yes. Yes," I said. "No one saw me come up here."

"Okay. You said it looks like he just died in his sleep, right? Nothing looks out of order?"

"Yes. I mean, he must have had a heart attack. I don't know." I was getting more and more worked up.

"Okay, here's what I need you to do," Fran said. "Pull yourself together. Clean up any sign that anyone else was ever there. Did you order room service?"

"No."

"Did anyone else see you together at all?"

I thought about that. "The bartender did. But that's it."

She exhaled with apparent frustration—that obviously wasn't the answer she was hoping for. "Well, as far as the bartender is concerned, you could've been some random chick at the bar."

I let her continue working this out. I was useless to help plan this cover-up. I stood in the bathroom, watching the lifeless body of my one true love. All I could think was my world was coming to an end.

"Just wipe down everything you think you might have touched. If they think the cause of death is natural, there won't be an investigation. But wipe down everything, just in case," Fran instructed.

At the mention of a possible investigation, my heart started racing again. I noticed my hand was trembling beyond my control. "What am I supposed to do?"

"Just like I said, clean it up and get the hell out of Dodge."

Fran wanted me to just up and leave? "Shouldn't I at least call for help?"

"No! Housekeeping will be there soon. Let them find him."

"No! This is just too much!"

"Do I need to come over there and help you?"

Of course, I didn't want Fran to clean this mess up. Through the doorway I stared at Steven. He no longer wore the euphoric look he'd had when we finally went to sleep. All of that was gone. Forever.

I felt like I couldn't stay in that room one second longer. "No, I want to get out of here now."

"Okay, then do like I said. Go home and act like nothing ever happened. Wasn't that what you two planned to do anyway?"

"Yes, but—"

"But nothing," she said, cutting me off. "You don't have any other choice. Now, get up, because I know you're crouched in a corner, crying, and get to cleaning this mess up."

I did what she said and started vigorously wiping down everything in the bathroom. I felt like a criminal. I had visions of police bursting through the door at any moment. "What am I supposed to do when Paula calls and tells me what happened?" I asked as I wiped the toilet handle, the shower, and everything else I might have touched.

"You're going to be the supportive friend and be there to help her grieve," my sister said like that was a no-brainer.

That was so easy for my sister to say. She was the take-no-prisoners, hard-core one of the family. I was the emotional one. That's why I had no idea how in the world I was going to get through this.

I hung up with Fran, promising to call her as soon as I reached my car. After I wiped down everything I could've even possibly breathed on, I gathered all my belongings, triple-checked to make sure I wasn't leaving anything, then tiptoed toward the door. My heard disintegrated into a thousand pieces as I took one last look at Steven. In a voice strangled by years of regret, I whispered, "I'm sorry. I love you. God forgive me," before easing out of the room.

8

Paula

IN ALL THE YEARS THAT WE HAD BEEN MARRIED, Steven had never stayed out all night. We'd had arguments before—some pretty ugly ones —but he'd always come home.

Until last night.

What do you expect when you told the man you wanted a divorce? I heard my mother's voice in my head. I truly hoped Steven knew I was just mouthing off. That was a bad habit of mine, saying things I didn't really mean. It had been a source of contention throughout our marriage. I was pretty good about not saying crazy stuff to the kids, but Steven had seen the brunt of my verbal fury on several occasions. I only hoped this time I hadn't gone too far.

When he came home today, I promised myself, I wasn't going to be mad about him staying out all night. I wasn't going to hurl accusations at him, like I'd been prone to doing lately even though he'd never given me reason to suspect he was cheating. I was going to explain why I was so unhappy. We would fix this. As soon as he got home.

With a renewed positive attitude, I made my way into the kitchen and noticed the mess as soon as I set foot in the spacious area.

"What in the world?" I mumbled.

All four of my children stopped and turned to me, looking like I had walked into something major. Then I noticed my favorite tray with the giant sunflower.

"We were trying to make you breakfast," Stevie said dejectedly, like I'd ruined their surprise.

"Yeah, we know they've been a handful," Tahiry added, pointing at her brothers, "and so we wanted to do something nice for you."

Twenty-four hours ago, I'd been dreaming about what it would be like to be childless, and now my kids were reminding me why I loved being their mother.

"Don't be mad at the mess. We're going to clean it up," Tahiry hurried to add.

I couldn't help but smile as I walked over and hugged each one of them. "I'm not mad. I'm actually very happy"

"You don't seem happy," Mason said.

I squeezed him tight. "I am," I replied. "Let's just enjoy breakfast."

"You don't want to eat in your room?" Tahiry asked.

I pulled out a chair at the kitchen table, where my mom was sitting, reading the newspaper. "No, I want to eat right here with my family."

"Where's Daddy?" Marcus asked, climbing into the chair next to me.

"He had to go into work early."

My mom side-eyed me. She could tell I was lying. But we all sat down, and they filled me in on the latest news from their school. The meal was less than stellar, but the fact that my kids had cooked it made it feel like a gourmet breakfast.

After we finished eating, Tahiry gathered the boys and announced that she was taking them upstairs to play on the Wii and watch a movie. She would make sure they were quiet so I could enjoy the rest of my day. I studied my daughter and my three sons, who were all standing there looking angelic, and I wondered what they were up to.

"Okay, what's going on?"

"Nothing. Granny just told us that you were sad and so we're going to be on our best behavior today," Tahiry said.

"Yeah, but we can't make any promises for tomorrow," Stevie added.

I laughed as Tahiry shuffled them out of the room. I picked up my cell phone and called Steven again. I'd already called him twice this morning. He still didn't answer, but this time I left a message.

"Hey, babe. It's me. I'm so sorry about last night. I want to talk to you about what's going on with me and figure out how we can fix this. Okay? Love you. Please come home."

I hung the phone up and wandered into the living room to watch TV. I started flipping through the channels until I came across the movie *Love & Basketball*. I smiled because that was Steven's favorite movie. As the familiar scenes appeared on the screen, my mind drifted back to our first date. He'd done the cooking as we watched *Love & Basketball*.

"So, how was the food?" Steven had asked.

I smiled and patted my stomach. "You don't meet many college students that can cook."

"Yeah, I wanted to be a chef, but my parents weren't trying to hear that at all." He grinned. "But I like cooking, and I like having someone to cook for."

"Well, aren't I the lucky one?" I had come to his tiny Georgetown apartment. It was sparsely decorated—a sofa, coffee table, TV, and a Muhammad Ali picture on the wall. But that didn't faze me. I was just enjoying his company.

"I'm trippin' that we never got to meet in the entire four years I was at UT," Steven said. "Felise said you guys used to be the best of friends."

I shrugged. "We are from DC, but my dad moved us to Houston when I was little. Felise and I became best friends in middle school. But then she went to UT, I came back up here to Howard, and we kinda drifted apart. Once my dad remarried, I didn't go back to Houston much. But that's the good thing about real friends. You can go forever without talking and still pick up like you were together yesterday."

Steven and I chatted all evening. He told me about him and Felise, and it sounded like he really cared about her. I recalled the times she'd told me about him, and she'd always made it clear that they were just friends. Watching him, though, I don't know why she wouldn't want more with him. He was intelligent, funny, charismatic, handsome, and just an all-around good guy. I made a mental note to get the real deal from her, but in the meantime, I was going to hit him up for all the information I could get.

"So, are you and Felise really just friends?"

He hesitated, long enough that I didn't know what to make of it, but then he said, "Yeah, we really are. I guess I took your best friend slot. Besides, she has her man now."

"You talking about Greg?"

"Yeah, she loves her some Greg."

He had a look cross his face that I couldn't make out, which led me to ask him, "Are you sure?"

"Oh, yeah. What did Felise tell you?"

"She told me that you guys were just friends. That you were like a brother to her."

He forced a smile. "See. A brother."

"So, that means you're on the market?"

He shrugged. "I'm not trying to get in a serious relationship right now. I want to focus on law school. But I wouldn't mind having a good friend to hang out with and whip up my meals for."

I leaned back and nibbled on a raspberry soufflé he'd cooked for dessert. "I wouldn't mind being that friend."

Before long our friendship escalated into something more, and before I knew it, we were sleeping together on a regular basis.

When I got pregnant with Tahiry, just two months after we started sleeping together, we decided to do what was right—and that had been the story of my life ever since.

I SHOOK AWAY THE MEMORY. I NEEDED TO FOCUS ON the positive and stop thinking about what-ifs and what could've been. This was the life God had given me. It was time that I learned to appreciate it.

I lay back on the couch as I made all kinds of mental promises of how things were going to change as soon as Steven got home. I could be happy as a wife and a mother if I took my mother's advice and found something outside my home that gave me purpose. Yeah, I thought. I had a good life. And getting an outside life was all I needed to get myself back on track.

9

Felise

I DON'T KNOW HOW I GOT DOWN THE HALLWAY, DOWN the elevator, and out of the hotel to my sister's apartment, but here I was, in her living room, trying desperately to pull myself together. I was pacing back and forth across her Berber carpet. The tears hadn't stopped coming.

"Okay, would you relax?" Fran said.

"That's easy for you to say. You're not the one that committed a crime," I said frantically. I was *so* not a criminal. I'd forgotten to pay for a bracelet when I was fifteen, and I had an anxiety attack until I got my mom to take me back to the store to pay for it. How in the world did I think I'd be able to live with leaving a dead man without reporting it? "I'm such a lowlife," I moaned.

"Oh, stop being dramatic," Fran said. "What crime did you commit? I don't think having a lethal kitty is against the law."

I stopped and stared at her. That was not what happened between Steven and me. "This isn't the time for jokes."

"Okay, okay," Fran said, raising her hands apologetically. "Sorry."

I fell down onto her sofa. "I just can't believe this."

Fran shook her head. "Me either. Because I can't understand how Dolly Do-Right," she said, using the nickname she had given me after the bracelet incident, "would do something so scandalous."

That had always been a source of contention between Fran and me. I was the perfect one. The one who always did what she was supposed to, and was always where she was supposed to be. Even our older sister, the ultra-religious Mavis, got in more trouble than I did. But Fran was the wild one, and our parents—God rest their souls—never let us forget who they preferred: me.

"I can't believe I did it either." I sighed. "I was just so mad at Greg for forgetting our anniversary, and I was so sick and tired of being neglected, and then I bumped into Steven at the bar, and he was mad at Paula, and we both had been drinking and . . . and . . ." I buried my face in my hands. "What have I done?"

Fran leaned back and inhaled. "Well, I'm not surprised that you finally stepped out on Greg. The way he neglects you, I'm surprised you hadn't done it already. But I just can't believe you did it with Steven."

"I've got to come clean," I said with finality. I didn't have any other option. I couldn't carry this guilt around.

"And why would you do something stupid like that?" Fran asked, perplexed. "You cleaned up the place, right?"

"Yes, but I should have called for help."

"Why? You said yourself that he was dead. He was still

going to be dead whether you reported it or not, so why should you get in trouble, too?"

We were interrupted by the doorbell. I froze as images of police bursting in to take me into custody flashed in my head.

I jumped up. "Who is that?"

"Calm down. It's just Mavis." Fran got up and headed toward the door.

Now I really was ready to run. My older sister was as bad as the police. Since our parents died in a car crash when I was in college, Mavis had taken over the role of mother and, most of the time, had taken it way too far. "Mavis? Why didn't you tell me she was coming over here?"

"Because I didn't know you were coming over. You were supposed to be going home, remember? Mavis was already on her way over to pick up some money I owe her. You know she's like Tony Soprano when it comes to getting her money back."

I took a deep breath, trying to calm my nerves. "Don't tell her," I said. "I can't take her judging me."

Fran put her hand to her mouth. "Oops, too late."

"Ugh, do you have to tell everybody everything?"

"I was on the phone with her when you called, and she wanted to know what was wrong. I tried to tell her nothing, but she didn't believe me. I told you, she's Tony Soprano. She strong-armed me."

The doorbell rang again, and we heard Mavis's muffled call. "I hear y'all in there. Open this door!"

Fran shrugged at me, then opened the door.

Mavis didn't even speak to Fran as she rushed toward

me. She looked so much like my mother it was eerie—full-figured, beautiful smooth skin, and a head full of naturally curly hair. If I didn't know better, I would think it was my mother coming to be by my side.

I took a step back because my sister had been known to smack me back in the day, and I didn't need her having any flashbacks. But she just grabbed me and hugged me tightly. "Oh, Lord, Felise. What have you gotten yourself into?"

I couldn't help it. Being in my sister's arms felt safe, even though I knew I was far from that. "I messed up, Mavis," I cried.

"Yes, you did, baby girl," she said, stroking my hair, "but it's going to be okay." She pulled back and examined me. "So, what did the police say?"

I looked over at Fran and didn't respond.

"See, my mouth isn't that big. I didn't tell her everything."

Mavis's eyes grew wide. "Tell me what? What is there to tell?"

Neither Fran nor I said a word. Mavis's hands went to her hips. "I know somebody better get to talking." She narrowed her eyes at me. "What did the police say?"

"I–I . . ."

"She left without reporting it, okay?" Fran said.

"Excuse me?" Mavis asked in horror. "You left the scene of a crime?"

"Mavis, leave her alone," Fran snapped. "There was no crime. He died in his sleep. I got this handled."

Mavis threw up her hands in exasperation. "You don't need to be listening to Fran. You know she got the devil in her."

Fran gave Mavis the hand. "You better go somewhere with that, or you're about to see the devil rear its ugly head."

"So, you really think I should tell that I was there, Mavis?" I asked.

"Girl, don't listen to Mavis," Fran said. "Tell for what?"

Mavis sat down next to me. She had a way of adding things up quick, and I could see that turning myself in was no longer her first option. "I can't tell you what to do, Felise," she replied, taking my hand. "I'd never be in that situation because no way I'd get involved with my best friend's husband—"

"Way to make her feel better, Mavis," Fran said, cutting her off.

"I didn't mean it like that," Mavis clarified. "What I'm saying is I can't tell you how I would react, but I can tell you one thing: what's done in the dark always comes to light."

"Not always," Fran said. "Because nobody still knows about that time you and Elijah Reynolds—"

"Fran, would you shut up," Mavis snapped. "This isn't about me." She turned her guns back on the guilty party. "Whatever you do, sis, you need to take to your knees and repent."

"Okay, on that note, I need to go," I said, rising. I felt bad enough as it was. The last thing I needed was Mavis preaching to me.

"See," Fran said, "you always bringing God into the equation. Now you got her all spooked."

"Honey, God is always in the equation," Mavis replied, "whether I bring Him or not."

I knew how this was going to go, and I couldn't do the two of them bickering right then. That's all they've been doing for as long as they've been alive. Usually, I played the peacemaker, but I was so not in the mood.

"Okay," I said. "Both of you are right. Mavis, I need to pray. And Fran, I do need to pull it together."

They both nodded their heads in agreement.

"So, do you want to tell me how you ended up in the hotel room with Steven?" Mavis asked.

I shook my head. I wasn't standing for Mavis's opinion on what happened between us.

"She just finally got fed with the neglectful husband of hers," Fran replied.

Fran liked Greg, but she'd been telling me for years that I deserved better. She couldn't stand his obsessive ways and how he devoted so much time to work.

"So how long have you and Steven been having an affair?" Mavis asked.

"We weren't having an affair," I protested. "We both happened to be in the same place. We both were upset at our spouses. We had been drinking."

Mavis tsked. "Unh-huh, that devil's juice will do it every time."

Fran rolled her eyes as I continued. "I tried to turn away once I got to the room, but it's like this little voice was pushing me forward."

"Unh-huh. Satan has a little voice," Mavis said.

"Okay, Pope Mavis," Fran interjected. She turned to me. "Seriously, pray about it, ask for forgiveness, and move on. You're not doing anyone any good if you keep beating yourself up about it."

"I agree," Mavis said sternly. "I'm not going to tell you what you need to do, but you need to come clean."

"No, she doesn't," Fran said.

"You know it's the right thing to do," Mavis continued.

"You don't need me or Fran to tell you that." She patted my arm. "But whatever you do, I'm by your side, okay? Even if it's seeing you through divorce court and your trial."

"Mavis!" Fran exclaimed.

Mavis quickly apologized. But she was right. That's exactly where I'd be if Greg ever found out.

10

Paula

I'D FINALLY GONE TOO FAR. IN ALL OUR YEARS OF MARriage, Steven had never gotten so mad that he'd stayed out all night, let alone all the next day. But as I rolled over and saw my husband's untouched side of the bed, I realized that's exactly what had happened.

After spending the day with the kids, I'm come into my room to lie down, hoping Steven's warm body would wake me up as he eased into bed next to me. He'd apologize. I'd apologize. Then I'd show my husband how much I really loved him.

I threw back the covers and stood up. It was almost ten p.m. I couldn't believe I'd been asleep all evening. I eased downstairs, hoping that Steven had come in and didn't want to wake me. But to my dismay, the living room was empty, the space where he normally dropped his keys was clear, and when I opened the garage door, my heart sank when I realized that his car still was AWOL.

I fell back against the wall in the hallway. I couldn't

take the suspense anymore. I had the strangest feeling in my gut that I had truly messed up this time, and I didn't know how to make it right.

I said a small prayer for God to deliver my husband home. I'd adopt a new attitude permanently. My mom was right. I had been such a jerk, and the blowup I had was completely uncalled for.

I was just about to pick up the phone to call him again when my mom appeared in the kitchen entryway.

"Oh, hey, Mom," I said dejectedly. "What's going on?"

"Heard some movement in here and came to see what was going on, since I knew the kids weren't here."

"Where are the kids?" I asked.

"Tahiry went over Liz's so they can practice for their cheer competition. Rodney came and got the boys and took them to a movie," she said, referring to Steven's cousin, who often took the kids. "I figured it was okay and a way to get them out the house. He'll bring them back early in the morning on his way to work. And Tahiry will be back whenever you go get her."

I nodded, grateful for her making the arrangements.

"Are you okay? Is Steven home yet?" my mom asked.

I fell down in one of the seats at the kitchen table. "Mama, I really messed up," I cried. "Steven has never stayed away this long."

"Maybe he was really upset. I mean, the threat of divorce is pretty major."

"But I didn't mean that. I was just angry," I confessed. "I was having a serious I-hate-my-life-moment and thinking things would be better without him."

My mom patted my hand sympathetically. "Yeah, that's

usually the way things work. Everyone always thinks the grass is greener on the other side. But it's not. You got a good man, honey, and you have to realize that before it's too late."

"Steven wouldn't go anywhere, would he?" I don't know why, but I no longer believed that.

"Baby, a man can take only so much. When he doesn't feel loved in his own home, it's just a matter of time before he seeks love somewhere else."

I buried my face in my hands. "I don't know what's wrong with me."

My mom was quiet for a minute, then gently said, "Well, I was talking to this lady at bingo and I think you're suffering from postpartum depression."

I cocked my head at this unexpected remark. "Really, Mom?"

"Yes, really. I mean, you were unhappy before, but it seemed to go to a whole different level after the twins were born."

That reminded me all over again of my fight with Steven. "I know, Mama. I love them, I really do, but I can't shake this." *Postpartum depression?* I had never thought about that. But it would definitely explain my mood swings.

"You gotta find a way to shake it," my mom said. "Maybe even see someone professionally. Or go to your primary care doctor. I'm sure they got some pills for it." She turned her attention to a picture of our family, which was displayed prominently on our refrigerator. "And explain it to your husband. I'm sure he'll understand and even help you through this."

I nodded, praying that she was right.

"Just get some rest. I'm sure you're still tired, so go lay

back down. That was a pretty heated argument, so just give Steven a minute. You got a good man. He's not going anywhere. You asked the man for a divorce. Maybe he just wants to make you sweat. I'm positive he'll be home tonight." My mom kissed my forehead before walking out the room.

I hoped that she was right, but I still needed to talk to someone else. I needed to call the only other person who understood my pain. I picked up the phone and called my best friend

Felise and I went way back. She was my ride or die. We drifted apart when we went to college, but our bond was never broken. The only time things got a little shaky with us was when I first started dating Steven. She seemed distant, like she was trying to avoid me. Some people would say I broke the girlfriend code by dating him, but she assured me that they were merely friends. I made it very clear that I wasn't going to do anything without her blessing, and she gave it to me. I'd even fought my feelings for Steven in the beginning. But when Felise found her own happiness with Greg, what was holding me back?

Felise didn't answer, and my heart sank. I needed to talk to her. So I dialed again. And again. She knew if I called back-to-back, it was an emergency.

I was grateful when she finally picked up the phone. "Hey, Felise, I'm sorry to be blowing up your phone, but I need to talk to you."

She hesitated, then said, "You want to talk to Tahiry? Her and Liz are upstairs turning flips."

I didn't know why she would say that. If I wanted to talk to my daughter, I would've called her cell phone. "No. I need to talk to you."

She still sounded brittle as she said, "What's going on?"

I opened my mouth to talk, and a sob came out instead. When I recovered from the outburst, I said, "I think I really messed up this time."

"What do you mean?"

"Me and Steven had a huge fight. He hasn't come home since. I haven't even heard from him," I said.

"What do you mean, you haven't heard from him?" she asked.

"He didn't come home last night or all day today, and you know that's not like him. The fight was really bad."

"Maybe he's somewhere trying to cool off."

"Do you think he left me?" I asked pointedly.

"Wh-why would you say that?" she replied.

"Because I asked him for a divorce."

"A divorce? Why would you ask him for a divorce?"

She was sounding too cool, like she already knew all about it. But I didn't have time to decipher her demeanor. I was in the middle of a crisis. "I know it's crazy. I was just frustrated and upset. I don't want a divorce. I love my husband."

Felise continued to sound distant as she said, "Well, I'm sure everything is fine. He'll probably be home in a little bit."

Even she didn't sound like she believed that. "You know this is completely unlike him," I continued. "Even when he's mad, he still comes home. I think I might have gone too far this time. What if he's with a divorce attorney right now?"

"Don't be silly," she replied. "It's ten-thirty at night. He's not with a divorce attorney. And no, you didn't go too far. I mean, he's probably— He's probably somewhere, you know, just cooling off."

I shook my head, desperation setting in. "His phone is

going straight to voice mail, and he didn't even call to check on the kids. He's gone. My gut is telling me he left me."

"Come on, don't think like that," Felise said. I could tell my best friend was trying to pacify me, prepare me for the worst, because she sounded like she knew that I'd finally pushed Steven over the edge. She'd been trying to tell me to ease up on him, and I wouldn't listen.

"Everyone has fights," Felise continued in a flat monotone. "You guys, umm, you are gonna be fine."

She didn't sound like she believed that. And now neither did I.

11

Felise

I TOOK A DEEP BREATH AS I DROPPED MY CELL PHONE down on the kitchen table. *Keep it together*, I said, repeating what I'd been telling myself all day. I'd been doing okay until now. That phone call from Paula had shaken me to my core. I'd tried to ignore her calls, but she was relentless, and I knew if I didn't answer, she'd get in her car and head over to my house. No way could I see her face-to-face. When Greg had returned from his coffee run this morning and he had Tahiry by his side, I thought I would pass out from guilt. I couldn't look my godchild in the eye. No way would I be able to face her mother. Greg had tried to talk to me about last night, but I was saved by a call from my supervisor. Two nurses had called in sick, and she asked me to cover their shifts. I changed into my scrubs and was out the door so fast I could have been running in the Olympics.

I breathed a sigh of relief when I came in the living room and saw it was empty. Greg's car was in the driveway, but maybe he was asleep. Yet as soon as I felt myself try to relax, I heard his voice behind me.

"Babe, I am so sorry."

I spun around to see him standing in the hallway, an apologetic look on his face, a bouquet of roses in his hands.

"I was so scared you weren't going to come home." He held the flowers out toward me. "I know this won't make up for me being a jerk, but I want to make it up to you."

My body trembled as I fought back tears, which made Greg pull me into his arms.

"Baby, don't cry. I'm so sorry. I'm gonna work on being a better husband. I promise."

I knew I needed to pull myself together, so I nodded dutifully.

"How about I take you out tomorrow night?" he asked.

An entire evening alone together? "No," I sniffed. "I have to work the four-to-twelve shift."

I dropped my purse on the floor. Like clockwork, Greg immediately picked it up and set it on the counter.

That was the least of my concerns. Right then I just wanted to get away from him, shower, and try to pull myself together. I made my way upstairs and had another urge to cry when I walked into the bathroom. Greg had taken Post-it Notes and posted messages all over my bathroom mirror.

I pulled one off.

I'm sorry.

Then another.

I love you.

And two more.

Please forgive me.

I'm trying.

The fact that he'd cluttered up the whole mirror meant a lot. Seeing the clutter had to drive him crazy. And that deviation from his strict routine made me cry even harder.

Feeling miserable, I shed my scrubs and stepped in the shower. The hot water mixed with my warm tears as I tried to cry everything out of my system. All day I had wondered if the maids had discovered Steven yet. I played out all kinds of scenarios, from it being ruled a simple death by natural causes to the FBI coming in and taking me down.

When I got out the shower, I knew I was a wrinkled prune, but I did feel a little bit better. Fran was right. I was going to have to get past the guilt. I was going to have to learn to live with what I'd done.

I dried off, slipped into my lounging gown, and walked back into the bedroom. "What are you doing?" I said when I noticed Greg sitting up on the bed with his laptop.

"I was just looking at some tickets to a comedy show. Mike Epps is at Reliant this weekend and, well, I was hoping I could take you."

I forced a smile. I loved comedy shows, and any other time I would've been thrilled that my husband had taken the initiative. However, I was in no mood to laugh. But I knew if I protested, Greg would continue trying to make up for last night, and that would only make me feel even more guilty. Right then I just wanted to be left alone.

"I'd like that. Why don't you go get the tickets in person? You know, if you buy them online, they have that ridiculous surcharge. Plus, I'd really like some ibuprofen."

He looked up in concern. "What's wrong?"

"I just have a headache. And we don't have any pain medication," I said, praying he didn't go check the medicine cabinet.

"Okay. I'll go pick up the tickets and get you some Advil." He had researched the subject thoroughly, and that was what we had to have in the house. He closed the laptop and came over to kiss me. "I hate when you stay away overnight. Promise me that no matter what kind of jerk I am, you won't stay at Fran's again."

I nodded but didn't say anything. He assumed I'd spent the night at Fran's because that's where I usually went when we argued, which lately had been quite frequently. I was actually surprised that he hadn't called Fran's looking for me, but I know he hated people being in our business. Greg's obsessive ways were driving me insane. The worst of them was, we had to have weekly meetings to review where every dime was spent. He calculated, down to the penny, how much money we were blowing by letting the faucet drip, or leaving the bathroom light on. All he did was work, nitpick, then work some more.

As soon as Greg left on his errands, I went to his laptop and typed in "what happens when you leave the scene of a crime?" I had been searching for ten minutes when my cell rang. Fran's name popped up on the screen. She'd tried to call earlier, but I was working and I'd forgotten to call her back.

I answered, "I'm fine, Fran."

"You know I have to check, girl. So, are you holding up okay?"

"As well as can be expected," I replied with a heavy sigh. "I worked today so I didn't have to be around the house. I was scared I would confess."

"Good grief, remind me never to rob a bank with you," Fran said. "Your conscience is eating at you, and it hasn't even been twenty-four hours."

I added a little steel to my voice. "I'm sorry, I don't know proper etiquette for killing someone."

"You didn't kill him, not literally, anyway. But I am gonna start calling you the kitty slayer." She laughed. I didn't.

"Fran, would you stop playing around? This is serious. I just know Paula is going to call me any minute now and tell me the police have showed up at her house."

She sighed like I was spoiling her fun. "Fine, and when that phone call comes, you need to fall down on the floor and scream, 'Oh, Lawd, not Steven. Don't tell me Steven is gone home to glory!'"

I knew my sister was being her usual silly self, but I was so not in the mood. Steven was dead. A man I'd loved without even realizing how much I loved him was gone. And I had no idea how I'd live with that. Or the guilt of bringing on whatever killed him.

"Bye, Fran. I'll talk to you later," I said.

"So what did Greg say?" she said, ignoring my good-bye.

I closed the laptop. "He's apologizing for being such a jerk."

"Oh, wow. I know that's not helping your conscience."

"You know it's not. But look, I need to go. I'm fine, okay?"

If Fran kept trying to keep me on the phone, I was going to hang up on her. But luckily, she said, "Okay, sis. But seriously, relax. Everything is going to be all right."

"Okay. Bye."

I hung up the phone. Fran was dead wrong. Something told me it would be a long time before everything was ever all right again.

12

Felise

I FELT AWFUL, YET THE LITTLE VOICE IN MY HEAD KEPT trying to convince me otherwise.

He was yours first.

I shook away that thought. I'd let Steven go, all but handed him to my best friend with my blessing. I'd denied that I had any feelings, and now I was paying the ultimate price. Fran joked about me killing him, but the more I thought about it, maybe she was right. I knew he had a heart condition. Paula had told me that years ago, but I didn't think it was that big of a deal. Still, I knew it. Why didn't I think about that?

That was not the only burden I had to carry. Now that I knew he had never stopped loving me either, I had to spend the rest of my life wondering what would've happened if I never had let him go.

As I sat alone in the empty bedroom, my mind drifted back to the time that I had made such a terrible mistake.

• • • • • •

"Hey, you," I said, racing into Steven's arms as I picked up him from the baggage claim. I hadn't seen him in six months, and I was surprised at how happy I was. "You got a beard and everything." I rubbed his chin. "I send you to DC a boy, and you come back a man."

He gave me a quick peck on the cheek. "What you talking about, girl? I was a man long before I set foot on DC soil."

"You look good." I squeezed his biceps. "Muscles and everything. I guess Paula and Ms. Jean feeding you good up there."

"Yeah, they're taking care of me."

Yet the look on his face had me uneasy. I knew Steven well, and I could tell when he was hiding something.

"What's wrong with you?" I asked.

He flashed a smile. "Naw, I'm cool. Just a long flight."

"Well, all that hard work will be worth it soon because you're going to blow up. You're about to be a bona fide attorney."

"Yeah, I hope so. Law school is kicking my butt, so I just hope that I can make it."

Something unspoken was still wrong. "Boy, please. You graduated with a 3.7. You know you're acing law school."

"Nah." He laughed. "Didn't I tell you? I'm thinking of dropping out and going to barber school."

I gave him a playful push. We laughed some more as he tossed his luggage in the back of my car. "You hungry?" I asked as we pulled off.

"Starving," he replied.

"Cool, I figured we'd go to Beef N Bun," I said, referring to our favorite eatery.

On the ride over, we fell back into our comfortable groove, laughing and talking about everything under the sun.

At the restaurant, we got our food, settled in, and I made more small talk. I didn't know what had changed, but Steven once again didn't seem himself.

"Okay, now that we've said our hellos and shot the breeze, tell me what's really going on," I said, looking him dead in the eye.

He shrugged. "Same ol', same ol'. But what's going on with you? You still dating Rain Man?"

I cracked up, laughing at his name for Greg. "He's not Rain Man, he just has a few obsessive tendencies."

"So when am I gonna meet Mr. Good Guy? Since you're raving about him all the time."

"He's actually going to meet us here." I glanced at my watch. Greg wasn't feeling me coming to pick up Steven alone. He had no appreciation for our friendship, so I'd tried to ease his worries by having him meet us.

He said jokingly, "Cool, but you know if I don't approve, you have to dump him."

"Oh, is that how we're doing it now?"

He nodded. "Yep, you had to have a say in who I'm dating, so I have to give my stamp of approval."

My eyebrows rose in shock. "Dating? So you and Paula are dating *now?"*

The expression on his face said he felt like he'd put his foot in his mouth.

"Yeah, we're kinda kicking it," he admitted.

I don't know why, but that put my stomach in knots. "Kickin' it, like we're-having-a-good-time kickin' it?" I clarified. "Or kickin' it, like we're-really-feelin'-each-other kickin' it?"

He didn't respond, and he lost his smile.

"Steven, what's going on?" I said. "I can tell you're keeping something from me."

He took a deep breath, then said, "I don't know how to say this."

His tone made me set my fork down. "How about you just come right out and say it?"

Steven released a heavy sigh. "Paula is pregnant."

The knots in my stomach twisted in a tight fist. I couldn't even get words to come out of my mouth. "Wow," I finally managed to say.

"I mean, I don't know how it happened."

I raised an eyebrow. "You don't?"

"I mean, of course I know how it happened. She's just, well, she's as shocked as I am," he stammered.

"Is she keeping it?" I asked bluntly. I know Paula and I weren't as close as we used to be since she moved back to DC but I couldn't believe that she hadn't shared that with me.

"What?"

Steven narrowed his eyes, and I immediately felt bad.

"No, I'm not saying she should have an abortion," I said, trying to backpedal. "I just thought, you know, with school and all, all I was saying . . ." I didn't know what I was saying, so I let my words trail off. All I knew was this had to be the most devastating news I'd ever heard.

"So, what are you going to do?" I finally asked.

"Well, I came home to break the news to my parents, and you know what they're going to want me to do."

I held my breath as I waited for the next words.

"They'll want me to marry her."

"Marriage?" I said, trying to keep my voice steady. "How do you feel about that?"

"How should I feel?"

We stared at each other. I didn't know what to say. Not

until that very moment—when the thought of Steven's happily-ever-after with someone else was about to become a reality—did I realize that I wasn't being honest with myself about Steven. Because the pain I felt was overwhelming me.

Tears began welling up in my eyes, but before either of us could say anything, Greg walked in.

"Well, this must be the great Steven," he said, approaching our table. I immediately willed my tears back and swallowed the lump in my throat.

"And you must be Mr. Wonderful himself, Greg." Steven stood to shake his hand. "It's a pleasure to finally meet you. I've heard a lot about you."

Both Steven and I managed fake smiles. Greg put his arm around me and pulled me close. His hug didn't feel warm at all. In fact, it felt tight and possessive. Suddenly, I was glad that I'd never told him that Steven and I had slept together. Steven and I had both agreed that since it was a mistake for us to cross the line, we needed to forget it ever happened.

"Well, that's good because the way she raves about you, I was beginning to wonder if I should be worried," Greg said, pulling me even tighter.

Steven laughed uneasily. "Naw, she's like my little sister. Nothing going on here but the best of friends."

Little sister? Best of friends? Who would've ever thought those words could be so painful?

I wriggled to get Greg to let go a hair. I said, forcing a smile as I glared at Steven, "See, I told you, baby. We're just like brother and sister. And besides, Steven was just sharing the good news with me."

"What good news?" Greg asked.

"Looks like him and Paula are about to have a baby."

"What? Congrats, man." Greg extended his hand again.

Steven shook it. "Yeah, it's not the ideal situation with me being in my first year of law school, but life happens."

"I feel you, but from what Felise has told me, if anybody can make it work, you can. Y'all getting married?"

I waited for that answer.

"Yeah, probably."

It took everything in my power to keep my knees from buckling.

"Well, let me know, man. Maybe I can chip in on the bachelor party." He leaned in and kissed me on the lips, like a dog staking its claim. "And who knows? Maybe we can have a double wedding."

STEVEN HAD RETURNED TO DC AFTER THAT VISIT, AND the distance between us began, both literally and figuratively. Paula started calling me more. A part of me sensed that she was trying to make sure that I was okay with everything. But she was pregnant with his child, so what was I supposed to say at that point? I'd given her my blessing, and I definitely couldn't take that back now. So I continued to assure her that I was happy for her and for Steven.

I couldn't take Steven's calls, though. He called often, trying to gauge where my head was. The few times I did take his call, I was abrupt and I could tell that he knew my excitement was fake. Thinking of Paula and Steven married with children hurt my heart to the core. And I never told a soul.

But that's why, one day, when Greg made a haphazard proposal at Joe's Crab Shack, I jumped to accept. We had been dating for nine months, and besides his few obsessive tendencies, he was a good guy, so I said, "Sure." That was the extent of our proposal.

He bought me a miniscule ring from JCPenney. I almost died when he turned away from the one-and-a-half-carat ring I was eyeing, pointed at the smallest diamond in the case, told the clerk we'd take that one, then handed her a 20-percent-off coupon. When I started making wedding plans, he took one look at my budget and decided that it made "absolutely no sense to spend that kind of money on a wedding." I protested at first, but then Paula emailed me a photo of her elegant wedding dress. I knew I'd never have a dress like that, so why bother? Greg and I went to the justice of the peace three days later.

I took great pride in telling Steven that I was married. His long silence told me that my declaration of love for Greg stung, and I was glad. I wanted him to feel the same pain I did. He never let on, though. And I took my place as a bridesmaid at their wedding. I fought back tears as I watched them say, "I do." I led the toast for the married couple to have a lifetime of joy. And I convinced myself that I wasn't in love with my best friend's husband.

13

Paula

I WAS BEYOND WORRIED NOW. IT WAS NINE THE NEXT morning. I still hadn't heard from Steven. I'd logged on to AT&T and seen that he still hadn't made any calls since we talked, which only intensified my worry.

I was about to break into a full-fledged panic when my mother appeared in the bedroom doorway.

"Umm, Paula." She looked extremely nervous as she fidgeted with her hands. "The police are here."

"The police?" I said, jumping up off my bed. "For what?" In my distracted state I hadn't heard the doorbell ring. "Are the kids back? Where's Tahiry?" I asked as I slipped on some pants.

"I went and picked up Tahiry last night. She and the boys are downstairs."

"Well, what do the police want?"

My mom didn't answer as she followed me out. I had barely reached the bottom of the stairs when the first officer said, "Mrs. Wright?"

"Yes?" I replied, taking slow steps in their direction.

The first officer glanced at Tahiry and her brothers, who were all standing in the middle of the living room, staring at him.

"Ummm, is there somewhere we can go talk in private?"

"Private? Why do we need to talk in private?" I asked, my voice squeaking. "Is this about my husband? Did something happen to Steven?"

"Please? It'll just take a few minutes," the officer said.

I didn't like the way this was sounding. "Mom, can you take the kids in the other room?"

Tahiry wanted to protest, but the look on my face must've told her that now wasn't the time. My mother took Mason and Marcus's hands and led them out. Tahiry and Stevie reluctantly followed.

"What's going on?" I asked as soon as they were out the room.

"Well, it is about your husband"—he glanced down at his notepad—"Steven Wright."

My heart immediately sank. "What about him? He's fine, right? Where is he? Has he been arrested?"

"Ma'am, unfortunately, there's been an accident."

I fell back against the wall. I had to hold on to the railing to keep from losing my balance. "What kind of accident?"

The officers exchanged glances; then the second one, a compassionate-looking man, stepped forward. "I'm sorry to have to inform you of this, but Steven's body was discovered in a local hotel this—"

"Wh-what do you mean, body?" I said, cutting him off. Surely this had to be some kind of mistake. I felt my mom ease to my side and take my arm, trying to keep me from collapsing. "Where's my husband?"

"Sweetie, calm down," my mom whispered, her voice shaking.

I jerked away. "No, what are you talking about?"

The second officer looked pained. "Ma'am, there's no easy way to say this. Your . . . Your husband was found dead in his hotel room this morning. One of the housekeepers found him in his bed unresponsive. Of course, the coroner will give the final report, but it looks like he just died in his sleep."

All of the breath inside me escaped, and I fell to the floor. I didn't realize that I was screaming until Tahiry came running out.

"Mom, what's wrong?" she cried.

"There has to be some kind of mistake," I heard my mother say.

"Mom, what's going on?" Tahiry frantically repeated.

"Get her out of here!" I screamed at my mom.

Tahiry jerked away as my mom tried to take her arm. "No, I'm not going anywhere! What's going on?"

I looked at my daughter, then opened my arms to hug her. "They said your dad is gone," I sobbed when she didn't move.

"Gone where? When . . . when is he coming back?" She stammered, turning her gaze from me to the officers.

"Ma'am, I'm so sorry," the first policeman replied.

"What happened?" I heard my mom ask. I don't know exactly what he told her. Honestly, how on earth could it even matter? My husband was dead. Whatever they said elicited agonizing screams from Tahiry. Then my whole world went black.

14

Felise

MY MANIC HUSBAND WAS WORKING EVERY NERVE IN MY body. He was going all out trying to make up for the anniversary fiasco and driving me straight to the mad house.

"... So I was thinking that maybe this weekend, instead of going to see Mike Epps, we could catch a plane to Vegas for a late anniversary celebration," he said. "I know the tickets are last minute, but I think we deserve it."

I was sitting on the bed, thumbing through a magazine, not digesting a single word on the pages. I just wanted everyone to leave me alone to mourn.

I definitely didn't want to hear any chatter about Vegas. Steven used to love going there. His favorite . . . I caught myself and had to fight back the lump in my throat. Was I going to spend the rest of my life thinking about Steven? I struggled to keep down the tears. I couldn't cry. Greg knew I was upset about the anniversary, but tears would bring a whole other set of questions.

Still, a part of me wanted to cry in my husband's arms.

He'd grown to love Steven, too. After Steven and Paula got married and he saw how close Paula and I were, he let down his guard. Steven and Greg would've probably never been friends on their own—they were too different—but they had developed a mutually respectful friendship over the years.

That made my betrayal even worse.

My cell phone rang, and I saw Paula's name pop up on the screen.

I couldn't do it. I couldn't talk to her yet. I knew that I was going to have to at some point. But I was sure that she had gotten the news by now, and I didn't know what to say.

"You're not going to get that?" Greg asked when I tossed the phone back on the bed.

"I don't feel like talking," I snapped. "Period."

"Okay, hint taken," he said, standing. "I guess I'll leave you alone."

"That would be nice."

Greg stood over the bed, staring at me. "How long are you going to stay mad at me?"

I took a deep breath and slapped the magazine, trying to pretend I wanted to keep reading. "I'm not mad, Greg. I'm over it, okay?"

"It doesn't seem like it."

"I'm just not in the mood for conversation." I would have given everything to just disappear right then. Go to a dark land where no one could talk to me.

"Well, you haven't been in the mood for conversation since you got home. You slept on the sofa, and if you say that you're not mad anymore, then I don't know what it is," Greg said.

We were interrupted when Liz came rushing into the

room with her Samsung Galaxy extended toward me. "Mom," she said frantically, "it's Tahiry. She's on the phone crying. She said Ms. Jean has been trying to call you because Uncle Steven died."

My daughter didn't call Paula her aunt, but for some reason she'd taken to calling Steven uncle. Maybe because he was always doing stuff for the girls and they absolutely adored him. Right then, hearing her call him that sent daggers through my heart.

I slept with my daughter's "uncle."

"What?" Greg said in shock. "What do you mean, Steven died?"

Liz thrust the phone toward me. "Here, she wants to talk to you."

I could not get around this with my husband and daughter standing there, staring at me. So I slowly took the phone. "Hello?"

"Nana!" Tahiry cried, which was another punch in the gut.

"Yes?" I said.

She was sobbing hysterically. "They say my dad is dead."

Both Greg and Liz were staring at me, so I knew I had to sound shocked. "Oh, my God," I said. "What happened?"

"I don't know. Some cops just showed up at our door. Mom passed out, she's up now, but she's moaning and nobody can get through to her. Granny's going crazy. Oh, my God! What am I going do? The boys are crying, and I . . . I just can't believe this."

"What's going on?" Liz whispered in the background.

"Can you come over?" Tahiry sobbed. "We need you, Nana."

How in the world could I say no? "Okay, I'll be there right away."

When I hung up, Greg and Liz were standing there, waiting for answers.

"Something horrible has happened," I said, getting out of bed. "They found Steven dead."

Greg let out a loud gasp and Liz screamed "No!" as Greg took her into his arms.

"Come on, honey," Greg said, motioning for me to get up. "You told them we're on our way over there, right?"

I looked at him and wanted to say "*We?*" But I just nodded. I knew I had to go through this. I had to go face my friend. Not only did I have to face her, I had to give her a shoulder to cry on. While my husband stood at my shoulder. How in the world was I ever going to live with myself?

15

Felise

IF I COULD HAVE BEEN ANYWHERE ELSE RIGHT THEN, *I would have been.* I felt like the scum of the earth as I stood in the living room of my best friend's home. A somber Stevie had opened the door for us. Greg had hugged him, and Tahiry came racing into my arms.

"Nana, why? Why did my dad die?" she cried, squeezing me tight, like she didn't ever want to let me go. "Whyyyy?"

I held her as my own tears streamed down my face. "Baby, sometimes we don't understand things."

"What am I going to do?" Tahiry sobbed.

My guilt aside, my heart broke for Tahiry. She was so much like her father it was eerie, from their beautiful hazel eyes to the dimple in their left cheek to their caring, witty personality. I don't know if that's what drew me to her over the years, but I loved Tahiry like she was my own daughter.

"Oh, Felise!" I looked up to see Paula come barreling toward me. I didn't want to let Tahiry go because I didn't want to hug Paula. But Tahiry moved aside and into Liz's arms so the two of them could weep together.

Paula threw her arms around me, and all I could do was stroke her hair as she sobbed and asked, "Why? How could this happen?"

I wished that I could answer that for her. I had no idea why Steven had to die. And certainly not why he had to die at that time and that place. With me.

Greg came up behind Paula and rubbed her back as I held her.

"Paula, I'm so sorry. What happened?" he asked.

Paula stepped back and swiped at her tears. "That's just it," she said. "I don't know. The police said that he was found in his hotel room. All they said was it didn't look like foul play or anything."

"I didn't know he was going out of town," Greg said.

She buried her face in her hands and sobbed some more. Her mom came and stepped up on the side of her. "He wasn't. It was the hotel downtown—the Four Seasons."

Paula sniffed as she tried to explain. "We had a fight, and he spent the night at a hotel. They said he just died in his sleep."

Greg looked bewildered. "Was he sick?"

"No! I mean, not to my knowledge."

This thought made Paula wobble like she was about to faint. Greg took her arm and led her to the sofa. While he was cordial to Steven, Greg had a genuine affection for Paula. "Come on, sit down. You don't need to overexert yourself."

After he settled her on the sofa, they both looked like they were waiting for me to say something, so I turned to my daughter. "Liz, why don't you take Tahiry in the kitchen and get her something to drink?"

Tahiry looked at me like she wanted nothing more than to climb into my lap like she used to do when she was a little girl. I nodded to tell her it was okay, and she let Liz lead her out.

Greg eased down next to Paula. "Now, tell us what happened."

Paula shook her head. I could tell she couldn't make any sense of what was going on. "They said a maid found him in his hotel bed dead. He must've been there all day. They said the Do Not Disturb sign was on the door, so the maid hadn't cleaned the room. Not until late last night, when they realized that he hadn't checked out, did they find him."

"Oh, my God," Greg said.

I had completely forgotten about the Do Not Disturb sign. The thought of this small detail sprang up like a billboard in my mind, reminding me all over again of how horrible that morning had been. I stood with my hand covering my mouth, tears in my eyes. I didn't need to act. Watching Paula, I truly was heartbroken. "I just don't understand it," I managed to say. Which was the truth.

Greg said, "What did they say was his cause of death?"

Paula dabbed her tears as she pursed her lips to stifle more cries. Her mother, Ms. Jean, stepped up. "They haven't said yet," she replied. Her eyes were puffy and red as well. "All they told us is that it doesn't look like foul play. I think it may have been his heart, but we won't know until the medical examiner releases his findings."

"He had a bad heart?" Greg asked. "I didn't know that."

Paula looked at me strangely. I had never mentioned that to Greg because I didn't see the need. And I never knew his condition was bad enough to kill him. Maybe if I had . . .

Paula sniffed again as she told Greg, "Steven had a heart murmur. That's why he had to stop running marathons. But we thought he had it under control. I just don't understand. How does somebody just die in their sleep?"

Greg patted her hand. "I'm sure the medical examiner will have some answers for you. In the meantime, is there anything we can do?"

"I guess I need to notify Steven's mom and begin planning . . . planning his . . ."

I stepped up when she couldn't finish. "You don't need to do anything right now."

Paula extended her hand toward me, and as much as I didn't want to, I reached out and took it. Her hand felt all soft and flabby, like Steven's death had sucked everything strong out of her.

"I don't know how I'm going to make it through this," she said.

I finally sat down on the other side of her. As guilty as I felt, my grief was real, so I did what I was supposed to do—I let her cry on my shoulder.

"Well, one thing you don't have to worry about is going through this alone. We are going to be right there for you," Greg said. "Right, Felise?"

My stomach twisted in another sharp knot. "Right."

I had never in my life felt as low as I did then.

16

Paula

I DIDN'T KNOW HOW LONG I HAD BEEN DRIVING AROUND. I just needed to get out of the house. I needed to escape the nightmare that my life had become. I would give anything to turn back the hands of time, to go back just two days. I wouldn't fight over frivolous things. I wouldn't make my husband so unhappy that he didn't want to come home. And most of all, I would push him to go see the doctor. My mind raced back to about exactly this time last month. Steven had canceled his doctor's appointment because a meeting came up. I had brushed it off.

If only I had pushed him.

But *would, could, should*—none of those words mattered now. All that mattered was that Steven was gone.

My ringing cell phone snapped me out of my daze. I saw my mother was calling again. She'd been calling me nonstop for the last hour. I knew she was worried sick. I was supposed to be lying down, but the thought of lying in the bed that I had shared with my husband was suffocating and heartbreaking. I pressed Ignore again and continued driving. Before I knew it, I was pulling into the circular driveway of the Four Seasons Hotel. I had no idea what I was looking for, but I needed to come here. I needed some answers, and this seemed to be the only place I could get them.

I parked, then walked to the front desk and asked to speak to a manager. They brought me a curly-haired boy who looked like he couldn't have been more than twenty-two years old.

"Can I speak to the manager?" I said softly.

He flashed a wide smile. "Um, yeah, you've got him."

"Hi. Uh, I–I . . ." I stammered. "I'm sorry to bother you, but my husband was found here yesterday."

He lost his smile. "I'm sorry, I don't understand."

"He died here yesterday," I said, my voice cracking.

A look of compassion immediately crossed the young man's face. "Oh, I am so sorry. I was off yesterday, but everyone's talking about it. My condolences to you and your family."

I didn't want his condolences. I wanted answers. "Thank you"—I shook as I spoke—"but I'm trying to figure out what happened. When did my husband book the hotel room? Was he here with someone? Did you all find anything out of the ordinary in his room?"

The guy looked at me sadly. "I'm sorry, I can't give you that information."

"He's dead!" I snapped. "What do you think he's going to do? Come back and sue?"

"Ma'am, calm down please."

I slammed my hand on the counter. "I will not calm down! I need some answers!"

He looked around. Several people had started staring, but I didn't care. "Hold on," he said. He began tapping on one of the computers behind the counter. "Your husband didn't get the room until late Friday night, and it looks like there was nothing out of the ordinary. Housekeeping said that he was just in the bed, like he'd died in his sleep."

"Was he alone?"

"Like I said, I wasn't here, but the room is just in his name." He checked the screen again, then turned to the girl at the end of the counter, who was trying to act like she wasn't listening to our conversation. "Lori," he said, then waited for her to approach. "You checked in Mr. Wright, didn't you, the other night? The guy they found dead?"

Her hand moved to her heart. "Yes. That is so sad."

Her sympathy looked genuine, so I asked her, "Was he alone?"

Her eyebrows rose in shock, and she looked over at the manager like she didn't know what to do.

"It's okay," he said. "This is his wife, and as you can imagine, she's obviously upset. But I told her, we show that he checked into the room by himself, right?"

Lori still looked apprehensive, but she nodded her head. "Yes, he was by himself," she replied. "He looked a little tipsy and said he was going to get a room to sleep it off."

I don't know why that didn't give me the relief I'd thought it would.

"He had been at the bar drinking," Lori added, trying to help.

"Maybe he got some kind of alcohol poisoning at the bar," I said. I knew I was grasping at straws, but I needed something to make sense.

The manager tensed up, and all compassion left his face.

"I'm sorry, that's all the information we can give you. I could lose my job giving you that much."

"Thank you," I said as I spun around and headed toward the bar.

I found a lot of people in the bar area: laughing, flirting couples oblivious to my pain. I immediately marched to the bar.

"Excuse me! Excuse me!" I called out, waving to get the bartender's attention.

The male bartender was in the middle of taking an order, and he said, "I'll be with you in just a minute."

"No!" I said, slamming my palm on the bar counter. "This can't wait. I need to know something." I fumbled in my purse and pulled out a picture of my husband. "This man, he was here the other night. Do you recognize him? Were you working?"

He sighed, then excused himself from the customer in front of him and walked over to me. He glanced down at the photo.

"Yeah, I served him. Why?"

"You gave him a lot to drink, and then he died in this hotel. What did you do to him?"

"Whoa, slow down, lady," the bartender said, holding up his hands in defense. "I didn't do anything. I don't do anything but serve drinks."

"Was he drunk? Did you keep serving him? Did you give him alcohol poisoning?" The words were rushing from my mouth. I'm sure I looked like a madwoman, but I felt like desperation was swallowing me whole.

"Whoa," he said. "You need to chill out, lady!"

I couldn't help it. I started losing it, yelling at the bartender, accusing him of killing my husband, until I felt a hand on my shoulder.

"Paula?" I turned around to see Felise's old college roommate Sabrina. We'd all hung out when I came back to Texas over the holidays freshman year. I'd seen her a few times over the years. The last time, I was at this hotel for a cheer camp for Tahiry. I'd forgotten that she worked as a bartender here.

"Sabrina!" I said.

"What is going on? What's wrong?" she asked.

I couldn't help it. I started crying as I buried my head in my hands.

"Shhh, it's okay, calm down." She looked at all the people staring at me, including the bartender, who looked pretty mad. "Hey, Zen, I got it," she told him. "I'm sorry, she's upset. Just go on, I'll handle it."

Zen still had an attitude, but I couldn't be concerned with him as I let her lead me into the ladies' room.

"Now, tell me what's going on."

"Steven died here the other night," I cried. "He was at the bar, then he got a room, and then he died in the room, and I just don't understand. I don't understand what happened. I don't know if he got some type of alcohol poisoning or if somebody killed him or what."

"Okay, calm down. I assure you, Zen is our best bartender. If he thought Steven was anywhere near drunk enough to get alcohol poisoning, he would've stopped serving him."

I wiped the warm moisture flooding my eyes. "They said it was Steven's heart. But it just doesn't make sense!"

She wet a paper towel and handed it to me. "Here. Wipe your face."

I took it and dabbed my tear-streaked face.

"Look, I will find out what I can for you, okay?" she said. "But Zen is a good guy, and he wouldn't have poisoned your husband. So just relax, and let me see what I can find out, and I'll get back in touch with you, okay?"

I sniffed, nodding as I balled up the paper towel and tossed it in the trash.

"Look, this is all too fresh. You go home, get some rest. I'll get your number from Felise, and we'll talk soon, okay?"

I knew she was right. I needed to get out of there. But I also needed to figure out what was going on before I lost my mind.

17

Felise

THIS ISN'T ABOUT ME. THAT'S WHAT I HAD TO KEEP telling myself as I gathered up the strength to knock on Paula's door. I had to focus on my goddaughter, who needed me right then. Nothing else mattered.

"Hey," Paula's sister said, opening the door. Although I had known Charlene for years, I didn't think she cared too much for me. Paula always said that Charlene was jealous of how close she and I were. Her sister was never rude or anything, but she wasn't overly nice either.

"Hi, Charlene. When did you get in?"

She gave me a polite hug. "I just got in. Trying to get everything situated." She stepped aside to let me in.

"Tahiry called me. I was worried about her, so I came over," I said as I cautiously advanced into the living room. I was praying that I didn't see Paula.

"Yeah, she's not doing too well," Charlene replied.

"Where's Paula and the boys?"

"The boys are upstairs moping around, too. Paula is asleep. Do you want me to wake her up?"

I wanted to breathe a sigh of relief. "Nah, let her sleep."

"Hey, Nana."

I looked up to see Tahiry's long figure coming down the stairs. She had on some cut-off jeans and a tank top. Her long natural hair was pulled back haphazardly into a ponytail. Over the past year Tahiry had sprouted into a young woman. Today, though, she looked like a helpless little girl.

"Hey, sweetie. I just came by to check on you. Maybe get you out of the house," I said, trying to will a smile to come.

Her eyes were swollen and sunken. She leaned up against the railing. "And go where?"

I shrugged. "I don't know. Wherever you'd like to go."

She thought about that for a moment, then said, "I want to go back to the past. When my daddy was home."

"Oh, honey." I opened my arms, and she all but fell into them. She cried silent tears as I led her over to the sofa.

I let her cry for a while before I leaned back and dabbed her face. "You know what? Why don't we go get something to eat? How about we go to that new seafood restaurant downtown?"

She grew solemn again. "My dad had promised to take me there soon."

"Well, then that's definitely where we need to go. We need to go in his honor," I announced.

She managed a faint smile. "Really?"

I nodded. "Yes, really."

"Can we also go find me something to wear? I don't have a dress to wear to the funeral, and Mom . . ."

"And your mother is distraught," I said, finishing the sentence. "That's why I'm here. We'll let her rest, and I'm going to do whatever I need to do to help you through this."

She hugged me again. "Thank you, Nana. Just give me a minute to change," she said before darting up the stairs.

Charlene had remained at the entrance to the living room, saying nothing. To relieve the tension of our mutual silence, I asked, "Will you be okay with the boys?"

She nodded. "They're my nephews. I can take care of them." But then she let her attitude go and added, "Sorry. Everyone is so stressed. The boys are upstairs just watching TV, not really saying anything. You know, none of us are used to that."

I walked over and hugged her. She was caught off guard but finally hugged me back.

"I know I'm not there for Paula like I should be. It's just . . . so hard," I said.

She gave me a genuine smile. "Well, you're there for Tahiry, right? And that's good because I'm not the greatest with teens."

"She'll be okay," I said. "You take care of Paula and the boys, and I'll make sure Tahiry makes it through this."

Charlene seemed happy with this proposal. So was I. Taking care of Tahiry was at least one promise that I could keep.

18

Paula

HOW IN THE WORLD DO YOU BURY THE MAN YOU LOVE, especially when he's only thirty-six years old? How was I supposed to smile as person after person came to offer condolences?

My house felt like Grand Central Station. I didn't even know who all was here. The last few days had passed in a blur. I know Steven's mom and brother had arrived yesterday. They'd gone to take his suit to the funeral home this morning. I simply couldn't do it. My sister, Charlene, had come up from DC, but really, I couldn't entertain any of them. I felt like I was just going through the motions.

Steven's mother, Lois, a very poised, put-together woman, approached me. She was wearing a navy St. John pantsuit, her hair pulled back into a tight bun. Even in her grief she looked like royalty. I sat at the kitchen table with the blank piece of paper in front of me. I'd yet to formulate one word. "Sweetie, you should really let me do this," she said gently.

"No, I need to," I said, tugging the paper toward me. I didn't mean to sound harsh. I liked his mom, I really did. And I knew she was grieving just like me, but I didn't want her around right then. I didn't want anyone around when I wrote my husband's obituary. Well, except for the one person who understood my pain because she understood me. I couldn't understand why she wasn't here.

"I was just trying to help," Lois said.

"She knows that," my mom said, stepping forward to play peacemaker. "You know she's stressed."

Lois nodded, flashed a sympathetic smile, then walked off.

"Mom, did you call Felise?" I asked before she walked away as well.

My mom nodded. "I did. She said she'd be by here later. She sounded broke up herself."

"She probably is. They did use to be best friends in college."

My mom raised an eyebrow. "Umph." I knew she never liked how close they were, but you'd think by now, she would have gotten over it. She didn't believe in "man sharing," as she'd called it. But I wasn't sharing Steven. He was mine. He *had been* mine.

I understood if Felise was broken up, but she couldn't be mourning nearly as much as I was. And I needed her here with me. We could share in our grief together.

"Let me see the phone." I motioned to my cell phone, which was sitting on the counter. "I'm going to call her."

"I just don't understand," my mother said, reaching for the phone. "You're the one grieving, but you got to call her?" She rolled her eyes as she handed me the phone.

I called Felise and it actually rang three times, and just before it went to voice mail, Felise picked up.

"Hey, Paula, how are you?" Felise asked.

"Not too good. Trying to do this obituary." I released a long sigh. "It would be nice if I had some help."

She didn't respond right away. "Where is your mom?"

"She's here. Where are you?"

"I'm at home."

Usually, I would've gotten an attitude with Felise, but I didn't have the energy, so I said, "Felise, this is so hard. I can't do this. I need you here. Where are you?" I cried. I knew I sounded like a blubbering fool.

"I, ah . . ."

"Please, Felise. I know this is hard on you, too. But you're the only one who knows what I'm going through. His mom doesn't know about the fight, and I . . . I just need you."

She held back for a moment, then said, "Okay, okay. I'm on my way."

"Thanks, Felise. See you in a bit." I wiped away my tears, a sense of relief filling me because my best friend was on the way.

My mother stood there, a chastising look across her face. "What kind of friend do you have to beg to be there for you in your time of need?"

"I'm not begging her, Mama." I waved my mom off. I wasn't in the mood for her either. "Just please, go check on the kids, or make sure the guest room is ready for Lois, something."

My mom threw her hands up. "Fine," she said, stalking off. "But I'm gonna give Ms. Felise a piece of my mind."

I hadn't written more than a sentence in the obituary when my doorbell rang. I don't even know who let her in, but I looked up to see Felise standing awkwardly in the doorway to the kitchen. At the sight of my best friend, I jumped from my seat and raced over to her. I couldn't help but fall into her arms.

"Shhh, come on, sweetie. It's going to be okay," she said, stroking my hair.

"It's never going to be okay again," I cried, clutching her tightly. She let me cry for a few moments, until finally I pulled back and said, "How am I going to make it without him? I haven't worked in years. Shoot, I don't even know how much money we have in the bank!"

"I'm sure Steven had insurance money. You guys will be taken care of," Felise said soothingly.

For the first time, I realized I didn't care about the money. I just wanted my husband.

"I know." I sniffed. I sat back down at the table and pointed to the mostly blank piece of paper in my hand. "Trying to do this obituary is killing me. I just can't believe he's gone. And the way he died, it's just not adding up."

She blinked, like she was spooked. "What are they saying?"

"They still think it was his heart. They're doing an autopsy now." The police officer handling Steven's case was getting tired of me. I called that man four to five times a day. And every time I got the same answer: nothing.

"There was no investigation because police said, as of now, it appears to be natural causes," I added.

My mom shook her head as she walked over. I didn't fail to notice that she didn't bother speaking to Felise.

"Ain't nothing natural about a man dying so young." She squeezed my hand. "But you be strong. I know you may not believe me, but you will make it through this."

I heard what she was saying. I just couldn't, for the life of me, see how I'd ever be able to do it.

19

Felise

I GROANED AT THE SIGHT OF MY SISTER, MAVIS.

"What? Don't give me that look," she said, pushing past me and into Fran's living room. I knew that she wouldn't be able to keep her nose out of my business. After all, Mavis made her living minding other people's business.

"Have you come to your senses and confessed yet?" She glared at me through judgmental eyes as she plopped down in the recliner.

Fran took my arm and pulled me inside since I was still standing there with the door wide open.

"Mavis, don't come over here starting nothing," she said. "If I had known you were going to be doing all of this, I wouldn't have even invited you."

I glared at Fran. "Why *did* you invite her?"

"Because Mama's gone and I have to be the voice of reason," Mavis said, cutting her eyes at Fran. "Because obviously your little sister is not."

"Whatever. Don't try to make me feel guilty."

"You *are* guilty," Mavis said. "And you are going to end up in the pen right along with Felise."

"I'm too cute for the pen," Fran said, striking a pose. "The guards *and* the prisoners would be fighting over me—men and women. Unh-unh, I can't be doing all that. Shoot, I can't even visit the pen, which is why we need to make sure Miss Guilty Conscience sticks to the plan."

Mavis crossed her legs like she was getting comfortable, which wasn't a good sign. I'd come over here to get my head together. If Mavis was here, that meant I was in for a long lecture.

"So for real, Felise. What are you going to do?" she asked.

"She's going to do exactly what she's been doing," Fran said, snuggling back into her seat on the sofa. "Play it cool."

"How can you live with yourself?" Mavis asked. "I know the guilt has to be eating you alive. I mean for God's sake, you're the godmother of her child."

"Thanks for reminding me, Mavis," I mumbled. "I can always count on you to make me feel better."

"You know how I do," Mavis replied. "I am going to make you feel better. But I'm going to make you feel worse first. Maybe that will keep you from making this mistake again."

That elicited a painful laugh. "Trust me, I won't be sneaking up to my best friend's husband's hotel room ever again. I won't be sneaking to any man's room, not after last time," I said.

Fran frowned and pointed a narrow finger at Mavis. "Don't start beating her up! She beats herself up enough. Now, here you come. That's why don't nobody like having your judgmental self around! Every time you open your mouth, you always want to talk about somebody else."

"Don't get mad at me because the two of you act like you don't have any common sense!" Mavis snapped right back.

I couldn't take it anymore. I let out a groan. "Ugh! Would you two shut up already?" I looked at Mavis. "Of course the guilt is eating me alive. I feel awful. I never planned for this to happen. I can't imagine how Paula would feel if she ever found out."

Mavis raised an eyebrow. "If? No, honey, that's *when* she finds out, because I'm sorry, but she *will* find out."

"Not if Felise plays her cards right," Fran said.

"I'm sorry, Ms. *CSI*. You watch a couple of episodes and think you know the perfect way to cover up a murder."

"First of all, it's not a murder. Secondly, yes, I *do* watch *CSI*, which is why I know—"

Mavis cut her off. "Why you should know that the criminal *always* gets caught."

"I'm not a criminal," I muttered. Mavis looked at me, her eyebrow raised again.

"She's not," Fran reiterated.

"Honey, I know you're not a criminal," Mavis said, reaching out to cover my hand. "But this whole cover-up *is* criminal, and even if leaving him there wasn't criminally wrong, it was morally wrong. Being there with him was morally wrong!"

"Okay, and so what do you want her to do about it now?" Fran said. "Seriously, she made a mistake. In your perfect world, she should just go tell her husband, tell Paula, tell the police. Then they'll all pray on it, forgive her, and let her go on her merry little way, right?" Fran tsked in disgust as she fell back on the sofa. "You and that fantasyland you live in drive me crazy."

Mavis ignored her and continued talking to me. "Fefe," she said, calling me by the nickname my mom used to call me whenever I was in trouble, "I know that you didn't mean for this to come out the way it did. I just am worried because I don't want this to blow up in your face. And my gut is telling me that's exactly what's going to happen."

"What do you suggest I do?" I said. Her words were really starting to get to me.

"A web of lies eventually gets tangled," she replied. "As difficult as it is, come clean."

Fran jumped up like she could tell Mavis was getting through to me and she needed to nip this in the bud right away. "And say what? 'Hey, Paula, I know I helped you through the funeral and let you cry on my shoulder and everything, but I was with your husband the night he died. We were getting it on, and it must've sent his heart into overdrive, but if it makes you feel better, he died feeling good.' Really, Mavis? Is that what she should do?"

Mavis sighed like that sounded ridiculous even to her.

"I just know right is right," Mavis muttered.

"All I'm saying," Fran continued, turning her attention to me, "is you have to pull it together and *keep* it together. That's all you have to do."

"And what's going to happen when the guilt keeps eating at her?" Mavis pointed my way. "Because I can see that it already has."

At that moment, I caught my reflection in Fran's ceiling-to-floor mirror. I looked a hot mess. I had on a pair of tattered leggings and a long, dingy T-shirt with a hole in the front that I hadn't noticed until I was in my car and on my way over here. My hair actually looked like it hadn't been combed in a couple of days. I had no makeup on. My lips felt dry and crusty, and my eyes were swollen because I'd cried the whole way over here.

"That's what she's going to work on," Fran said. She ran her eyes up and down my body. "And she will never, ever, ever wear that outfit again, looking like she's going to work on a Habitat for Humanity project."

I hated that they were talking about me as if I wasn't there, but they both were right. I needed to keep it together, and I needed to come clean. But I knew if I came clean, I would lose everything. Greg would not forgive me. Shoot, his mother had pawned him off on a relative when he was eleven, returned two years later, and spent the next twenty-five years trying to get him to forgive her. To this day, Greg refused to have anything to do with his mother. And Paula, if she didn't try to kill me, she'd never forgive me either. Then I thought about Tahiry and how much I loved her and how close she and Liz were. My betrayal would kill them both.

No, I decided, there was no way I was coming clean. I needed to learn to get over what I'd done. I'd asked God for forgiveness, and I meant it from the bottom of my heart, so I hoped that He forgave me. Now I just needed to figure out how to forgive myself and pray that it was enough to help me move on.

20

Paula

THANK GOD FOR FELISE. THAT'S ALL I COULD THINK AS I watched her straighten Mason's little tie. I don't know how I would've made it these last few days if Felise hadn't taken part of the load. At first, I was a little worried. She didn't show up until I called, begging her to come, but since then she hadn't left my side. I was glad that she was devoting more of her time to my children, especially Tahiry, than to me because I didn't have the strength to comfort them right then. After I put my husband in the ground today, I was going to have to pull it together for my children. But first I had to get through the funeral.

"So, are you ready?" Felise asked. She looked more like the widow than I did. We both had on simple black dresses, but Felise wore a small pillbox hat with a netted veil hanging over her face. Any other time I would've talked about that hat, but today—on the worst day of my life—her attire was the least of my concerns.

"Hold on before we go," I said, taking her hand. "I just

want to tell you how much it means to me that you're here."

Her eyes filled with tears. "Where else would I be?"

"I'm lucky to have a friend like you. I know my mom is trying to be strong, but she's more emotional than I am. So is Steven's mom. I don't know how I would get through this without you."

She shifted, like I was making her uncomfortable, then said, "Come on, let's go."

I draped my arm through hers as my children, my best friend, and I headed to bury my husband.

"BEAUTIFUL SERVICE, PAULA. STEVEN WAS A GOOD MAN."

I smiled as Steven's boss looked at me through sorrow-filled eyes. We had come back at my house for the repast, along with just about everyone from the service. People were wall to wall.

"Just know that if you or the kids need anything, I'm here."

I patted his hand, which covered mine. "Thank you, Mr. Chimere. My friend Felise will be staying with me a few days. She'll make sure I'm taken care of."

Felise's eyes bucked. I knew I hadn't talked to her about that, but I knew it wouldn't be a problem.

"It's so wonderful to have great friends," Mr. Chimere said to her.

"Thank you," Felise said, her voice soft.

I greeted more people until I simply couldn't take it anymore. "I gotta get out of here. I'm going to lie down. Come with me for a minute," I said, taking Felise's hand and pulling her down the hallway. As soon as the door to my bedroom closed, I collapsed. "I don't know what I'm going to do," I cried. "How am I supposed to make it through all the days to come?"

"You're a strong woman. You're going to pull it together and keep moving," Felise said matter-of-factly.

Her eyes looked wracked with pain, reminding me once again that I wasn't the only one grieving.

I sat up on the bed. "I'm sorry. You were close to Steven, and I know you're hurting, too."

She forced a smile. "This isn't about me. This is about you and the kids. So you have to be strong for them."

"I know. It's just the guilt is killing me. My last words to him. I didn't want a divorce."

"Shhh," she said. "Now's not the time. Tell you what, why don't you lie down? I will take care of everything out there. You just rest, okay?"

I nodded. Flopping down on the bed did feel like the best thing in the world right then. "Where's my mom and Charlene?"

"Your mom is already lying down, and Charlene is keeping the boys entertained. Tahiry and Liz are in her room."

I hoped my mom was fine. She'd actually passed out at the service, but I didn't have the stamina to deal with anyone else right then, so I was grateful for Felise for taking on that task.

Felise headed toward the door. I stopped her just before she opened it. "Felise?"

"Yeah?" she said, turning toward me.

"I love you."

She hesitated, and a slow tear escaped from her eyes. "I love you, too, Paula. I really do."

I smiled and crawled under my covers, confident that my friend would make sure everything was handled.

21

Felise

"ARE YOU OKAY?" GREG SAID, APPROACHING ME. I NODded as I slowly massaged the back of my neck.

"Yeah, I'm fine," I replied. "It's just been a stressful day." I know Paula hadn't wanted so many people back at her house, and I surely didn't either. We both wanted people to pay their respects and leave us to our grief. But Steven's mom was a true Southern matriarch, and according to her, "Steven wouldn't be able to rest in peace unless he got a proper sendoff, and that includes a repast."

"I just got Paula to lie down for a while," I said. "This is really hard on her."

He pulled my chin up and looked me in the eye. "It is hard on you, too. You don't look good."

I snatched myself away from his grasp. I didn't need him making me perfect today. "How am I supposed to look?"

He drew back in shock, and I sighed. I had to stop snapping at him.

"I'm sorry," I said. "I'm just . . ."

He put a finger to my lips. "It's okay, honey. No apology needed." I was grateful for the reprieve and changed the subject as soon as I could.

"Those were nice words you spoke at the service today," I said. Putting Steven in the ground had to have been one of the most painful things I'd ever done in my life.

"I am surprised you didn't want to say anything."

"Nah, I think you represented well," I replied.

Greg continued to study me. I must not have been making the right responses. "Do you need anything?" he asked. "I'm worried about you."

The last thing I needed was him reading anything extra into my grief. "I'm fine," I said, "really I am. But I could use some water."

I wasn't really thirsty. I just wanted Greg to leave me alone.

"Okay, one water coming right up," he said, squeezing my hand before heading into the kitchen.

I watched my husband walk away so purposefully, and I wondered how we would ever fix us. Amidst my mourning I had come to realize a truth that should have been apparent to me long ago. I had put up with so much for so long because honestly, I think I lived vicariously through Paula and Steven. Even if I couldn't be with him, I wanted to be a better wife because of him. How could I continue to do that with Steven gone?

"Very nice ceremony."

I turned toward the voice coming from behind me.

"Oh, hey, Sabrina," I said, leaning in to give her a hug.

Sabrina Fulton was my roommate from freshman year of college. We'd fallen out right before school ended, and then she didn't come back sophomore year. I'd seen her several times over the years, and we were both cordial to each other.

I was just glad that we'd put our petty spats behind us. "I didn't know you knew Steven."

She leaned back against the wall and shrugged. "I didn't. But remember, Paula used to hang out with us when she was visiting you in college."

I tried not to frown in confusion. I didn't know they still talked.

"It's so beautiful how you're there for Paula," Sabrina said.

"Thank you," I replied. "Just trying to be there for my best friend."

"Yep," Sabrina said, taking a sip of her drink. "Good ol' Felise. Always the good girl of the group. The one everyone wanted to be like, who could do no wrong."

Her tone made me uncomfortable. "Ah, are you going somewhere with this?"

"Nah, I just want to compliment you." She flashed a tight smile. "I love to see women sticking together."

"Oh, okay." I didn't really care for Sabrina anymore, so I said, "Well, if you'll excuse me, I need to go check on the kids."

"Yeah, that's right. You're godmother to the oldest."

I smiled and nodded. "Yes, Tahiry."

"Well, you go take care of them and I'll talk to you later." She turned to walk off, then stopped. "Oh, yeah," she said, turning around. "Zen told me you were at the bar the other night."

The mention of a bar put me on my guard. "Who's Zen?"

"The bartender," she said, looking me directly in the eye. "You know, at my job, at the Four Seasons. I introduced you to him the last time you and some of your sorority sisters were there for happy hour a few months ago."

My mind started churning as I recalled that day. We'd already been at the bar an hour when Sabrina started her shift. She'd made personal introductions, and Zen hooked us up with drinks the rest of the night.

I couldn't believe I'd forgotten that. That's why Zen had greeted me like he knew me when I first sat down at the bar. I thought he was just being friendly to get a bigger tip. Maybe if I had remembered meeting him before—shoot, if I'd remembered that Sabrina worked there—that would've kept me from going to Steven's room.

Sabrina continued, "He told me that you were upset and getting pretty toasted, but luckily," she added slowly, "you had someone to help you get over whatever was bothering you."

I couldn't move as she kept talking. "I hate I missed you, though," she said. "Hate I was off that night, period. I heard there was quite a bit of action that night. There was a fight in the bar, and then of course the stuff with Steven."

I was still frozen as Greg walked up. "Here, hon."

Sabrina broke out in a huge smile. "You go on and see about those kids now." She set her glass down and turned to Greg. "Hi, I'm Sabrina Fulton. You must be Felise's wonderful husband."

Greg smiled and shook her hand. "Greg Mavins, nice to meet you. Are you a friend of Paula's?"

"Kinda sorta, by way of Felise here," she replied. "Felise and I used to be roommates our freshman year, and we all would hang out whenever Paula came to town. I hadn't seen her in a while, but I work at the Four Seasons, so I'm trying to help Paula figure out what happened to her husband."

I sucked in air and tried to keep from passing out. Greg didn't seem to notice, but Sabrina smirked.

"Such a shame," Greg replied. "They say it was his heart, so I don't know what else there is to find out, but I know Paula is just looking for some peace."

"Yep," Sabrina said, "and I'm hoping I can help her find it." She turned her malicious smile on me. "Well, I must get going. Give my condolences to your BFF." She actually reached out and hugged me, and it took everything in my power to hug her back.

As she backed away, I had to lean against Greg to keep from losing my balance. Sabrina was a hood girl who had landed at UT on a track scholarship, and I knew all about her survival instincts. Her street ways would mean major trouble for me, if she knew anything about that night.

She doesn't know anything, I told myself.

"Greg, it was nice to meet you." She took out her iPhone. "Felise, give me your number so we can . . . catch up."

"Uh . . ." I began.

"Oh, I know today isn't a good day. I can call Paula later and get it from her if you prefer."

I quickly took her phone. "No, I'll put it in."

She stood there with a stupid grin on her face as I programmed my number in her phone.

"Cool," she said, taking the phone when I was done. "I'll be in touch."

She flashed one last smile before she took off. As she walked away, Greg put his arm around me and said, "I sure hope she can help Paula get some closure."

I hugged him tighter, but only because I realized what Sabrina wanted. She knew. The question now was exactly what she planned on doing with that knowledge.

22

Paula

MARTIN LAWRENCE DANCED ACROSS MY TELEVISION screen. He was in rare form playing his neighbor Sheneneh Jenkins. That used to make both me and Steven crack up laughing. But now I stared blankly at the television. Even if I did find it funny, was I supposed to laugh? Was I supposed to laugh ever again? How could I watch our favorite shows? How could I find joy in the little things we used to do together? How could I do any of that ever again?

My door eased open and Tahiry peeked her head in. "Mom, Grandma Lois said she's about to head out. She needs to get to the airport."

I knew that I'd been a horrible host to my mother-in-law, but hopefully, she understood. Steven's father had passed several years ago, so she knew the pain of what I was going through.

Lois peeked her head in. "You don't have to get up."

I was already on the edge of the bed. "No, I need to see you out."

Lois walked in the room, and the look on her face told me it pained her to enter her son's bedroom.

"Are you sure you're going to be okay?" Lois asked.

"I'll be fine," I replied.

Concern blanketed her face. "I'm really worried about you."

I managed a smile, even though I was so unhappy. "My mom is here. Seriously, I'll be okay."

"I feel like I need to move back here. We still have the house on Danforth." Lois had moved to Florida after her husband died, and I knew how much she loved living there.

"No. I'm fine. You don't need to be worried about me or the kids," I told her.

She nodded in acceptance. "Okay. I hope I'll still be able to see the kids."

I squeezed her hand. "You know I would never keep you away from your kids. You're their link to their father."

She seemed relieved. She had always been cordial to me, but we'd never had the relationship I'd envisioned having with my in-laws. I think part of the reason was because she was disappointed in my getting pregnant before we were married. But thankfully, she'd never treated me with ill will. And regardless of how she initially felt, she loved her grandchildren and had always played a vital role in their lives.

"Well, I'm going to keep you in my prayers. I know your mom is here, but you let me know if you need anything," she replied.

I stood up and hugged her. "I will, and I'll let you know if I hear anything else about Steven's death."

That caused her to stop in her tracks. "What else would you hear?"

It suddenly dawned on me that I hadn't shared my concerns with her. "I meant when I get the autopsy results."

"Autopsy? But he died of heart failure. Why are you doing an autopsy? You think it's something else?"

"No, I just want to be sure, that's all."

That seemed to pacify her, and she squeezed my hand one last time. "You let me know if you need anything."

I waved good-bye and returned to my bed. I tossed and turned, but was unable to go back to sleep.

Five endless days had passed since we put Steven in the ground. They say the pain is supposed to get easier, but it hadn't. I didn't know how I was going to find the strength to move on. Having a job might have helped. I needed something to take me away from sitting around here, wallowing in self-pity.

I finally gave up my quest for sleep and picked up the phone to call Felise. Maybe we could go have lunch. Her phone bounced to voice mail. I hadn't seen her since the funeral, which was pretty frustrating. I know that she was grieving, too. I know that she was hurt by losing Steven. But we would heal better if we grieved together.

I hung up and made my way downstairs. The kids were in the kitchen, sitting quietly at the table.

"Hey," they muttered in unison.

Every one of them looked sad.

"Do you guys want me to fix you something to eat?

"Grandma Lois cooked for us before she left," Tahiry said.

"Tahiry's food tastes nasty," Mason said.

"Forget you," Tahiry replied.

"Where's Charlene?" I asked.

"I don't know. She went out."

I sighed. "Where's Mama?"

"In her room, same place you were, in the bed," Tahiry said. It seemed like she had an attitude.

"I'm sorry, guys. This is just hard."

"We know," Tahiry said.

I rubbed Marcus's hair. "Just bear with me, okay? It's not going to be like this forever."

"I miss Daddy," Mason said.

Unexpectedly, in the middle of playing his handheld video game, Stevie let out a huge sob and laid his head down on the table. He had been so strong. He'd cried silent tears at the funeral and, at one point, tried to comfort me by telling me he would now be the man of the house. I realized at that point I wasn't the only one grieving. And if nothing else, I needed to find the strength to help my kids get through this as well.

23

Felise

I KNEW THAT PAULA NEEDED ME. SO I HAD TO PULL myself together so that I could be there for her. Fran was right. It would start to look suspicious if she kept turning to me and I shunned her.

"Mom, can I—?"

"What?" I snapped. "Why aren't you in the bed?"

My daughter flinched. "I just wanted to ask you something. Never mind."

I took a deep breath. "I'm sorry."

My precious daughter stared at me through innocent eyes. Even though she was thirteen, she wasn't like a lot of her friends—she was mature for her age. With her long, naturally curly hair, underdeveloped chest, and long, athletic legs, she hadn't come into her looks yet, and that was fine with me.

"I was just asking if I could go over to Tahiry's house in the morning," Liz said.

"No," I replied. In the week since the funeral I hadn't

been back over there. Liz had been over there every day. But between trying to figure out Sabrina's sarcastic comments and stewing in my own guilt and grief, I hadn't been able to make the trip myself. "There's a lot going on right now."

"But Mom . . ."

"What did I say?" I snapped. "When I say no, I mean no!"

She took a step back as Greg eased into the room.

"Liz, sweetie, go on to bed. We'll talk about it tomorrow," Greg said.

"What is there to talk about? I already said no."

He waited for Liz to disappear down the hall, then closed our bedroom door. "I understand that Steven's death is weighing heavily on you. But taking it out on your child is not the answer."

I rolled my eyes. With his work schedule, he was hardly the one to lecture me about our daughter. "I'm not taking anything out on anyone."

"Yeah, you are." Greg sat down on the edge of the bed. "I know you're upset, but you are taking it out on us and that's not fair. We all are sad about what happened."

I couldn't disagree with him about that. "I'm sorry," I said. "I'm not trying to be difficult."

"It's understandable. You're going through a lot." He scooched closer on the bed and began massaging the back of my neck. His touch felt like an invasion, and I flinched, then ducked away from his touch.

He held his hands up. "Sorry."

I let out a long sigh. "No, I'm sorry."

"I understand, baby. You got a lot going on." I sensed the edge in his voice. He had thought he'd won out over Steven, but now he could see how deeply I was affected. His phone rang, and he reached into his pocket to cut it off. "I was just saying, I know you are going through a lot right now, but I want us to be able to pick up the pieces and move on."

That sounded less like comfort and more like a threat. Or maybe I was imagining things.

The phone rang again. This time Greg glanced at the display and said, "I'm sorry, babe. Gimme a second. Hello," he answered.

I narrowed my eyes at the sound of the woman's voice.

"Hello . . . Um, yeah, I'm in the middle of something. Okay. Will do. I'll call you back."

It took everything in my power not to go off as he hung up the phone.

"Who was that?"

"What?"

"I didn't stutter."

"That was Donna from work." He had the nerve to look appalled that I was questioning him.

"Who is Donna?" I snapped.

"*Really?*" he said. "You know me better than that, Felise."

"I know I'm not going to let you make a fool out of me," I said, snatching the phone from him. I glanced down and saw several text messages on his screen. *Need u now*, I read. I looked up at him in shock. " 'Need u now'? Who the hell is Donna, and why is she talking about needing you now? Tell your hos not to call you in the middle of the night!"

He stared at me in disbelief. "Wow. My *hos*? Donna is my supervisor."

"You must think I'm stupid. I know your boss, and *she* is a *he*." I was so not in the mood for Greg trying to play me. He'd had a brief affair nine years ago, and I'd found out this exact same way—from him ignoring her phone calls. Granted, Greg and I had gone to counseling and worked through that, but I wasn't about to travel down that road again. I pushed Donna's name on the phone and put the phone to my ear.

"May I speak to Donna?" I snapped as soon as the woman answered. I half expected Greg to snatch the phone away.

"This is she," the woman said.

"Yes, Donna, this is Felise Mavins, Greg Mavins's wife. I'm trying to understand why you're texting and calling my husband at almost one in the morning. News flash, he's married."

Silence filled the phone before the woman said, "Umm, I know that."

"And I guess you just don't care."

"Umm, wow, okay. This is Donna Langley—I'm one of the new partners. I don't think we've had the pleasure of meeting as I just transferred in two weeks ago. I wasn't trying to cause any problems, but my computer crashed and I lost a report Greg did and we need it for a presentation in the morning. That's all."

I swear, if I could've made myself disappear in a tiny hole in the earth, I would have.

"Ah, ah, I . . ."

Greg snatched the phone away. "Donna, I can't apologize to you enough for my wife. As you can imagine, she's very upset about her friend's husband, and that's the only reason I can imagine that she would do something like this. So please accept our sincerest apology for disturbing you." He let her respond, and I could only imagine what she was saying. "I'm sorry, I was just trying to be by my wife's side, I was going to call you back . . . Yes, ma'am. I will email you over another copy of the report right away."

Greg hung up the phone and glared at me. "I know that you're going through a very difficult time, and for that reason, and that reason only, I'm going to give you a pass. But don't ever, ever do some anything like that again."

"But I mean Miranda . . ."

"Miranda was almost ten years ago. We went to counseling. You said you forgave me. And I have never given you reason since then to believe that I am unfaithful." He was steaming, and now he had another reason to be upset. "You know I don't do that ghetto foolishness of calling and confronting someone." He stood, then walked toward the door. "It's obvious you need some 'me' time, so I'm going to sleep in the guest room. Hopefully, when you wake up tomorrow, you'll be in a better place because this is absolutely unacceptable."

Greg walked sternly out the room. *Well*, I told myself, feeling helpless, *at least I got him to go away.*

24

Paula

I WANTED TO SCREAM AT THE SOUND OF SOMEONE TAPping on my bedroom door. I wanted everyone to leave me alone. I didn't want to come out from under these covers. I knew my mother was as much of a basket case as I, so I knew she wouldn't be much help. But hopefully, my sister was holding it down. I couldn't deal with her over-the-top behind either, but at least she was handling my children. I'd tried to spend the day with them yesterday after I saw how they were grieving, too, and although I'd made it through the day, today I had retreated back to my safe place: under my covers.

"Hey, Paula, someone's here to see you," Charlene said, easing my door open, despite the fact that I hadn't bothered to answer.

"Ugggh," I groaned. I didn't feel like visitors. Why did people always feel the need to come visiting you when you'd lost a loved one? Didn't they say everything they needed to at the funeral?

"Who is it?" I moaned.

"You need to get up and come see," she replied. "They have on plain clothes, but I can smell a cop a mile away."

I sat up in bed. "Cops?"

"Yeah, I think they're detectives or something."

"What do they want?"

"I don't know. You?"

"Maybe they have some news about Steven." I threw my covers back and stood up. I knew I looked a hot mess, so I ran my fingers through my hair. I threw my robe over my pajamas and made my way downstairs.

"Where's Mama?" I asked.

"Same place you were, in the bed."

My heart was racing as I spotted the two men standing in the living room. I hoped that they had some information, that my husband had been the victim of a brutal robbery gone wrong, something other than that he had died from a heart condition. A condition I knew about when I told him I wanted a divorce.

"May I help you?" I asked.

"Hi, Mrs. Wright, I'm Detective Clark Aimes. We wanted to let you know that we have concluded our investigation." He handed me a sealed envelope. "Since the autopsy confirms that your husband did die of heart failure, we're closing the case. All the details are in that letter."

The other detective handed me a box. "We also wanted to drop off his belongings. A few things that were in the hotel room."

When I didn't make any attempt to move, Charlene stepped forward and took the box. "I don't understand. Why are you closing the case?" I asked.

"There's nothing else to look into. Everything appears to be in order."

"In order? How could a thirty-six-year-old man dying be in order?"

"I'm sorry." He squeezed my hand, and then both of them headed out the door.

I sat heavily on the sofa, the box set on the table in front of me. My sister was standing by, looking uneasy, while I set the official report down, then pulled the box toward me. I pulled out my husband's wallet and fingered it while I tried to keep a tear from escaping. I could not believe this. It was over.

"Umm, Paula, I know that you're dealing with a lot, but . . ."

"But what, Charlene?" I wasn't in the mood for my flighty sister. I just wanted to sit here and go through my husband's belongings.

"I don't know how to say this," Charlene said, fidgeting with her hands.

"Say what?" I asked, not trying to hide my irritation.

"Okay," Charlene shifted from side to side, "but you're going to be really mad."

"Mad about what, Charlene? Just tell me. I don't have time for games."

She was biting her bottom lip, which was not a good sign. "Tahiry isn't here."

A prickle of alarm made me sit up straighter. "What do you mean, she's not here? Where is she?"

My sister ran her fingers through her hair but didn't answer as her eyes darted about, like she was looking for a way to escape.

"Where is Tahiry?" I demanded.

"I–I don't know," my sister stammered. "I let her go to this party last night, and, ah, she didn't come home."

I stood up abruptly, nearly knocking over the box. "What do you mean, she didn't come home? What party did she go to? She's fourteen! She doesn't go to parties!"

"How am I supposed to know that?" my sister cried. "You were so out of it, the boys were driving me crazy, and Mama was a basket case." She started talking real fast. "Tahiry was stressing out and wanted to go to that party, and . . . and I thought it would make her feel better."

"Oh, my God, where is my daughter?" I yelled.

"I don't know. I tried calling her cell phone, but it's going straight to voice mail." My sister looked more frazzled than I was. "I can't handle this. I don't do kids. Where is Felise? She needs to be here helping with this stuff."

"I don't know. I don't know. I just need to know where my child is," I cried, shaking my sister. "Call Felise—see if she knows where Tahiry is. Just find my daughter, do you hear me?"

I fell back on my sofa. "I just can't take any more." I continued crying as I buried my head in my hands.

25

Felise

I WAS STANDING IN THE MIDDLE OF THE KITCHEN, getting ready to go, as my husband entered. He gave me a strange look. I hoped that he wasn't going to grill me about that Donna fiasco. I'd overacted. Big deal. I wasn't about to get into another argument about it.

"What?" I finally said as I stuffed a bottle of Aleve into my purse.

Greg pointed to my scrubs. "So, you're going to work?"

"Where else would I be going?" I looked around for my bottled water. I'd been off for a week and a half, and I needed to show up before I lost my job. Besides, I'd made up my mind last night that I wasn't going to wallow in sorrow anymore. Maybe going back to the busy ER would keep my mind off my loss.

"Where else would you be going?" Greg asked. "I don't know, maybe to see about your friend? She called me yesterday, concerned because she hadn't talked to you."

"Why is she calling you?" I rolled my eyes in disgust.

"Fine, I'll call her on my way to work. Does that make you feel better?"

He held up his hands in defense. "Sorry, I just . . . I don't know, I mean Liz has been going over there every day, and it seems like you'd be trying to go over there, too."

I tossed my purse over my shoulder, not bothering to hide my agitation. "So now you're planning my schedule, too? Isn't your own schedule full enough?"

"Okay, okay. Don't bite my head off," he said. "I was just asking."

I huffed as I snatched my keys off the counter. I felt like I was slowly falling into a horrible abyss and I needed to escape.

"I have to go to work."

"Fine," Greg said, shaking his head as he turned to walk away.

"I don't understand what everybody wants from me," I mumbled.

He stopped, spun back around. "I don't want a thing, okay? I just asked." He was agitated now, too. That was how he worked. Whenever he felt on the defensive, he got mad about it.

I left without saying another word. I had just pulled out of my garage when my cell phone rang. Paula's home line popped up. I found myself wishing she had other friends.

"Hello," I said, answering only because I didn't need her calling Greg and creating more drama.

"Hey, um, yes, Felise, this is Charlene, Paula's sister. Um, is Tahiry at your house?"

I frowned. "No. Liz wants to come over to your house."

She sighed like that was not the answer she was hoping

to hear. "Well, Tahiry didn't come home, and we don't know where she is."

"What do you mean, she didn't come home?"

Charlene rushed the words out. "She went to a party last night, and oh, my God, I can't do this! I don't handle kids!"

I quickly pulled over to the side of the road so I could give her my full attention. "Okay, just calm down. What's going on?"

"I let her go to a party last night."

"Tahiry? To a party? Where?"

"I don't know. Look, she was upset, and I thought it would help her feel better."

I couldn't believe Charlene. She always had been ditzy. Who lets a fourteen year old go to a night party and doesn't get details?

"Let me call my daughter. Maybe she knows something. I'll call you right back." I hung up the phone and called Liz.

"Hey, honey," I said when she picked up.

"Hey, Mom." Her voice was cold, and that made me sad. Liz wasn't like most young teenagers. She really was a good kid, and I know she was trying to understand why I'd been snapping at her so much lately. After I managed to lift myself out of my misery, I was going to have to do something nice to make up for how I'd been acting.

"Have you talked to Tahiry?" I asked.

"No, why?"

"She didn't come home last night." Liz didn't offer a helpful response. "Do you know where she is?" I continued. When she still didn't say anything, I said, "Liz. I need you to tell me where she is."

"Mom, she's just upset."

"Elizabeth, where is she?"

"She spent the night over Kayla's house," she finally admitted. "That's why I wanted to go over there this morning. She really needed me to be there for her."

I groaned. Kayla was a fast-tail girl that neither Paula nor I liked our daughters hanging around.

"What is she doing with— You know what, never mind. Call her and tell her I'm on my way over to get her right now."

I didn't think as I made a U-turn in the middle of the street. I called Charlene back to tell her I was going to get Tahiry and would be to their house in a half hour.

Less than ten minutes later, I was knocking on the door to the home Kayla shared with her six siblings and her grandmother.

The older woman, complete with pink hair rollers and a bent cigarette dangling from her mouth, answered the door.

"Who you is?"

I fought the urge to correct her English. "I'm looking for Tahiry. I'm her godmother."

The woman looked me up and down as if she was trying to gauge whether I was telling the truth. As if some random woman would show up claiming a teenage girl. I wanted to berate this old woman for letting Tahiry stay here in the first place, but I held my tongue until she let me in.

"She back in the back." The woman stepped aside.

Once I was in the tiny, dirty living room, I couldn't help complaining. "You didn't think to call her mom?"

The woman's hands went to her hips. "Look, I got a hard enough time keeping up with that hot granddaughter of mine and her little crumb-snatcher brothers. I'm watching

Wheel of Fortune and *Family Feud*, and I ain't got no time to be asking her who she bringing in and out her room!"

I decided it would be useless to have a conversation with this woman. *Just get Tahiry and get out of here.*

She turned toward the TV show and screamed, "Drinks and food! How you not gon' say drinks and food? Chimney?" she shouted. "Now, that's the dumbest question ever!" She turned to me. "The question was, name something that's on the house. A chimney, really? Look! Even Steve thinks it's crazy! Look at him rolling his eyes!" she said, pointing at the TV. Then she had the nerve to lick her lips. "Mmm, mmm, mmm, I tell you, if I was a few years younger, back in my heyday I woulda had that man. But now I'm waiting on them to invent some Viagra for women before I get back on the dating scene." She cackled.

"Tahiry, please?"

She rolled her eyes, annoyed that I didn't find her humor entertaining.

"Kayla!" she screamed. "Someone is here for your friend."

After a teenage minute, Kayla finally walked in, Tahiry lagging behind her. Kayla was wearing a pair of Daisy Duke shorts and a fishnet tank top with her bra showing. She looked like a cheap hooker, especially the way she was smacking on her gum. I couldn't for the life of me understand why Tahiry or my daughter hung around this girl.

"Tahiry, your mother's worried sick," I said.

"She ain't worried about nobody but herself," Tahiry said, her eyes betraying her sadness.

I took a deep breath. "Tahiry, this is hard on everyone."

"You think it's not hard on me?" Tahiry cried, like she was bursting out of a shell. "My daddy's gone! And I can't talk to my momma or my granny! I'm just supposed to deal with this by myself!"

I took her into my arms and hugged her. "I am so sorry, honey. But you know you can always come to me."

She sobbed as she clutched me for dear life. "What am I going to do, Nana?" she said as I stroked her hair. "What am I supposed to do without my daddy?"

"Excuse me?" Kayla's grandmother said. "They 'bout to do the lightning round. Can you take her on home and y'all finish that conversation in the car?"

Kayla actually laughed.

I took Tahiry's hand. "Gladly," I said, leading her to the door.

"Bye, Kayla," Tahiry said, sniffing as she followed behind me.

"I'll call you, girl," Kayla said as she blew a big bubble.

When Tahiry and I were settled in the car, I said, "What are you doin', honey? Don't ever do that again. You had us all worried to death."

"Liz told you where I was?" she said.

"Yeah," I said gently, "and the fact that you told her must have meant that you wanted me to know."

She looked away, and I knew that had been the case.

"Why did my daddy have to die?" Her tears had subsided to a slow trickle.

I didn't know what to say, so I just took her hand and said, "I don't know, but you can rest assured that he's in Heaven right now looking down on you." I touched her chest. "And he's going to live on right there in your heart forever."

"It's just so . . . I don't know . . . tense around our house. Why can't I come live with you?"

I felt awful. If I thought it would help, I would push aside any feelings I had to let Tahiry stay with me. But I knew Paula needed her daughter, even if she wasn't acting like it. "Tell you what, promise me you'll never run off like that again, and I will talk to your mom about chillin' with us for a little while. Deal?"

"Deal." She sniffed.

She looked out the window as she wiped her tears. We rode in silence until we pulled up into her house.

"Tahiry!" Paula said, swinging the door open and meeting me on the porch.

A part of me wondered if she was going to haul off and smack her daughter upside the head. But she grabbed her tightly, and they both broke out crying.

"Baby, don't do ever do that to me again. I would die if something happened to you, too." While still holding her head tight to her daughter's, she looked up at me. "Thank you, Felise."

"You're welcome. Tahiry is just very upset and trying not to worry you because she knows how hard this is for you."

Paula pulled away from her daughter, wiped her eyes, and kissed her on the cheek.

"I'm so sorry, baby."

"No, Mama, I understand." She reached out to include me in the hug. "Nana made me feel better."

"She always does." Paula smiled and then reached over to enfold me as well. "I don't know what I'd do without you."

I inhaled sharply, grateful that she couldn't see my eyes because I'm sure the guilt would've given me away.

26

Paula

"YOU KNOW THOSE THINGS AREN'T GOOD FOR YOU."

I looked up to see Tahiry standing over me, her arms folded across her chest, her lips poking out.

"So, what, you're the cigarette police now?" I tried to say with a smile as I dropped the cigarette down by my side.

"No, it's just that I've already lost my dad. I don't want to lose my mom to lung cancer."

Wow. That was a low blow, but it was enough to make me squish my cigarette out.

"Okay, babe." I held up my hands in defeat. "I'm done." *At least I'm done smoking around her*, I thought. But my cigarettes were the only thing keeping me calm these days.

"What are you doing?" I asked her. I'd tried to spend the last two days giving Tahiry some extra time. Yesterday, we'd lain in bed together, watching old movies. The together time was good for us both. I'd come out here on the deck to try and steal a moment of "me" time—and a smoke.

"I'm trying to straighten up the living room," she announced.

I raised an eyebrow. "*You* straightening up the living room?"

Tahiry shrugged. "Keeps me busy. But I wanted to see what you wanted me to do with a box."

"What box?" I asked.

"I don't know. It looks like it has a few of Dad's things in it. Why is it in the living room? Are you packing his stuff up already?"

"Of course not," I said, trying to figure out what she was talking about. "Oh, my goodness, that's the box the police brought over," I said, when it dawned on me. "Go get it. Bring it here. I haven't paid it any attention since they brought it here."

"Oh, okay." Walking back inside, she returned with the box and set it at my feet. "What is that stuff?"

"It's just Dad's belongings."

"Oh." She turned like she couldn't bear to see me go through it.

His portfolio was placed on top, so I took it out and shuffled through it. I didn't find anything unusual: some paperwork with Kevin's signature, business cards, a notepad, and his iPad. I set the portfolio to the side and then slowly fingered his suit and his tie, his socks. But I stopped when I saw his underwear. I couldn't think why, but something didn't feel right. And then I figured out what was puzzling me. Why would his underwear be in this box and not on him? My mind started churning as I tried to figure that out. I never asked the police what he was wearing when they found him.

But why would they have removed his underwear before the coroner came? I jogged my memory, and I was right. This box came from the hotel, not the coroner.

I was so engrossed in my thoughts that I didn't hear my sister walk out onto the deck.

"Hey," Charlene said.

I glanced at her, then quickly turned back to the box. "Hey."

"What are you doing?" she said, walking over to peer in the box.

"Just going through some of Steven's stuff," I said. I was annoyed that she was messing up my thought process.

"Ugh, are those his drawers?" she said, eyeing the briefs I was holding in my hand.

"Yeah."

"Yuck. Why are they giving you back his underwear? Did you take him some clean ones to be buried in or something?"

"No," I said, shaking my head. "That's what I'm sitting here trying to figure out. Why is his underwear among his belongings? They only returned what they found in the hotel room."

She shrugged. "I don't know. Maybe they took his underwear off?"

I narrowed my eyes at her. "But why? I mean, he died in his sleep."

"I don't know," she replied. "I guess he wasn't wearing any underwear when he went to sleep."

"That's just it," I said as my puzzlement started to come into focus. "Steven *never* sleeps in the nude," I said. "The *only* time he does . . ." I paused as the words formed on my lips. "The only time he sleeps naked is when he's having sex and he falls asleep."

My sister's mouth fell open. "You don't . . . You don't think . . ."

My mind started churning. I knew my husband well. There was no other explanation as to why he'd be naked when he died. Acting on instinct, I dug in the box until I pulled out his wallet, which I remembered dropping back in when I'd first gotten the box. I sifted through the wallet until I found a receipt. Several Coronas, hot wings, and that's it. The bill was fifty-seven dollars. I tossed that receipt aside and continued going through his stuff. Then I noticed another credit card receipt. This one had two vodka and cranberries and then two apple martinis.

"Hold up," I said.

"What? What?" my sister said, leaning in as she sat down next to me.

"This receipt paid for apple martinis."

"And?"

"What man do you know drinks apple martinis? Certainly not my man."

My sister grabbed her chest. "You're not saying . . . You really think Steven was with somebody else?"

"Of course I don't want to believe it, but that would make sense. That's why he was naked in the bed. That would explain this." I held up his underwear as realization swept over me. "My husband was with another woman when he died." The words hurt just coming out of my mouth.

"Do you think she killed him?"

I took a deep breath as I tried to process what I'd learned.

"I don't know. The autopsy said he died of a heart attack, but maybe someone caused the heart attack."

We sat in silence, shocked by this new revelation, before my sister said, "You know what? I think you're letting your mind get the best of you. Steven was one of the good guys, and I'm sure there's an explanation. I mean, he would buy some woman a drink and never have to see her again. You know, just to be nice. That doesn't mean anything."

I nodded as I took in what she was saying. My heart didn't want to believe that Steven had been in that hotel room with someone else, but everything was pointing to that. Including my gut. Now I had an entirely new problem. I had to find out who that woman was.

27

Felise

THIS WAS THE FIRST TIME THAT I HAD FELT HALFWAY okay about being around Paula. Fran was right. I had to push the guilt aside. I'd never forgive myself for what I'd done, but I needed to help Tahiry and Paula. So when she'd called me this morning, telling me she needed to talk, I didn't ask about what. I told her I'd come over as soon as my shift ended.

"Knock, knock," I said, slowly pushing open the front door.

"We're back here," Paula called out from the den.

I headed down the hall and to the spacious den in back.

"I brought you some—" I stopped when I saw Sabrina sitting there, holding a teacup in her hand.

"Well, hello, Felise. So good to see you," she said with an evil smile.

"Hey, Sabrina," I slowly said. Sabrina had been more my friend than Paula's, so why she was sitting here in Paula's living room was beyond me. Unless . . .

"Hey, Felise." Paula stood up and gave me a hug. "Sabrina surprised me and stopped by. I asked her to look into Steven's death, to ask around the hotel to see if she could find out anything."

I had yet to call her since she gave me her number, so I had no idea what Sabrina was up to, but the way she was watching me, like a predator, was not good. "Paula here was just telling me what a blessing you've been to her and her family," Sabrina remarked.

Paula draped her arm through mine. "Yes, Felise has been a lifesaver."

Sabrina clicked her lips. "Good ol' Felise. Always saving lives," she said with a smirk.

"Soooo, you just dropped by?" I asked. My tone told her she could now pick up and go.

"I did." Sabrina stood and took Paula's hand. "I can't imagine the pain of losing your husband, the man you love from the bottom of your heart. It's almost like—" She turned her wide eyes on me. "It's almost like a betrayal, wouldn't you say so, Felise?"

If I'd had any doubt that her snarky comments the day of the funeral were just a coincidence, they were gone. Sabrina knew. The question was, had she come here to tell Paula?

"It is very difficult," Paula said, sadness overtaking her once again. "I was just telling Sabrina how Steven and I had a fight before he died."

I looked at Paula like she was crazy. Why in the world was she sharing her personal information with loudmouthed Sabrina?

"Yes, she did," Sabrina said, "and I told her, all couples fight, so there was nothing for her to feel bad about."

Just then we all heard a loud crash upstairs. "I'll be right back," Paula said hurriedly. "No telling what those boys have gotten into." She dashed toward the stairs.

Sabrina and I were left alone. "Such a tragedy," she said, making a mocking face of sympathy. "And can you believe Paula has to carry that burden of knowing her last words to her husband were during a fight?" She stopped, as though a question had popped into her head. "Do you think her husband sought comfort in the arms of another woman? Because, for some reason, she now seems to think so."

What? Did Sabrina know something I didn't? I kept my cool as I stared at Sabrina. "I don't know why Paula would think Steven was with someone else," I managed to say. "He was one of the good guys."

"You would know, right? I mean, you guys were really close back in the day. I mean, you were never home because you were always spending the night at his place."

"We were very good friends," I clarified.

"*Friends.* That's right. Nothing more." She made another face, to show me how ridiculous that sounded. "I don't know why Paula's all worried. Steven probably went to the hotel to drown his sorrows at the bar. I see it all the time. He was probably too drunk to drive, so he got a room."

Her tone was the exact opposite of her innocent words. I was tired of playing games with her.

"Sabrina, what are you doing?" I asked.

"What do you mean?" she replied.

"You're not Paula's friend. So, what are you doing?"

"Ohhhh, can you school me on how a real friend should act?"

Paula walked back in. "Girl, these boys are going to be the death of me. Stevie has been acting out, and as bad as his behind was, I can't afford for things to get any worse."

Sabrina turned to her and smiled. "Aww, honey, it's going to be difficult for everyone. I know you have Felise here in your corner, but don't hesitate to call me if you need anything."

"Thank you, Sabrina."

She flashed a fake smile my way. "Well, I guess I'm going to give you two some BFF time."

"Remember what we discussed," Paula reminded her. "Let me know what the hotel security concludes with their investigation. I'm going crazy here, and any little bit of information helps."

"Oh, I'll definitely be in touch," Sabrina said.

She gave Paula a hug, then flashed another tight grin at me. "I'll see you later, Felise. I know you probably want to try and help Paula deal with this awful tragedy."

I didn't say anything as Paula walked Sabrina to the door. So she hadn't told Paula anything. But the gnawing feeling in my gut told me I didn't have long before she did. And only one thing could stop someone like Sabrina Fulton: money. I made a mental note to call Sabrina tomorrow to find out just how much it was going to take to shut her up.

28

Felise

AS SOON AS THE DOOR CLOSED, I STARTED IN ON PAULA.

"What was she doing over here?" I asked. "Since when are you two friends?" The last thing I needed was Sabrina cozying up to Paula. Wherever Sabrina went, trouble wasn't too far away, and I had enough trouble in my life.

Paula made her way back over to the love seat. "Don't tell me you're still trippin' over the beef you two had back in college."

"No," I protested. "I just don't understand. She's not your friend, so I'm trying to figure out what she's doing over here."

Paula smiled, something I hadn't seen her do in days. "Are we having friend envy?"

"Paula, I'm serious."

"Calm down, girl. She came by because I had her looking into some stuff for me."

I'd been a fool to think that night would recede into the past. "Looking into what, and why?"

She folded her arms to show me just how serious she was.

"I told you. I'm not comfortable with this theory that Steven just died in his sleep. Even if it was his heart, why did it suddenly give out?"

"You said yourself, his job was stressful." I quietly drew in a big, long breath to keep from getting worked up. If I protested too much, I might make her suspicious. "All I'm saying is I don't see how Sabrina can help you."

"She can help me get some answers."

"Help you how?"

"I don't know. She works at the Four Seasons. It's obvious those people don't want to talk to me. Maybe she can get them to talk to her. Maybe she can find something out that I can't. Like who was with him the night he died."

I froze. "Wh-why do you think somebody was with him the night he died?"

"I just do." She had a determined look on her face, which wasn't a good sign.

"I told you that you're letting your imagination get the best of you."

"And I told you that I'm not crazy." She stomped over to the corner, and picked up a box, then brought it over and dropped it on the table in front of us. She pulled out a pair of men's underwear and held it up.

"What is that?" I said, though I believed I knew all too well.

"Steven's underwear."

My heart plummeted to the pit of my stomach. I had a vivid flash of taking them off him. "Wh-why do you have those?"

She pointed at the box. "This is the box of stuff that police brought from the hotel room."

My heart started beating faster. I tried to recall if I had retrieved everything that belonged to me. I instantly dismissed that thought, though. I was confident that I hadn't left anything behind.

"So his underwear proves that he was there with someone else?" I asked, trying to make sure I kept the shakiness out of my voice.

"Believe it or not, it does." She tossed them back in the box.

"Okay, Paula, you're seriously reaching."

"No, hear me out." She turned to face me like she wanted to convince me of her theory. "Steven never went to sleep in the nude."

"What?"

"He never slept in the nude," she repeated. "So for them to say he was found naked in bed raises a red flag. This box is all the stuff they removed from the room after the coroner removed the body. The naked body. The only time Steven went to bed with no clothes on was after sex."

I had to grab the back of the recliner to keep from falling over. How was I supposed to know that? Did I ever know that? "Paula . . ."

"No. I was married to the man for fourteen years. I know him. He never went to bed in the nude unless he just finished having sex. It's the one habit he was anal about."

"Paula, I really think this is just your imagination going into overdrive." I actually felt sick, like I was going to throw up. "I know you're searching for some answers, but this is a stretch." The fact that I had to try to convince my best friend to stop searching for the "other woman" was making me feel worse than I already did.

My mind raced as I searched for explanations as to why he'd be naked.

"Paula, you said yourself that the people at the hospital told you that he was drunk. He probably went to the room, took off everything, and passed out in the bed."

She paused like she hadn't thought about that, so I seized the opportunity.

"You know he didn't drink that much. And if you two were arguing, he got toasted."

"He wasn't a big drinker," she said and I prayed that my words were getting through to her.

I continued, "So, if he drank as much as they say, he probably barely made it up to that room, stripped himself of all his clothes, and fell out in the bed."

"But I also saw a receipt for two apple martinis and two vodka and cranberries."

Hearing the exact drinks I'd had nearly knocked me off my feet. "And? So he got a martini." She raised an eyebrow at me. "Or he bought someone a martini at the bar. You know Steven was always the life of the party." I could see her mind churning, so I knew that I couldn't let up. "Him buying the drinks is nothing new. Remember you got mad when he went to that Jack and Jill event last month and paid the whole tab at happy hour? I'm sure that's all this was."

"You think so?" she said, hopeful.

I felt like a heel as I took her hands. "I know so."

I saw her relax, so I gave her a hug, then said a quick prayer for God to forgive me for the lying snake that I had become.

29

Paula

I MISSED MY HUSBAND SO MUCH. WHEN I WAS A LITTLE girl, my grandmother used to say, "Neither date nor time is promised, so treasure each day like it's your last." I wished that I had listened to those words. I wished that I had not fought over such trivial things. I wished that I hadn't pushed my husband into the arms of another woman—if I actually had. But most of all, I wished that I had taken my husband's heart condition seriously. Maybe if I had made sure he kept up his doctor's visits, they would've detected that his heart condition had advanced enough to kill him. Maybe they would've put us on notice that he had to change his lifestyle. And maybe he'd still be alive today.

But I couldn't think like that. Steven used to always say, "Life is what you make it, and you can't live in a world of maybes."

As I sat on the foot of our California king bed, my mind drifted back to the first time Steven had uttered those words to me.

• • • • • •

I had never cried so much in my whole life. The trash can positioned at my feet was overflowing with balled-up Kleenex. I felt like I had been crying for two weeks.

"I can't believe I let this happen," I said for the thousandth time. "Maybe if we had just been more careful . . . Maybe if I hadn't been over to your place all the time . . ."

Steven had been pacing back and forth in front of me. "It is what it is. And we can't live in a world of maybes now."

"I just can't see myself struggling with a kid."

He looked sternly at me. "Paula, you didn't do this alone, so you're not going to go through this alone."

His words were so comforting to me and hammered home what a great guy he was. I had never planned to get pregnant. I took my pill religiously. Shoot, I had big dreams. I had recently landed a new part in a stage play, and based on opening weekend's sales, it looked like we were going to take the show on the road for several weeks. How could I do that if I was pregnant?

"I don't believe this."

"We've been through this over and over. I thought when I left to go home for the weekend, you were okay with everything," he replied.

I was, but images of Steven never returning had swamped me all weekend. I kept envisioning his "I need to go back to Houston" as an excuse to leave me and our unborn child. The thought of being a struggling single mother made me sick to my stomach. When he'd walked in my house that evening, I'd burst into tears.

"I told you, everything happens for a reason," Steven said. We were in the bedroom of my mother's house, where I was living. Usually, she didn't play that being-up-in-the-bedroom-

with-your-boyfriend mess, but she knew about the pregnancy and knew that Steven and I had serious business to discuss.

"Being somebody's baby's mama was not in my life's plan," I admitted.

That brought Steven up short. "You're not going to be my baby's mama."

He got down on his knees in front of me and said, "Hopefully, you're going to be my wife."

If I hadn't been sitting down, that surely would've knocked me over.

"Wife?" *I said. Steven had told me that he'd broken the news of my pregnancy to his parents. Of course, they weren't happy about it, but he said, like everyone else, they would learn to get over it.*

Nowhere in that conversation did he mention marriage.

He fumbled in his pants pocket and pulled out a small ring. "My mom gave me this ring. It's my grandmother's ring." He held it out to me. "It means a lot to me. And I want the mother of my child, the woman I want to be my wife, to have it. I want you to have it. Please say you'll be my wife."

The sight of the ring made me want to cry even more. I needed a magnifying glass to see the diamond. When I had dreams of my proposal, they did not include me with a baby in my belly and a microdiamond ring.

"Steven . . . we can't do this," I managed to say.

"You can and you will," my mother said, popping up out of nowhere to come stick her nose in my business.

"Mama, please."

"No." She walked in my bedroom and directed her attention at Steven. "I think it's so admirable what you're doing. Do you love my daughter?"

He looked at me and then back at her. "Yes."

"And I know she loves you. And you two are going to do right by this baby. Bring her or him into this world with a mother and a father married and living under the same roof. I didn't raise you any other way," she told me firmly.

I felt like I was fifteen years old. But she was right. I knew plenty of successful people who were single mothers, but that's not the life I envisioned. Abortion wasn't an option, and neither was giving up my child for adoption.

"So, what do you say?" Steven said.

"She says yes," my mom repeated.

I side-eyed her, and she stepped back and made a zipper motion over her lips.

"Are you sure this is what you want?" I asked, even though I wasn't sure myself.

He placed his hand on my stomach. "I am."

I took a deep breath. Do the right thing, the little voice in my head said. So I responded. "Then yes, the answer is yes."

"WHAT ARE YOU DOING?" MY MOM ASKED, WALKING INTO my room and snapping me out of my trip down memory lane. My microdiamond had been replaced by my wedding day with a three-carat princess-cut diamond, compliments of Steven's father, who refused to let his son "shame the family with that little ring." I think that Steven was a little insulted that I had sided with his father, but with the two rings side by side, that was a no-brainer.

"I'm just thinking."

"I'm thinking that you're thinking too much." She gave me a soft smile.

"Mama, Felise says I'm searching for something that's not there."

"Baby, you lost your husband. That's understandable." My sister had filled my mom in on everything, and I was surprised she had taken so long to give me her two cents.

"I think you're reading too much into the underwear thing. I mean, I was there—you had a big argument on the phone. You think this mystery woman was just sitting there, being quiet?"

That was easily explained. "She knew to shut her mouth when the wife calls."

"You've been watching too much Lifetime." My mom picked up the remote and clicked the TV off. "I think you're trying to make sense of something that doesn't make sense."

"I guess." I shrugged.

"You're going to drive yourself crazy, replaying and overthinking everything. I'm sorry this had to happen, but his death is not a reflection of your relationship or anything of the sort, so you've got to let it go."

I nodded but merely to get my mom to leave. She would never see eye to eye with me. My gut was telling me that no matter what any of them said, I couldn't rest until I got some answers.

30

Felise

THE SOUNDS OF TEDDY PENDERGRASS MET ME AT THE door.

"Hey," Greg said, greeting me as I walked in.

"What's this?" I asked, dropping my keys on the counter. The kitchen was spotless, and dinner was laid out on the table, which was decorated like it sat in the middle of a five-star restaurant.

Greg leaned in and kissed me before flashing a seductive smile.

"I cooked dinner. Liz is over at her friend's house, and I thought we could have a quiet evening at home."

I groaned. I wanted a quiet evening, all right, but by myself. It had been a rough day in the ER, I had been madly trying to figure out what Sabrina was up to (I'd called, but she hadn't returned the call), and I just wanted to get home and lay down.

"Wh-what's this?" I motioned to Greg's shoes, which were in the middle of the floor. He eyed the shoes and smiled, not making any attempt to pick them up. "So, you're really just going to let them sit there?" I asked.

Now I was getting nervous. Shoes lying around might have seemed normal for the average person, but for Greg not to pick them up? I needed to take his temperature because he obviously was running a fever. "Why are your shoes in the middle of the floor?"

"It's an experiment," he said. He put his hands over mine and led me to the kitchen table, where he sat me down. "I know I'm not the easiest person to live with, but one thing's for sure: I love you with all my heart. I know I need to relax and get this OCD under control, so I've been seeing a therapist."

"What? Since when?"

"Since the night of our fight, the day after our anniversary. I've only had a few sessions, but I can feel some progress."

"You're going to see a therapist?" That in and of itself was major because Greg was old school, and while he knew that something was wrong with him, never in a million years did I think he'd seek help. He only agreed to counseling after his affair because he didn't want me to walk out the door.

"I don't want to lose you, and I saw in your eyes the night of our anniversary that I was on the verge. I couldn't risk that. So, yes, I've been seeing a therapist, and she gave me an exercise today." He looked over at the shoes again, and his cheek twitched at the violation they represented. "Whew, it's been hard. I stepped out of them when I got home, and I've been wanting to pick them up ever since."

I couldn't help but smile.

Greg continued. "Felise, I want our marriage to work,

and I know these last few weeks have been difficult. Your having to be there for Paula hasn't been easy either."

I heard the words, but I didn't believe him. After all, I'd heard all of these promises before. And my husband would try. He'd try to put me first, but the effort never lasted. I think the record was nine days.

He stroked my hair and then leaned in and nuzzled my neck.

"I love you," he whispered. "I miss us. And I want everything to be all right." As music softly filled the room, Greg bent down and lightly bit my shoulder, which used to turn me on. Now it made me tense up.

"What are you doing, Greg?" I said, ducking away from his touch. I stood and tried to walk away, but he came up behind me.

"I want you, baby," he said. "I *need* you. It's been so long." His voice was husky as he turned me around and forced his tongue into my mouth. "Please, Felise," he moaned. His hands went inside my pants as he grasped my behind and tried to lift me onto the kitchen table.

"Greg, don't," I protested.

"Come on, baby," he said as his hands pulled at my panties.

I knew that I needed to be with my husband, but as he kissed me, I saw images of Steven lying deathly still in that bed and I yelled, "Stop it!"

Greg backed away in shock. I grabbed my underwear and pulled them up. "Just stop!"

"I'm sorry," Greg said, stunned.

"I . . . I just can't do it," I cried.

We stared at each other like two strangers. "Felise, what's going on? Have I lost you?" he said.

"No, no, it's not that," I replied more quietly, trying to play it off. "I'm just . . . I'm just not in the mood."

"It's been over a month."

"I know, but I can't. Why can't you understand?" I snapped.

"I *have* been understanding!" he snapped back. "I understood the night my wife stormed out and spent the night somewhere else. I'm understanding every time I touch you and you flinch like I disgust you. I understand that you haven't looked me in the eye since our anniversary. Was that our breaking point? Did I lose you that night?"

I adjusted my scrubs and tried to calmly reply. "You're overreacting, Greg. I have a lot on my plate right now."

He huffed as he ran his hands over his head. "Okay, Felise. Whatever."

I inhaled. Exhaled. "Why don't we sit down and eat?" I glanced at the counter by the stove. He'd made blackened tilapia and garlic mashed potatoes. "The food looks delicious."

"You eat it," he growled. "I've lost my appetite." He grabbed his cell phone and headed upstairs.

31

Paula

I HEARD THE DOORBELL RINGING, BUT I COULDN'T MOVE to answer it. I hoped my mom or sister did because right then the only thing that mattered was this piece of paper in front of me. I sat on the sofa, tears trickling down my cheeks as the paper shook in my hand. I didn't realize how unsteady my hand was until I saw the paper waving back and forth.

"Hey," Felise said, walking into the living room. I'd had Charlene call her as soon as I opened this. "Are you okay?"

I shook my head but didn't say anything. I didn't know if I'd ever be okay again. I didn't know if my family would ever be okay again.

Felise eased onto the sofa next to me. "What's going on?"

I mutely handed her the piece of paper.

She read the top line. " 'Death Certificate.' "

We sat in silence as she scanned the rest of the paper. I could've told her what it said because in the hour and a half since I'd received it, I'd committed each word to memory. According to this piece of paper, my husband was officially gone. Stricken from the records of the living, ripped from our lives by heart failure.

"Well," Felise said, folding the paper in half, "not that it's any consolation, but now you know." She handed the paper back to me. "Now you know without a doubt what happened."

"Well, I know the official cause of death, but I still have so many unanswered questions," I managed to mumble. "What if my asking him for a divorce stressed him out so that he had a heart attack? That would mean I killed him."

She patted my hand. "That's absurd. You didn't kill your husband. And you probably will always have questions about his death. But it's time to let him go."

"I keep trying to tell her that." I looked up to see my sister, who had appeared in the doorway. "But she keeps talking about how A plus B isn't equaling C," Charlene added as she walked in.

"There's a part of me that thinks I should keep digging," I told Felise.

"Digging for what?" Felise asked.

I shrugged. "I don't know—answers?"

Felise lightly pointed at the paper. "But you have your answers right there, sweetie."

That caused the tears to start up. "I know. I just want my husband," I said, breaking down in tears again. "Do you know he had a doctor's appointment?" I finally managed to say. "He had a doctor's appointment a month ago, and he cancelled it for work. I was having a really bad day with the kids and blew him off. I didn't make him go. I should've made him go," I cried, burying my face in my hands.

"Come on, you've got to stop beating yourself up," Felise

said, wrapping me in a big bear hug. "You can never let Steven's memory go, but you've got to let this uncertainty go."

She let me cry for a few minutes. After I was all cried out, I pulled myself up. "Do you think I should keep digging?" I asked. I trusted my best friend. She would be straight with me. "Or do you think my guilt isn't allowing me to let this go?"

Felise looked uneasy for a moment but then forced a smile. "No, I think what you're feeling is perfectly normal. You lost the love of your life. But I know one thing: Steven would not want you wallowing in this sea of worry."

I let out a long sigh. I was so glad I had Felise here because I had been ready to go storm the Four Seasons again to get to the bottom of what happened that night.

I sniffed and wiped my face. I felt a wave of exhaustion come over me. "I know you're right. It's just so hard."

Felise took the official report and my Bible off the table, and slid the piece of paper inside it. "Right now you stay focused on being the best mom for those children and know that Steven is right there for you."

"Thank you so much," I told her. I gave her a huge hug again, and watched as my sister rolled her eyes and walked out the room.

32

Paula

"HEY, MOM. DO YOU LIKE MY HAIR?"

I was delighted by my daughter's straight, flat-ironed hair. It looked really cute on her. I was raising a little beauty. As I'd been doing so often these days, I noticed how much like her father she looked. It brought a pang to my heart.

Tahiry stood next to Felise and Liz. They'd been out all day, and the sad part was I hadn't even realized it.

"Yes, your hair looks good," I said, running my fingers through her silky strands.

"Nana let me get a keratin treatment," Tahiry said, smiling at Felise.

"Don't worry," Felise put in. "It's all nonchemical."

I had never put chemicals in Tahiry's hair, even though she'd been begging for a perm since she was eleven, so I was glad Felise thought enough to take that into consideration.

"Come on, Liz, I want to show you something." Tahiry grabbed Liz's hand and dragged her up the stairs. "Thanks again, Nana!" she called out to Felise as they pounded up the steps like twin elephants.

"I hope you don't mind, I took her to Smashburger on the way home," Felise replied.

I shook my head. "She loves that place. She would eat there twenty-four seven if she could." I motioned for Felise to follow me into the living room. "I can't thank you enough for taking her to get her hair done," I said as I settled down on the sofa. "It's like I've been neglecting everything and everybody." I'd been really trying to spend more time with Tahiry, with all the kids for that matter. But it felt like I couldn't give my all to anything until I had some answers.

She sat in the love seat across from me. "That's understandable. Where are the boys?"

"They're with Steven's cousin Rodney. He's going to keep them for a little while, thank goodness. He took them to the park, I think he said. I needed some peace and quiet."

I was about to say something else when my cell phone rang. I didn't recognize the number and almost didn't answer because I couldn't deal with any more calls of condolence, but I went ahead and pushed Answer.

"Hi, may I speak to Paula Wright?" a lady on the other end said.

"This is she."

The woman didn't go on.

"This is Paula," I repeated.

"I really shouldn't be calling you because I could get in so much trouble," she began.

"Who is this?"

"This is Lori. I'm the clerk that was working the front desk when you came to the Four Seasons the other day. My manager was trying to help you get some information about your husband."

"Oh, yeah. With the long, blond pretty hair?" I sat up straighter as I tried to figure out why she was calling me.

"That's me." She hesitated. "I thought long and hard about whether I should tell you this, but my husband left me for another woman, and I just feel like . . . Well, I wish someone had told me. Everyone I knew covered it up." She took a deep breath like she was trying to get up the nerve to continue. "Your husband was with someone that night."

I inhaled sharply as I gripped the phone tighter.

"What?" Felise mouthed. "Who is that? What's going on?"

I held up a finger for Felise to wait.

"Do you know who it was?" I managed to ask.

"I have no idea. But they were at the bar for a while. I noticed them when I went on my break because I thought he was attractive. Later, he came and got the room, went back to the bar, then went upstairs. She followed shortly after. They were trying to make it seem like they weren't together, but I've been doing this job long enough to know when someone is creeping."

I choked back tears, although I didn't know whether to cry or scream.

"I really don't want to sully your husband's memory, and I hope that I don't make things worse by telling you, but I remembered everyone trying to make me think I was crazy when I told them my husband was cheating, and I was right. I just wanted you to know that your instincts were right."

"But you don't have any details?"

"No, like I said, she didn't come to the front desk with him."

"What did she look like?"

"Honestly, I didn't get a good look because her back was to me. But she was a tall woman, real pretty dark skin, beautiful hair. She was trying real hard not to be seen, which is why I noticed her in the first place."

Well, that didn't give me much. Based on her description, that could be practically anyone.

"Please don't tell anyone I called you," Lori said. "I could lose my job."

"I won't. Thank you so much." I hung up the phone and fell back against the sofa.

"What's going on?" Felise asked again.

"That was the hotel clerk at the Four Seasons. Steven *was* with someone."

Felise's mouth dropped open.

"I knew I wasn't crazy." I wiped away the tears that had once again started making their way down my cheeks. I hadn't even realized I was crying.

"D-did she say who it was? What she looked like?"

I shook my head. "She didn't get that good of a look at her."

Felise was in as much shock as me.

"Hard to believe your perfect friend wasn't so perfect after all, huh?" I managed to say, my voice a mixture of sarcasm and anger.

It took her a while to compose herself, but finally she said, "Why would that lady call you with that?"

"Because she knew I was going crazy and needed some answers." I don't know what good it did me, but I was grateful to at least know.

"So what answers do you have now?" Felise asked.

That was a good question. Yes, my suspicions were confirmed, but really, all I had now was more hurt.

"Exactly," Felise continued when I didn't respond. "Let this go and remember the man you loved and who loved you. That's all that matters."

Through tear-filled eyes I said, "I wish that it was as easy as that."

This time she didn't say anything. She took me in her arms and held me until the tears stopped coming.

33

Felise

I HAD TO PSYCH MYSELF UP TO STEP INSIDE THE ROtating door. I hadn't returned to the Four Seasons since that night, but Sabrina and her veiled comments were driving me mad. She sent me a text yesterday that said, *How's Paula?* When I replied, asking her what she was up to, she didn't respond. Just like she hadn't returned my call the other day. I really think she was trying to make me sweat. I needed to get to the bottom of what she knew and what she wanted and I didn't need to wait another day. Especially now that this hotel clerk had confirmed for Paula that Steven was here with someone else, I needed to nip this in the bud right away.

I pushed my shades up on my face and kept my head low. I didn't want to take any chances on anyone recognizing me.

I'd already called to make sure Sabrina was working tonight. I spotted her immediately, giggling as she flirted with two men at the end of the bar. She was good at what she did. Too bad she'd dropped out of school and hadn't taken her talents any further than this.

I slid onto a bar stool and waited until she noticed me.

"Well, well, well." Sabrina strutted toward me. "I was wondering when you'd come." She placed a coaster in front of me. "What can I get for the great Felise Mavins?"

"Hello, Sabrina. How are you?"

"I'm splendid," she replied with a sly smile.

A part of me wanted to believe she was being her usual snarky self, but my gut knew better.

"So, what brings you to the Four Seasons. *Again,*" she added with a smirk.

"I just, umm, I wanted to come by for a drink."

"Really? Okay. What can I get for you? Apple martini?"

I didn't know if she knew that was the drink I'd had the night I was here with Steven or if it was just a coincidence. Either way, the question cut just the way she'd intended.

"Sure. An apple martini is fine."

I waited for her to fix my drink, and when she returned and set it in front of me, she leaned on the bar and said, "Cut the bull, Felise. Why are you really here?"

"Why don't you cut the bull, Sabrina?" I replied matter-of-factly. "I'm just trying to find out what you think you know." I picked my drink up and tried to take a nonchalant sip, but my hand was shaking so badly, I lifted the drink only a few inches before setting it back down.

Sabrina laughed. "Oh, what I *think* I know, huh?" She stood upright and folded her arms. "Let me see. What I think? I *think* that Dolly Do-Right met up with her best friend's husband at the Four Seasons. Something went wrong: either she put it on him a little too hard, or she killed him. I don't know."

"I didn't kill anybody," I said defensively.

She replied, "So, you admit that you came here to meet up with Steven?"

"I didn't admit to anything. I didn't come here to meet up with anyone," I protested.

"What were your intentions then? Although I'm sure to Paula it would all be the same."

I glared at her through hate-filled eyes.

She grinned as she drummed her fingers on the bar. "You know, when Paula asked me to look into Steven's death, I never expected to find out you were involved."

"So, I guess you can't wait to tell Paula this little bit of news."

"If I couldn't wait, I would've already told her."

I knew what she was implying. Disdain was written all over my face. "I didn't have anything to do with Steven's death, nor was I with him," I finally said. "We had a drink at the bar, and I left it at that." Whatever she knew, I was going to admit to the bare minimum.

She gave me a broad wink like she knew I was lying. But no one had come into the room, so she couldn't prove anything other than that I was at the bar with Steven. I got my purse and removed my checkbook. "So what do you want? How much?"

She lost her smile. "Oh, so you think you can buy my silence?"

I couldn't believe she'd say that. If there was one thing I knew about Sabrina, it's that she worshipped money.

"I can't be bought," Sabrina said, much to my surprise. But then she leaned in again and said, "But since we are friends, I could use a loan of a grand."

I looked at her like she was crazy. I was an average

middle-class working woman. A grand would dang near wipe out my personal savings. And I didn't want to touch the joint savings I had with Greg because he watched the money so closely. But looking at the smirk on her face, I knew I didn't have a choice.

"Fine," I said as I started scribbling in my checkbook. "I'll give you a loan." If all I needed was a thousand dollars to make her go away, I'd gladly pay it.

She smiled.

"But this is it." I tore off the check. "The only reason I'm doing this is because I don't need the headache of anyone raising any questions."

"Of course you don't," she said, taking the check. "But I think I decide when this is over." She flashed a smile as she tucked the check in her bra. "Have a nice day. Don't pick up any more men in this bar," she added before going to wait on the next customer.

I couldn't get out of there fast enough.

In the car, I knew I was too frazzled to go home, so I called my younger sister.

"Fran, where are you?" I asked as soon as she picked up.

"About to go meet Mavis for lunch," she replied.

I debated hanging up because I didn't want to hear Mavis's mouth, but I needed Fran. Maybe I needed them both. "Where are you guys meeting?"

"Pappasito's on 59. Why?"

"I'm going to come meet you."

"Oh, okay, what's up?"

"I just need to talk."

"Okay, I'll see you there," Fran said.

Fifteen minutes later, I pulled into the Pappasito's parking lot. I spotted Fran pulling into a spot near the front of the restaurant. But she was driving a car I'd never seen before.

"What's up, sis?" she asked as she got out of the car.

"Um, where did this come from?" I asked, eyeing the silver Mercedes.

She grinned as she ran her hand over the hood. "Nice, huh? This is my man's car."

"What man?" I said. Fran couldn't keep a man for longer than two months, so I had no idea who she could be talking about.

"My new boyfriend." She smiled. "Actually, it's his wife's car."

"What?"

"Long story. I'll have to tell you about it some other time." She slid her shades on and pushed the remote to set the alarm.

"Girl, have you lost your mind? Are you trying to get killed driving some other woman's car?" I said.

"The car is at the center of an ugly custody battle, so I'm driving it until they work all of that out." She eyed me over the top of her shades. "But I know you're not about to judge me."

"You're right," I said. I had my own problems. I couldn't lecture my sister on her drama.

"So, what's up with you?" she asked as we made our way inside.

"I need a drink. I'll tell you in a minute so I don't have to repeat it for Mavis."

"I hope you're treating for the drink," she said, holding the door open.

We spotted Mavis, and she looked surprised to see me.

"What are you doing here?" she asked.

"Felise called and wanted to meet us," Fran said, sliding into her chair.

I hugged Mavis and had barely sat down before I instructed the waitress to bring me a Wave margarita.

"Okay, what's going on?" Mavis asked as soon as the waitress walked away.

"Someone knows I was at the hotel," I said, coming right to the point.

Both of their mouths gaped open.

"Who?" Fran said.

"Do either of you remember Sabrina Fulton? I went to college with her. She was my roommate freshman year."

"Oh, yeah, I remember her," Mavis said.

I then proceeded to fill them in. From the funeral to this morning.

"This is un-freakin'-believable," Fran said once I was done. She had that gleam in her eyes like she was ready to go jump someone.

"Don't even look like that," Mavis said. "We're too old for violence."

"So, I'm supposed to just let some chick blackmail my sister and I don't do anything?" Fran asked.

Mavis ignored Fran and turned back to me. "Did you make it clear that you won't be bullied into subsidizing her lifestyle?"

"I did, but somehow, I don't think she was paying me any attention." I sighed. "I gave her the grand to go away. I can't believe I'm in this position."

"Wow," Mavis said.

The waitress set my drink down in front of me, and I immediately began sucking it down.

"Hey, slow your roll," Fran said.

"Yeah. All that drinking is what got you into this position in the first place," Mavis added.

I rolled my eyes at her, and thankfully, she didn't say anything else.

"Well, maybe she really will go away," Fran said.

No sooner had the words left her mouth than my phone beeped, letting me know I had a text.

I didn't recognize the number it was coming from, but it appeared to have some kind of video attached. I almost deleted it, but then I saw the name: "Steven and Felise."

The entire back of my neck prickled, spreading up over my head, as I opened the video and pressed play.

"What are you looking at?" Mavis asked, leaning to look over at my phone.

"It–it's a video."

"What kind of video?" Fran asked.

I no longer could speak. I simply set the phone down and turned it so my sisters could see the video of me and Steven sitting a little too close for comfort at the bar. In the corner of the video was a date stamp: *06-01-2013*. None of us said a word as the next text came in. *This is just a snippet. The terms just changed. Stay tuned. SF*

An hour ago, I'd thought I was all cried out. But this video brought on a whole new onset of tears. I had suspected that giving Sabrina that money was a bad idea. At this moment I knew without a doubt that my nightmare was only going to get worse.

34

Paula

"KNOCK, KNOCK."

My sister lightly tapped on my door and pushed it open at the same time. "Are you okay?" she asked, sticking her head inside.

Charlene and I were so far apart in age (I was ten when our mom had her) that we were never really close. But she was "in between jobs as usual" so she'd come when I called and hadn't left since. Despite the fact that she didn't know a thing about raising kids, she was still a tremendous help.

"Hey, come on in," I said, sitting up in bed. "I'm okay."

"No, you're not. You still bummed about that call?"

I nodded. "You know, I never thought Steven was a cheater."

"Didn't Kevin come to the funeral?"

"Yeah."

"And he confirmed that Steven was with him."

I nodded again.

"You don't think Kevin would come lying to you at the funeral, do you?"

"No," I replied. I had thought this whole thing through. "I believe Steven met up with Kevin. I mean, I saw the paperwork in that box of stuff they brought. But apparently, when he was done with Kevin, he met someone else. I just want to know who and why and how he could do this to me."

Charlene crossed her arms over her chest, looking like she was the older, wiser sister. "Do you think he actually had someone come to the hotel? As far as you knew, he was coming back home, right? So maybe it was a one-night stand."

"As if that makes it any better."

My sister sat down in the chair across from my bed. "It does. A one-night stand just happens. It doesn't mean he loved you any less."

I rolled my eyes. My sister could go somewhere with that mess. In my book, cheating was cheating.

"Look, I agree with Felise that you need to let this go—even though for some reason I'm not vibing with her right now."

"Is that what the eye roll you gave her was about?"

"Just something about her demeanor. It reeked of desperation. But I probably just have an attitude because she hasn't been around. I mean, what kind of friend bails on you in your time of need?"

"She was close to Steven, too. She's grieving in her own way."

"Whatever." Charlene flicked my comment off, and I knew to drop it because I wouldn't be changing her mind.

"So, you really think I should just let it go?" I asked.

She nodded. "I mean, what good is getting all the details going to do? Steven is gone. Why wallow in hurt over what he's done—especially when you don't know for sure if he even did anything? That clerk could be mistaken. She didn't actually see them go in the room together. If her man cheated on her, she's probably paranoid and thinks all men are dogs."

I considered what she was saying. No, that clerk had seemed adamant. "I don't know," I finally said. "I just want to know who it is. I want to look her in the eye. I want to ask her about his last minutes. What did he do? What did he say? Did he talk about how much he hated me?"

"Steven didn't hate you," Charlene said, slipping onto the edge of my bed. "But it's understandable how you're feeling."

We sat in silence, both lost in our own thoughts. Mine kept spinning over and over again about who could have crept up to his room that night.

Charlene said, "Has that Sabrina girl found out anything else?"

"Let me call her," I replied. "Hand me my phone."

She reached on my nightstand and handed the phone to me before heading toward the door.

"I'm going to go take the boys over to Rodney's house this morning. He wants them to stay with him a couple of weeks. I told him I'd talk to you about it. But I think it's a good idea. I'm leaving in a few days, and Mama is no good right now. A few weeks will give you time to get your head together."

Rodney had a son Stevie's age, so they spent a lot of time together, and his wife made no secret of how much she adored the twins, so I had no doubt my children would be well taken care of.

"That is a good idea," I said.

"Good, he said he's going to enroll Stevie in the camp he's teaching this summer."

"Camp!" I said. "I forgot all about Tahiry's camp." My

daughter was scheduled to go to cheer camp next week, and I hadn't done a single thing to prepare her.

"Don't worry, your girl is good for something. Felise is taking her shopping today. Tahiry called her because she was worried that you wouldn't want her to go."

"No, she needs to go. But I haven't gotten her anything that she's supposed to have."

"Look, you know Felise'll get her whatever she needs. I'll take the boys out of your hair. You call Sabrina or do whatever you need to get some closure."

"Thank you so much. My purse is on the dresser. My Visa card is in my wallet. Can you go by the mall first and pick up Stevie some shorts? He's growing so fast and I'd been meaning to buy him some new clothes. Then you can take the boys to that new Marble Slab ice cream store before you head over to Rodney's."

"Oooh, the mall. Can I go in and buy me something?"

"You can buy you whatever you like—within reason," I added, forcing a smile. I was just grateful that she was picking up some of the slack, and I knew I was slacking with my kids.

My sister blew me a kiss on her way out. I picked up the phone and called Sabrina. Her voice mail picked up.

"Hey, Sabrina. It's Paula Wright. I was just wondering if you found out anything—" I hesitated. "If you have any idea on who the woman he was with could be, let me know, okay? Thanks a lot. And Sabrina, you have no idea how much of a help you've been to me."

I hung up the phone and prayed that she called me back soon. I wanted closure, and I knew I wouldn't be able to get it until I learned who the woman was who had been with my husband on his last night on earth.

35

Felise

WE NEEDED THIS TIME. AS I WATCHED TAHIRY ACROSS from me, devouring her ice cream, I couldn't help but smile.

Liz was supposed to be with us but decided at the last minute to stay home and finish her history project. That was my daughter, the brainiac. Her partner had bailed on her, and she was determined to pick up the slack so she could get an A. At first, I was nervous about being alone with Tahiry, but I told myself that was just the guilt.

I'd picked up everything Tahiry needed for camp. Now we were sitting in the food court at the mall, eating Marble Slab ice cream.

"Thank you for everything, Nana," she said.

I patted her hand. "It's my pleasure, sweetie. I know the past few weeks have been extremely difficult for you. But you've been so strong."

She gave me a sad smile. "Can I tell you a secret?"

"Of course, you can tell me anything."

She looked down at her ice cream, toyed with a minute,

then said, "I used to wish my mom and dad would get a divorce."

"What?" I said. What had Paula been telling her daughter?

"They still want to look at me like I'm a little girl, but I'm not. I know when someone is unhappy, and the two of them, they were in no way happy."

Wow. Everything inside me wanted to press her, ask her more questions. But I didn't believe in putting children in grown folks' business.

A slow tear trickled down her cheek. "How could I wish that for my own parents?"

"It's nothing wrong with how you felt. You just wanted them both to be happy."

"I love my mom. But she is the most miserable person. Dad tried everything in the world to make her happy, but nothing worked. I used to think she hated us."

"Tahiry," I said as she hunched her shoulders, "I know she doesn't. I saw this lady on TV one time say, 'If Mama ain't happy, ain't nobody happy.' That's us."

Sitting there with my goddaughter, I was relieved I could be there for her when her mother couldn't. At least I could give Tahiry some sense of normalcy, some place of refuge.

Will she love you when she finds out the truth?

I don't know where that voice came from, but it caught me off guard and I quickly shook the thought away.

"Nana, what's wrong?"

"Wh-what's wrong?" I said, struggling to draw a breath. "Oh, nothing. Entirely, absolutely, nothing at all."

"Let's change the subject," she announced. "I don't want to be sad today."

I smiled and Tahiry and I made small talk and it seemed like old times. I was truly enjoying our conversation. So much about her reminded me of Steven, from the way she ate with her ice cream (eating from the center out), to the corny way she laughed. A part of me wondered if that's why I was enjoying her company so much. But then, I knew that I always enjoyed being around my goddaughter. And right about now, she needed me as much as I needed her.

"'Hiry!"

Both of us turned toward the tiny voice yelling in our direction. Our eyes widened in surprise as Marcus and Mason came racing over.

"What are you guys doing here?" Tahiry asked, picking Marcus up and swinging him around.

"Auntie Charlene brought us for ice cream." Mason pointed across the food court at Charlene who was waiting in line at the Marble Slab Creamery. She was texting on her phone and hadn't even noticed that the boys had darted off.

"Boys you shouldn't run away from your aunt," I told them. Just as I said something, Charlene looked up, noticed they were gone, then frantically turned to Stevie, who was standing behind her engrossed in his handheld video game.

Fear filled her face as her eyes darted around the food court.

"Charlene," I called, waving at her.

She looked in my direction and relief filled her face when she spotted the boys.

"Oh, my goodness," she said, hurrying over to us.

"Wow, you're sure in the losing kids business," I said. I was joking, but the look on her face told me that she didn't find anything funny.

"I didn't lose them. They ran off," she snapped.

"That's because we saw 'Hiry," Mason said as Tahiry set his twin down next to him.

"Well, don't do that again, boys. You could've given your aunt Charlene a heart attack." I tussled Mason's curly hair.

Charlene grabbed their hands. "Come on, let's get this ice cream."

"How's Paula?" I asked before she walked off. "She was asleep when I picked Tahiry up."

Charlene stopped and glared at me. "She's fine, no thanks to you."

Her tone caught Tahiry and me by surprise.

"Tahiry, why don't you watch your brothers while I talk to your aunt real quick," I said, flashing a smile to let all of them know everything was fine.

Charlene didn't let go of their hands.

"Just for a minute," I said. I motioned for Charlene to step to the side, which she eventually did.

"Is everything okay with us?" I asked her. I was sure I knew the reason for her attitude—she was salty about me not being there for Paula like I should have been. But I needed Charlene on my side, not working against me.

She huffed. "Look, the boys just have my nerves frazzled. I don't know what I was thinking, bringing them to the mall. I'm not cut out for this kid stuff."

I gave her a reassuring smile. "You're doing a fantastic job."

"Yeah, losing kids," she said, rolling her eyes.

"But we all would still be lost without you." I took a deep breath. "I know I haven't been there for your sister, but it's just so hard." I don't know why I felt the need to justify my actions with Charlene. Maybe there was part of me that wanted her to make Paula understand my absence.

She actually seemed to relax. "I know. I'm sorry. I know this is hard on everyone."

"I'm just trying to help Tahiry cope."

"And I know Paula appreciates that."

"So, we're cool?"

She nodded and shrugged at the same time. "Yeah, we're cool."

It didn't feel like we were cool, but I knew I needed her on my side now.

"Are we still gonna get ice cream?" Mason said once we walked back over to them.

"I shouldn't get y'all's little bad behinds anything, running off like that," Charlene said and the twins immediately began whining. "Oh, chill out, I'm gonna get it." She waved goodbye to us as they dragged her back over to the ice cream shop.

"Here," Tahiry said, handing me my cell phone after they were gone. "Somebody named Sabrina called you."

My heart dropped. "You answered my phone?"

"It was ringing," she said, like it was no big deal. "I told her you were busy."

"What did she say?"

"She said get unbusy and call her back. She was really rude. You need to teach your friends some manners."

I managed a smile. "I need to teach little girls from answering my phone."

"I was trying to help you out."

I let the conversation drop but as soon as I dropped Tahiry off, I was going to call Sabrina, see what she wanted and do whatever I needed to do to shut this situation down.

36

Felise

I COULDN'T BELIEVE I WAS BACK HERE AGAIN. I WAS SITting in the back of the Four Seasons restaurant, praying that no one saw me. I think Sabrina liked torturing me by making me come here. Of course, she was late, which only gave me more time to ponder how in the world my life had come to this. I couldn't believe that I was caught up in a blackmail scheme.

After I dropped Tahiry off yesterday, I'd called Sabrina. This time, she'd answered like she was irritated that I'd taken so long to get back with her. Then she'd told me to meet her here. Of course, my initial reaction was to tell her absolutely not. When I told her that grand was a one-time payment, I meant it. Then she'd responded by sending me more of the video and I knew I didn't have a choice, so here I was.

Sabrina finally sashayed in like she wasn't thirty minutes late, then eased in the chair across from me.

"What's up, ol' buddy?" she said.

I so did not have time to play games with her. "What

do you want from me, Sabrina? You know I don't have any money."

"Mmmm, I beg to differ," she said, removing her shades and setting them on the table. "You have a nice house, a nice job. Your hubby makes beaucoup money, and you're a resourceful woman. Anything you don't have, I know you can figure out how to get."

"Again, what do you want?" I said. "Didn't we settle everything the other day?"

"You know, I really appreciate the thousand dollars that you gave me, but that was before I knew about this." She held up a jump drive she'd pulled from her pocket. "I mean, this changes things drastically, don't you think? And it got me to thinking, how much is someone's life really worth? You know, if someone wanted to keep their life from spiraling out of control, would they pay a million dollars? I know I would. So I got to thinking of the gold mine that I was holding." She fingered the jump drive.

"I don't have a million dollars."

"I know that, silly. I mean, I was there when you found out your parents had let their life insurance policies lapse so you and your sisters got nothing."

I couldn't believe she would bring that up, but I merely said, "So, if you know that, why am I here?"

"Well, you may not have a million dollars, but you aren't poor either."

"I can't do this with you for the rest of my life."

"Oh, you won't have to," she replied callously, "because here's how this is going to play out. You're going to give me enough money to go away. I'm going to move to Los Angeles and become an actress."

"Really, Sabrina? You're thirty-five years old, and you're going to become an actress?"

"Gabrielle Union is forty years old and getting all kinds of big offers. So is Angelina Jolie."

I was about to point out the obvious, but then it dawned on me, I didn't need to be discouraging her from trying to go after her dream in LA. I needed to be encouraging that any way I could.

"You're right. You have the total package to make that work."

She smiled like she knew I was BS-ing her. "But the way I see it, me and the whole starving artist thing—that doesn't work too well. So, I was thinking that you could give me seed money. Look at it as an investment into my career."

"Again, I don't have that kind of money."

"And *again*, I'm sure you can figure out a way to get it."

"I can't." I was not going to let her continue to blackmail me. And that little clip she'd sent me could be explained away.

"Did you not see the video I sent?"

I tried to play it cool, even though I was anything but. "Yeah, I saw it, and it looks like two innocent friends having a drink. Yes, Paula may be a little mad that I didn't tell her I was there, but she'll get over it." I hope I sounded more confident than I felt.

Sabrina gave a sly smile. "Will she, huh? Wonder if she'll get over this." She propped open her phone and pressed some keys, and then turned the phone around to face me. My mouth fell open as the video played of Steven looking nervously around as he went to the elevator. A few seconds later, I followed behind him. Then the image switched to a hallway: Steven went in a room, and seconds later, I went in the same room.

Sabrina pressed stop. "Now unfortunately, I don't have video *inside* the room, so I don't really know what went on. I'm sure you could convince Paula that you all just sat and talked about old times. I'm sure she'd buy that, right?" I was speechless as I stared at her. "Shall I keep going, because I do have the part where *you* leave the room in a panic the next morning—but Steven doesn't."

My eyes filled with tears at that terrible memory, but I refused to give her the satisfaction of seeing me cry. "How much?" I asked. "Because I know that's what this all boils down to with you."

"Twenty-five thousand," she said without hesitation. She held up a finger before I could say anything. "And before you balk, I think I'm being quite generous. My good buddy in security—he thinks I'm trying to catch my cheating boyfriend—gave me this digital file. Now, I could give it to the cops."

"I-I didn't kill him," I stammered.

"Don't tell me. Tell the cops. And your husband. And Paula," she said matter-of-factly. "I mean, I'm not sure what kind of time you can get for leaving a dead body, but I'm sure you don't want the hassle of an investigation and all. So that's why I'm coming to you first. The way I see it, you need to be thanking me."

"This is extortion," I said.

She handed me the phone. "Call the cops, then."

"I don't have that kind of money," I said again, my voice cracking this time.

"Well"—she cocked her head to the side—"guess I'll

have to see if Paula does. I'm sure Steven left her a hefty insurance policy. Wonder how much she'll pay for the tape. Probably more than twenty-five Gs, you think? Especially since she just called me to see if I'd found out anything. I haven't had a chance to call her back yet, but maybe I'll call her as soon as I leave here."

"I. Don't. Have. That. Kind. Of. Money," I repeated.

She lost her smile and turned serious. "Get it, or this little video here—there's a send capability. I'll be sending it to the cops. To the media. To your little sorority sisters. Your friends. Paula. Your husband. Your child—by the way, did I tell you I'm following her on Instagram now? Wouldn't her friends get a kick out of this?"

I fought back the lump in my throat. "I can't get my hands on that kind of money." My mind raced. We did have money in Liz's college fund. But I couldn't mess with that, could I? "Look," I said, already thinking that I could pick up extra shifts. "I can make payments. I get paid every two weeks. I can give you a thousand dollars a month."

She waved away my words. "Girl, ain't nobody got time for that. This isn't a two-year finance plan."

"Sabrina, please," I pleaded.

She paused, then broke out in a huge grin again. "You know what, since we go back, I'm going to be nice and give you three days to get my money. But look at it this way." She stood. "Once I get it, I'm gone and I won't bother you again. I'm a woman of my word. A woman of integrity." She slid her sunglasses on. "Of course, that's something that you wouldn't know anything about. Talk to you in three days, ta-ta."

37

Paula

I WAS GOING THROUGH SOME OF STEVEN'S PAPERWORK when I noticed the date. July 13. I couldn't believe our anniversary was coming up. As I checked the calendar, I remembered that our anniversary was a week after another special date.

"Oh, no," I said to my mom, who was sitting on the love seat across from me. "I've been so wrapped up in my own problems that I completely forgot about Felise's birthday."

"Honey, I'm sure no one will blame you for forgetting a birthday," she replied. She had finally been coming out of her grief and surprised me when she'd come and sat in the living room with me to read her latest edition of *Ebony*.

"Before all of this happened, Greg had mentioned a surprise party for her and I'd promised to help," I said.

"I'm sure he'll understand if you don't help," my mom said. "He knows you have a lot on your plate."

I thought about it—and about my continuing misery.

"No, it might help me get my mind off of things, and after all that Felise has done, it's the least I can do."

My mother looked like she didn't agree, but she decided not to protest and went back to reading her magazine.

I called Greg. He answered on the first ring.

"Hey, Paula," he said.

"Hi."

"How are you holding up?"

"As well as can be expected." I hated when people asked me that stupid question. I'd just lost my husband and the father of my children. How was I supposed to be doing?

I shook off those thoughts. There was no need to get upset with Greg. I was trying to get my life back to some semblance of order.

"I remembered you asked me a while back to help with the birthday party for Felise. Are you still going to do it?"

"I had planned to. We've kind of been going through a rough patch ourselves," Greg admitted. "And it probably would be good for us. Of course, I'm not expecting you to do anything."

"No, I want to," I replied. "I could use the distraction."

Greg considered that, and I could sense him going through his usual deliberations. "Well, I've already put the deposit down on the restaurant and invited some of Felise's friends. It would mean a lot to both of us if you came."

"You know I will. Is it still a surprise?"

"I don't know. With the way Felise has been acting lately, she might not want to do anything. But I kinda think she needs the distraction as well."

"Yeah, I've noticed she's been aloof with me as well."

He sighed heavily. "It's probably . . . You know what, never mind."

"No, Greg, what's up?"

"Paula, you have enough on your plate. I don't want to worry you with this."

"Like I said, I welcome a distraction." I managed a terse laugh.

"Well," he confessed, "I'm a little concerned about us. I know my obsessive behavior is pushing her to the edge, and I'm trying to work on it. I've even started seeing a therapist."

"What? You at a therapist?" I knew that was major. Felise had been trying to get him to get help for years.

"I had to because I could see it pushing a wedge between us. The anniversary was the final straw."

"What happened on your anniversary?"

He was stumped for a moment. "You mean she didn't tell you?"

"No."

"Oh, wow, that's strange. I thought she told you everything."

"I thought she did, too."

Greg then relayed the story of how Felise had laid our rose petals and he'd cleaned them up because he wasn't thinking and had forgotten all about their anniversary.

"She was really upset that night," he said once he was done with the story.

I didn't know whether to be upset or shocked that Felise hadn't told me. But then the significance of the date dawned on me. That was the same night Steven died.

"Oh, she probably was going to tell me, but everything

happened with Steven," I said. "I really hate to hear that you guys are having problems."

"So, you see how I wasn't in much of a party-planning mood, but I have booked the room, paid for it and everything."

"Well, don't worry. I got this, and we'll make sure she has a fantastic affair."

I was actually excited. For the first time in I don't know how long, I felt like my life had purpose outside of the home.

38

Felise

I WONDERED WHETHER THE BANK TELLER WAS PUSHing the silent alarm because I had to look like someone who was up to no good. My hands were shaking, and beads of sweat were trickling down my face.

"Yes, may I help you?" the teller asked, eyeing me suspiciously. I saw her cut her eyes over at the guard as if I were a bank robber. But I guess my nervous demeanor made her nervous.

"Yes, I'd like to make a withdrawal," I said.

"Do you have an account with us?"

"Yes." I nodded as I handed her my driver's license. She handed me a withdrawal slip, and I quickly scribbled down my information. She took the slip back, punched my info in, and relaxed as the account appeared the screen. That let her know that I wasn't a bank robber.

"Yes," she read my slip, "so you didn't write down how much you want. Are you withdrawing it all?"

"How much is in there?"

"Twenty-three thousand, one hundred and forty-six dollars," the woman said.

I took a deep breath. We'd been saving for Liz's college education since she was a baby. What kind of mother was I that I was about to wipe my child out in order to cover up my wrongdoing? How low had I sunk to be here about to do this?

"Ma'am, did you hear me?" the clerk said, once again looking at me strangely.

"Y-yes."

"So, how much are you withdrawing?"

I squeezed my hands together. Greg checked the accounts on the first of every month. That gave me twenty-two days to get the money back in. I shook my head. No, even if I worked triple shifts, I couldn't get the money back in in time.

"Ma'am?" The clerk was getting agitated.

"I–I'm sorry. Yes, I need to withdraw . . ." *My daughter's college fund.* The words would not come out of my mouth. I scribbled on the withdrawal form and pushed it toward her. "Just give me five thousand dollars," I hurriedly said.

She gave me a fake smile as she began counting out the money. "Would you like an envelo—"

I snatched the cash, along with my license, and hurried out of the bank. I just wanted to get out of that place. I wanted to forget how low I had almost sunk, wiping out Liz's college account. I told myself I would pay back the money in installments.

I prayed all the way to the Four Seasons. I couldn't believe Sabrina was making me meet her here, but leave it to Sabrina to continue torturing me. She'd texted me this morning and told me what time to meet her. I had to pray that she would take the five grand and let me send her the rest.

I made my way inside, only to find no sign of Sabrina. I sat in the lobby, nervously drumming my leg for about fifteen minutes.

I was about to take out my phone and call when she came waltzing in.

"Hello, my dear friend," she said with a big cheesy grin.

I wanted to slap that smile right off her face. "Save it. Where do you want to go?"

"Well, because it is a large transaction, I thought that we'd go somewhere private." She pointed toward the elevator. "Follow me. I don't need any of these people around here seeing what I'm doing and getting all in my business. And I definitely don't want anything caught on tape." She smirked.

I followed her in the elevator, wondering why we couldn't duck in a bathroom. This trick had the nerve to put her earphones in and belt out a Mary J. Blige song as we waited on the elevator to go up. Finally it stopped on the fifth floor. She didn't say a word as she got off the elevator. I followed and was just about to tell her how ridiculous this cloak-and-dagger thing was until she stopped in front of room 527 and put the room key in.

"What are you doing?" I stammered in horror.

"I'm going into a room so we can conduct our transaction."

"I'm not going in there," I said.

"What? Don't be ridiculous. Do you want to do this in the hallway?"

"I'm not going in there," I repeated.

She had the nerve to pretend to be confused, and then leaned back and looked at the door. "Oh, snap, my bad. I didn't even realize that this was the room that you killed your best friend's husband in."

"I didn't kill him," I said through gritted teeth.

"You got that lethal coochie!" Sabrina joked.

"Oh, my God, you are so disgusting!"

She giggled. "Girl, come on. They've cleaned the room up. No sign of a dead body."

"I'm not going in," I repeated.

"Okay," she loudly said. "We can stand out here in the hallway and you can give me the money for black—"

I covered her mouth. "Fine," I hissed as I motioned for her to go inside. She laughed like this was really entertaining.

As soon as we were inside, she turned to me and held out her hand. "May I have my money, please?"

I inhaled. Exhaled. Then said, "Sabrina, I couldn't get the money."

"Aww, hell naw," she said, starting to head toward the door.

I jumped in front of her to stop her. "Please, listen. I couldn't get it, but I did get five grand." I reached in my purse, pulled out the wad of money, and stuffed it in her hand. "It's all I can get."

She cut her eyes at me, then glanced down at the money. I was hoping it was more money than she'd ever held at one time, and it would be enough to buy me some time. She continued glaring at me as she said, "I thought you were resourceful. I mean, if you can steal my boyfriend and sleep with your best friend's husband, you're capable of anything."

I was surprised at this accusation. "Is that what this is about? You're mad over some stupid freshman-year relationship? For the thousandth time, I didn't know Earl was your boyfriend!"

"No, I'm mad because you get everything you want—including my boyfriend—because you think you are so much better than everyone else. You had this whole high-falutin, saddity attitude, and I was just the poor girl from the ghetto that you took under your wing—never hesitating to let everyone know when you'd given me a pair of shoes or some other hand-me-down."

"Are you serious?" I said. "I did nothing but try to help you, and I only let one person know that you were wearing some of my hand-me-downs."

"Yeah, but it was the person with the biggest mouth on campus—Shayla Green."

I couldn't believe that nearly two decades later we were having this discussion. "So, this is what you're ruining my life for? Some beef we had in college?"

"I'm not ruining your life. An opportunity just presented itself, and I took advantage of it." She shook her head. "You're a prime example of why people in glass houses shouldn't throw stones."

"I didn't throw stones!"

"Yeah, you did. You said if I was doing my job, I wouldn't have to worry about my boyfriend cheating."

"Sabrina, I was nineteen and foolish. And we were fighting. I seriously thought we had moved past that."

"No, *you* had." She rolled her eyes, thumbed through the money, then waved it at me. "What am I supposed to do with this?"

"Use it to get started. It will cover a couple months' rent in LA. I will work on getting you the rest." I knew that I never had any intention on giving Sabrina another dime, but I had to say something. "Please. Just take it for now."

I breathed a sigh of relief when, after a brief hesitation, she stuffed the money in her purse, which was crisscrossed on her body.

"Can I have the video?" I asked.

"Girl, you must be crazy," she said. "You get the video when I get my money. All of it." She started walking toward the door. "I can't appreciate you trying to play me."

"It's all I have," I said. I couldn't believe I was groveling to this woman.

"Fine. It'll do. For now. I won't send the video. This week," she added with a chuckle.

"Sabrina, don't play with me."

"Don't play with my money," she said, losing her smile. "I want another payment in two weeks."

I nodded, even though I knew that wouldn't happen. I couldn't live with her threat of blackmail hanging over me. I knew that I couldn't continue torturing myself, trying to come up with money. I knew that I couldn't sink any lower than stealing from my daughter. And that meant I had only one choice—it was time for me to come clean.

39

Paula

I WAS SO HAPPY TO HAVE SOMETHING TO DO OTHER than sitting around, wallowing in grief. I hoped that I hadn't stepped on Greg's toes, but I'd completely taken over the birthday planning.

"So, do you like this one or that one?" I asked my sister as I pointed at the small sample cakes in front of us. I'd dragged Charlene along to test out the different cake options for Felise's party. I was using this lady in Baytown who made fabulous cakes. Her bakery was a forty-five-minute drive, but the cakes were really delicious.

"This is some slap-your-mama cake," Charlene said, biting into another slice of the pineapple-kiwi cake.

"I'll give you five dollars if you do it."

"You're trying to get me killed." Charlene laughed. "So which one are you going to go with?"

"I don't know. They are all so good." My eyes scanned the six different samples laid out in front of me. The baker, Mrs. Barbara, was patiently waiting for us to decide which one we wanted. "I'm leaning toward the kiwi because Felise loves kiwi."

"Yeah, that one is definitely off the chain," Charlene said. "But really, I don't think you can go wrong with any of them."

I placed the order and paid the extra fee to have the cake delivered to the restaurant where Greg was having Felise's surprise party.

"So, Felise still doesn't know about the party?" Charlene asked once we were back in the car.

"No, it's a surprise."

She turned up her nose. She hadn't said much else about Felise, but my friend's absence had gotten under her skin. "Why are you the one running all over town?" Charlene asked.

"I offered to do it," I replied. "Felise has been a godsend to me, and this is helping me get up and get my mind off things. Besides, it's the first time you and I have had a chance to spend any time together."

As much as she could work my nerves, I loved hanging out with my little sister. She had a way of making me forget all my problems and just enjoy life.

"Yeah, I hate that I have to leave tomorrow," Charlene replied.

"Me, too. I've really enjoyed having you here, although I wish it had been under different circumstances. And thank you for everything you've done."

"Including losing Tahiry?" she asked with a grin.

"Yes, including letting my daughter go off like she's grown." I shook my head at that memory. I wasn't too mad at Charlene. Tahiry could be quite persuasive if she wanted to be.

"There's a reason I don't and won't have kids." She laughed.

We made more small talk on the long drive home. She filled me in on how things were going in New York. She was scheduled to start working as an apprentice for Vera Wang on the first of the next month. Since I knew how much she loved fashion design, I couldn't have been more proud.

"So, do you need me to take you to the airport in the morning?" I asked as I turned into my driveway.

"No, this guy I met last week is going to take me."

I shook my head. "Only you would come to town for a funeral and leave with a man. How did you . . . You know what?" I threw my hand up. "Never mind. I don't even want to know."

Of course my sister continued anyway. "Girl, I met him at the store the other day. He lives here in Houston, but he just got drafted by the Philadelphia Eagles. You know that ain't but a hop, skip, and a jump from New York. Baby sister is about to work her magic so I can become a football wife."

Charlene looked like a taller version of Kerry Washington, with the body of Serena Williams, which was funny considering the closest she got to working out was passing a gym on her way to the mall.

"Just be careful. You know some of those ball players are some big dogs," I warned as I parked and turned the car off.

"You don't have to tell me to be careful. I told you, I'm not like you. I believe most men are going to cheat. If you know that going in, you'll be all right when it happens."

That casual statement stopped me short. "So, I'm just supposed to be okay with what Steven did?"

"Nah, you ain't supposed to be okay," she said. "But it's

not the end of the world. If—and that's a big *if*—if he did do something, it probably wasn't his first time. And if he'd lived, it wouldn't have been his last. But I don't think it lessens the love he had for you. Men are driven by hormones. He probably saw some chick there, hooked up with her, she left, and he died in his sleep. I think you can take comfort in knowing that he wasn't in love with somebody else."

I didn't care what she said, that gave me no comfort.

"Cheater or not," Charlene continued, "one thing I do know is that Steven only loved one woman and it was you. Yes, he messed up, but I don't think that should change how you feel in retrospect."

I took in my sister's words. I'd never understood how a person could claim to love you yet cheat on you. But I did know that six weeks had passed since my husband's death, and I was getting tired of trying to make sense out of my heartbreak.

Charlene was right. In my heart, I knew that my husband loved me. I just needed to figure out how to make that my primary memory.

40

Felise

I COULD HEAR MY YOUNGER SISTER'S VOICE LIKE A roaring cannon.

Don't do it! Don't you dare do it!

As difficult as the prospect was, though, I dismissed her advice and prepared to face my husband. I know a lot of women would tell me to take this secret to my grave, but I couldn't do it. The guilt was killing me. The money I had given Sabrina had bought me some time, but I knew I wouldn't be able to come up with the rest, and even if I could, I could not continue living in fear of her deciding one day to tell Greg.

No, the only option I had was to come clean, pray my husband forgave me, and then begin repairing my marriage.

I eased the key in the lock and made my way inside. I had hoped to buy myself a little time. Some wine would help give me the liquid courage I needed. But as soon as I walked in, I saw Greg sitting at the kitchen table with a distressed look across his face.

"Hey, what's going on?" I said as I walked in.

He was in interrogator mode. "Where have you been?"

I frowned. Why was he acting like the police? "Out. Running errands. Is that okay?"

"Can you have a seat, please?" He motioned to the seat across the table.

This was not going the way I had planned at all. "For what?"

"Can you just have a seat?"

I eased into the chair because the tone of his voice was worrying me. He was already mad. Maybe I should come clean later.

"Do you want to tell me what is going on with you?" he asked.

"Wh-what are you talking about?" I asked. "Going on with what?" I hoped he wasn't about to start in on me again about the fact that we hadn't made love. I knew that at some point I was going to have to push images of Steven out of my mind and make love to my husband, but today wasn't that day.

"You. You just haven't been yourself lately," Greg said, eyeing me skeptically. "And I'm trying to figure out why."

I managed a weak smile. "You're exaggerating."

He shook his head. "No. No, I'm not. At first I thought my neglect was the problem, but it's not. You've been acting strangely for several weeks now." The way that he was dissecting me with his eyes was making me extremely uncomfortable. "Where's the negligee?"

"What negligee?"

"The one you bought for our anniversary. You keep all your lingerie in the second drawer."

I knew he was obsessive about his clothes, but now he was trying to regulate mine?

"Huh?" I said. I realized that was my opening. That was the hook I needed to tell my husband what really happened on the night Steven died. But when I opened my mouth, the harsh look in his eyes silenced me.

"Where is it?" Greg repeated. "I didn't see it anywhere. I saw the receipt in your jewelry box but can't seem to find the negligee you had on when you left here that night."

I didn't know what to say. I had tossed that negligee when I left the hotel. I knew that after what happened, I'd never be able to wear it again.

"So, you're snooping on me?" was all I could think of to say.

"Where. Is. It?"

"Greg . . ." I took a deep breath. The door to confession was wide open. All I had to do was walk through it. "Look, there's something—"

"I said, where is it!" He pounded the table so hard, it shook.

I jumped in fright. "I–I don't know. I was just upset, and I threw it away."

"You threw it away?" he said, looking at me crazy. "You want me to believe that you threw away a two-hundred-dollar negligee? Because you were mad at me?"

Now I was getting nervous because I didn't know where this line of questioning was going. "Why would you care? What is your problem?"

"No, I'm trying to figure out what your problem is," Greg replied. "Shoot straight with me," he said. "Are you seeing someone else?"

That accusation made me relax a bit. He didn't know anything. "Are you kidding me? No. Why would you ask me something like that?"

"I don't know. You don't want to be intimate with me. You're nervous and on edge all the time. You're snapping at me and Liz. And oh, yeah, you're a thief."

That took me aback. "Excuse me?"

"You're lying to me. I've been with you long enough to know when something is going on with you, and something is definitely going on. Because everything else aside, now you're stealing money."

"What are you talking about?" I repeated, only because it was the only thing I could think of to say.

He slammed a piece of paper on the table. "Liz's college money. Five thousand dollars is missing. Where is it?"

"Wh-wh-what are you talking about?"

"What do you think I'm talking about? I checked Liz's account."

"Why would you do that?" I asked, stalling as my mind raced, trying to come up with a response. "You don't do that until the first of the month."

"Is that what you were counting on? What? You'd planned to put the money back by then?"

I fought back tears. I couldn't take the drama. It seemed my life lately was one lie after another. I had to come clean—now!

"Greg, I have something to tell you . . ." I began.

"Oh, my God. You are having an affair!"

"Greg, would you just let me—"

"You dirty, filthy slut!" He rose out of his chair and grabbed me by both arms. His sudden aggression completely caught me off guard. "Is that why you stole Liz's money, to give to your broke boyfriend?" His grip tightened around my arms as he shook me.

"Owww, you're hurting me!" I was shocked beyond belief. In all our years of marriage, Greg had never put his hands on me. "Let me go."

"How could you do this to me!" he screamed. He caught himself, though, because he released me and pushed me roughly toward the wall.

I wanted to explain, tell him he was wrong, but I was so stunned, and he was so enraged, I couldn't get the words out.

"So, I guess this is payback?" he snapped. "You've been waiting all this time to pay me back?"

"Greg . . ." I finally managed to find my voice.

"I guess we're even now. You had your little fling." He took a deep breath, stood like he was pulling himself together, then added, "Tell your boyfriend I want my daughter's money back in her account on the first." He spun around and stormed out the room.

I knew that I needed to go after him. Convince him that there was no boyfriend and do what I had initially planned to do: come clean.

But with the way he'd just reacted—over an imaginary man he didn't know—telling him the truth would send him over an edge we would both regret.

41

Paula

MAYBE I'D FOUND MY CALLING—EVENT PLANNING—because I was having a ball trying to plan my best friend's birthday party. After all that she had done, I really wanted it to be a night that she would always remember.

Greg must have been super busy because I'd been calling him the last three days and hadn't been able to reach him. I didn't want to step on his toes or plan something he'd already taken care of. That's why I kept trying, and finally he picked up.

"Hey," I said. "It's Paula."

"Hey, Paula," he replied.

He sounded groggy and out of it.

"Are you okay?" I asked.

"Yeah, yeah. I'm cool," he said, although he sure sounded stressed out.

"Well, I know you said you were still having Felise's party, and since it's coming up quickly, we might need to finalize some things."

"Ah, yeah," he stammered. The tone of his voice was almost drugged, like he was taking medication.

"Greg, are you sure you're okay? You don't sound yourself."

"Nah, I just got a lot going on," he responded.

"Is everything okay?" I asked. The last time we'd talked he had been worried about his marriage. I hoped that wasn't holding him back now.

"It's work stuff, just work stuff," he said unconvincingly.

"Well, um, do you still want to do the party?"

A beat, then, "To be honest, Paula, my mind isn't in the right place to be planning a party."

I was a little shocked to hear that, especially because both of us had shelled out time and money. "I thought you said you already paid for the place."

"I did," he replied. "It's just . . . the planning. I'm not in the right frame of mind."

I relaxed. "Well, if the planning is an issue, don't worry about a thing. I got it."

"I could never ask you to do something like that."

"Please. Felise is my best friend and she's a really good woman." I swear I heard him laugh at that, but I kept talking. "Besides, I've done quite a bit of planning so far. I've sent out invitations. I got a cake. It's doing me good to keep my mind off of things."

"You're a good friend, Paula." He sounded so unbelievably sad, and it was breaking my heart. I knew now, more than ever, we *had* to have this party. Everybody needed the release.

"Felise has been a good friend to me. She really has. And

I know the two of you have had problems, but I know that she loves you and this party would do us all good."

The pause that filled the phone went on for so long, I thought he had hung up.

"Greg?"

"Yeah, I'm here," he softly said.

I don't know why, but I felt compelled to say, "Greg, if anyone can work through their problems, the two of you can."

I heard a loud exhale. "You know what? I don't want to talk about me. Have you found anything else out about Steven?"

It was my turn to pause. Should I tell him about the other woman? He and Steven weren't that close, but they were friends. Maybe he knew something about her. But I was in a good mood today. I didn't want to get myself worked up all over again.

"No, the autopsy confirmed that his heart gave out," I said.

"Just gave out, huh?"

"Yeah."

He tsked, then said, "Well, whatever you do, don't blame yourself. Steven was at that hotel because he wanted to be. Couples fight all the time, but they should always come home."

"You're so right." Greg was bringing me down, so I wanted to hang up and get back to the party planning. "But look, I know you have a lot going on at work and, well, I don't and I need the distraction. So, I'll take care of everything from here. You just get Felise to the Hyatt. Why don't you tell her you're taking her to dinner at the Hyatt Spindletop?

Make her think you're going to a quiet dinner for the two of you. Get a room and just make it a whole experience."

"You really have thought this through," he said.

"I have a lot of time on my hands. And I love doing this."

"Well, I really appreciate it."

"Cool, and Greg, what you two have is real love. I tell Felise all the time, you're a good guy." I laughed. "OCD and all."

He gave a terse chuckle.

"So, I'll take it from here," I continued. "I'll call you back when I've finalized everything."

He agreed, and we hung up. I hoped the rift between him and Felise wasn't serious. Over the years, despite everything they'd gone through, Felise had always been in Greg's corner. Even when he had his brief affair. Even when she felt neglected. Even when she wanted to give up, she hung in there. He couldn't be sounding defeated now. No, whatever they were going through, they needed to work through it. And I was going to do my part. I was going to help them both have a night to remember.

42

Felise

THE CHAOS WAS THE PART OF MY JOB I BOTH LOVED and hated. The hustle and bustle of the ER was on full speed tonight.

"We're losing her! Get me a working ventilator. Stat!" the ER doctor screamed as he stuck his head out of a drawn curtain.

"I'm coming!" I said, racing toward him. It had been a crazy night in the ER, and that was fine with me. I needed something to take my mind off my situation.

I hurriedly began removing the current ventilator, which we'd discovered wasn't working. I know it took me less than a minute to get the new ventilator hooked up, but just as I snapped in the final tube, I heard the sound that all of us in the ER hated: the droning tone of the machine indicating flatline.

The room grew eerily silent until the doctor removed his mask and said, "I'm calling it. Time of death, 9:46 p.m."

I inhaled deeply. I'd seen my share of murder and mayhem in the ER, but this one hit home for me. This one had happened right before my very eyes.

A young woman had come into the ER just after eight p.m., right after my shift started. She stumbled in with a stab wound to the stomach. She managed to mumble that her husband had stabbed her. I held her hand as she cried and pleaded with us to save her life. I managed to calm her down enough for her to say, "Please tell my kids I love them . . . Tell them d-don't hate him . . . and I'm sorry I caused this."

I didn't have a chance to learn any more information because her husband walked in and announced, "This is what happens to bitches who cheat." He fired two shots at her. One hit a nurse in the leg; the other hit the young woman in the stomach. After the shooting, the man dropped the gun and didn't resist as the emergency room security tackled him to the floor. I assumed the police had taken him away because he was nowhere to be seen.

By two in the morning, the ER began to return to normal and I was finally able to catch my breath.

"So what was the deal with that lady that was shot by her husband?" I asked April, one of the shift nurses. April was the ER reporter. If you wanted to know what was going on, she was the one to give you the scoop.

"Girl, her husband caught her cheating. Apparently, he killed the other guy, then stabbed her. She got away, then he followed her here," April said. "He just kept telling the police, 'I thought we were happy.' That's all he said over and over."

"Wow."

"Yep," she continued, shaking her head. "He tried to kill her." She stopped and looked toward the bay where the woman had died. "I guess he did kill her. That's why I try to tell folks, you playing with fire when you step out on your mate. You never know what someone is capable of until they've been wronged."

I was stunned. It's like she was sending me a direct message. But was Greg capable of murder? *No*, I told myself. Greg would never do something like that. But still, deep down, I knew, with a betrayal like this, I had no idea what my husband was capable of.

I had a hard time concentrating the rest of my shift. I had just clocked out when I saw Valerie Westbrook, our clinical psychologist, heading to her office.

I don't know what made me stop her, but I said, "Hey, Valerie. Can I talk to you for a moment?"

"Sure, Felise. What's going on?"

"You heard about what happened in the ER tonight?"

"Yes." She assumed her professional demeanor. "I got the All-text, which is why I came on in. Such a tragedy. And I understand you were with her. Do you need to talk?"

We had psychologists on staff because sometimes the trauma of the ER got to be too much.

"I actually do," I said. While the young woman's murder bothered me, that's not what I wanted to talk to Valerie about. I hated using tonight's situation to find out answers for myself, but I wasn't ready to admit to anyone else what I'd done.

"Let's step in my office." She led the way down the hallway. I followed her in and took a seat. She sat down behind her desk and got into therapist mode.

"So, you were with her when she came in?"

"I was. She wanted me to tell her kids she was sorry. It was so heartbreaking. She felt like she was to blame."

Valerie was listening intently. "I'm sorry you had to endure that, but I'm sure it was comforting to the woman to have you there."

"She said he'd never gotten out of control like that before. Do you think it's possible for someone with no violent history to snap?"

Valerie nodded. "Absolutely. Crimes of passion are often the result of rage, many times that no one saw coming. They're amplified when the person feels like the betrayal was significant."

"The lady was really remorseful, and she wanted to make sure her kids didn't hate her husband." She listened like she was waiting for me to continue. "I know you deal with mostly traumatic situations, but you do a lot of family counseling as well." I needed to make sure I was convincing, so I let myself look confused. I'd been trying to make sense of how I could've done what I did. Maybe Valerie could indirectly help me find some answers. "I guess I'm just trying to understand what makes a person cheat. I mean, she seemed like a sweet woman, and apparently the husband thought they were perfectly happy. Why would she risk everything?"

"No one who is perfectly happy in their primary relationship gets into a second one," Valerie said matter-of-factly.

"Hmmm," I said.

"Usually, they're missing or lacking something," Valerie continued. "Let me use this analogy. Imagine someone wandering around with a couple of empty wineglasses who suddenly meets someone with a bottle of wine. And so they want a little taste."

She narrowed her eyes at me. "Are you sure there's not anything more you want to talk about?"

"No, no. I just felt bad for the lady, that's all." I wanted to ask her more questions, talk to her about how I could get over the guilt, but I was too ashamed to let her in on what I'd done.

"Really, that was it," I said. "It's all just part of the job, I guess." I shrugged. "But thank you for taking the time out to talk to me."

"My door is always open, whenever you need me. You can come talk to me about anything, work-related or not."

I probably needed to come on a regular basis, but I knew I never would. I did walk away with one valuable nugget, though. This secret was a ticking time bomb. Greg had only rumbled the other day. If he stumbled upon the truth any other way, he would completely explode.

No, I had to put on my big-girl panties, tell the truth, and deal with the consequences—however frightening they might be.

43

Paula

RETURNING TO MY NORMAL HOUSEHOLD DUTIES FELT strange. With Steven gone, I didn't think that normalcy would ever return again. It had actually been quiet around here. My children still were away. I'd talked to them this morning. The boys weren't in a hurry to come home, and Tahiry wouldn't be back from camp for two weeks. I was going to do like my mom said and enjoy my peace, but honestly, I wouldn't have minded hearing the chatter of my children.

I was folding the last of the laundry and had just placed a stack of towels in the linen closet when the doorbell rang. I peeked outside and saw the UPS deliveryman.

"Hi," he said after I opened the door. "I have a delivery"—he glanced down at his clipboard—"for Steven Wright."

I was momentarily speechless. What was I supposed to say? "Sorry, Steven is dead"? Or, "Sorry, Steven can never sign for another package"? So I just said, "I'll take it."

Back inside, I opened the package. I couldn't believe the emotions that were flowing through me. What had my husband ordered? I slowly pulled the package open. My heart dropped when I saw the blue Tiffany's box inside.

"Oh, my God," I said, after opening the box. It contained a beautiful white-gold chain-link bracelet with a dangling heart and the most beautiful inscription: *I want to grow old with you. SW. Happy Anniversary.*

I fell to the floor in tears and didn't look up until my mom entered the living room.

"Are you all right?" she asked.

I managed a nod. "Yes." I held the box out toward her. "I just got this. Apparently, Steven was having it delivered to arrive in time for our anniversary."

"Oh, honey," my mom said. She took the bracelet out and examined it. "Oh, my God, it's beautiful."

I pulled myself up off the floor. "I guess this is a sign. Everyone keeps telling me to let the anger go, the quest for answers, everything. I prayed for God to send me a sign that that's what I needed to do. I wanted some kind of confirmation that I was doing the right thing."

She eased the bracelet onto my arm. "Well, you got your sign."

I put my hand over my mouth to stifle a sob.

"Paula," my mother said, "don't focus on what happened on the night Steven died. Look at the life he lived. And the legacy"—she handed me an envelope—"that he's leaving you and your children."

"What's that?" I asked, taking it.

"Came in the mail for you. It's from New York Life Insurance Company, so I thought it might be important."

I frowned as I pulled myself up off the floor. "That's strange. Our life insurance is through AIG."

I tore the envelope open and fell back against the wall in sheer shock at the sight of the check I was holding in my hand.

"What is it?" my mom said, leaning over. She clutched her heart. "Glory be to Jesus! Does that say two million dollars?"

I knew that Steven had insurance through his company. But I had no idea that he had taken out an additional life insurance policy.

"What . . . Who? I didn't even fill out the paperwork." I rifled through the envelope until I saw a letter. I was reading it when my mom nudged me and said, "Read it out loud."

I started reading: "'Hey, Paula. I know you are swamped, so I went ahead and processed your paperwork for Steven's life insurance policy. I know this can't bring him back, but he loved you and the kids so much and he wanted you to be taken care of. Let me know if you need anything. Love, Carl.'" I looked at my mom. "It's from Steven's friend, Carl. He's an insurance agent." I stared at the check again. "Oh, my God. I had no idea."

"Wow. I think that's quite a nice way to say 'I'm sorry.'"

"Mama!"

"I know that's bad, but it's the truth." She looked up toward the ceiling. "Steven, I don't know if my daughter forgives you, but I sure do."

"Mama, you are so foul." I actually managed to laugh through my tears.

"Whatever. Nothing says 'I'm sorry' like a two-million-dollar check."

I held the check to my chest. We'd already received five hundred thousand dollars in life insurance from Steven's job.

We would live off that. This, I'd use to pay off the house, then put the rest up for my kids. "This money is for my children's future."

"Okay, okay. It's for the kids. But let me hold twenty bucks for bingo. I'm feeling lucky."

I laughed as I pushed my mom out the door. I had so many questions and conflicting feelings about what had happened with Steven, but I felt a lot better. Not because of the money. I hated what he did, but the gift and the supplemental insurance policy announced his feelings loud and clear. My husband loved me—flaws and all. And that is the memory that I would choose to cherish.

44

Felise

YOU CAN'T CONTINUE THIS WEB OF LIES. MY OLDER SISter's words continued to ring in my ears as I watched Greg walk up the path to our house. I'd been watching out for him since he answered my call and agreed to come over.

I said a silent prayer asking God to give me strength to not back out at the last minute.

"Hey," I said, opening the door before he had a chance to unlock it. I stepped aside and motioned for him to come in.

"Hey," he dryly replied, walking in. "Where's Liz?"

"She's at her friend's house. I felt like we should talk alone."

He hadn't been home in a week. He'd been holed up in a hotel, and I felt like he was sinking into a depression. It was time for this madness to end. It was time for me to tell the truth.

"I don't know what there's left for us to talk about." Greg sighed heavily.

"Now that things have calmed down, I want to tell you everything."

He had a look on his face like he wasn't sure he wanted to hear it, so I motioned for him to sit down in the living room. "Please. Have a seat." He did, apprehensively, never taking his eyes off me.

I took a deep breath. *God give me strength.* "I asked you here because I wanted to tell you why I took the money," I began. "The real reason."

"I'm listening."

Don't do it—now Fran's voice was ringing through my head. I shook it away and continued talking. "I was being blackmailed."

I expected him to balk, drop his mouth in confusion, even call me a liar, but instead he only said, "By whom and for what?"

"By Sabrina Fulton. My old college roommate."

"Why would Sabrina be blackmailing you?"

I took another deep breath, and a lie slid to the edge of my tongue. But I'd done enough lying. I wanted to come clean. I *needed* to come clean if I wanted to save my marriage. Because one lie had spawned another, and the string of them was slowly killing me. My gut told me that the truth was going to eventually come out. I couldn't risk Greg opening his email one day and finding the video. I knew my husband. If our marriage could be salvaged at all, the truth had to come from me.

"There is no one else. I'm not having an affair. I swear." *Could what Steven and I did even be classified as an affair?* I shook away that thought. I needed to focus. "I want to be very clear about that."

He was studying me, trying to detect any lies. "Okay, if you're not having an affair, then what's been up with you?" he asked. "What did you do to allow someone to blackmail you?"

I thought about telling him that I did meet Steven and I did go up to his room, but that we didn't do anything. However, Greg knew that I didn't come home that night. That story would only infuriate him even more because of how implausible it sounded. He wouldn't believe anything but the truth. So I simply said, "The night of our anniversary, I was very upset and I went to the Four Seasons to go to the bar. I sat there and drowned my sorrows." I could tell Greg was waiting with bated breath. "Well, I bumped into someone while I was there."

"Who?"

I had to dig deep inside my soul to utter my next words. "Steven."

"Paula's Steven?"

I nodded, and his brow furrowed as if he was thinking. "Wait, that's the night he died. Did you . . . Were you? . . . You spent the night with him?"

I nodded as my eyes filled with tears.

"Are you kidding me?" he yelled, jumping up from his seat. "You had sex with Steven?"

Again, silence on my end. There were no words to justify my indiscretion, so I remained quiet.

"Paula is your best friend. Steven is . . . He's like family!"

"I know. I didn't mean for it . . . I mean, it just happened," I stammered.

"You don't *just happen* to fall into bed with your best friend's husband!" he screamed.

My shoulders trembled as the waterworks began. "Neither one of us intended for it to happen. We'd had too much to drink, and one thing led to another." I decided to leave out the information about all the unresolved feelings because my husband could handle only so much.

"Felise, how could you?" he cried. I didn't miss that, unlike the other day when he accused me of sleeping with some stranger, he didn't seem angry, exactly. Today, he seemed more hurt. And that hurt my heart.

"It just happened," I repeated. I did force out a lie when I added, "It meant nothing."

"So you cheated on me, you hurt me like this, and *it meant nothing*? Screwing him wasn't even worth it to you?" he questioned, his voice cracking. "You throw away everything we built over something that meant *nothing*?"

"We both knew it was wrong. We both swore it would never happen again. Please believe me," I pleaded.

"Believe you? I don't know how I'll ever believe anything you say again. Here I am trying to figure out what's wrong with me. What I'm doing wrong to the point that you can't even stomach my touch. And it wasn't even about me? You were feeling guilty because you slept your best friend's husband *on our anniversary*?" He stopped his rant and stood, pensive. "Wait, so . . . d-did you kill him?"

"No!" I exclaimed. "The next morning, I woke up to find he wasn't breathing. And I freaked out and just left."

"Oh, this just keeps getting better!" Greg released a pained laugh. "You sleep with him, you cheat on me, and then you leave him for dead? Did you even call for help?"

"He was already dead. I didn't know what to do."

He stared through me, totally repulsed. "I don't even

know you." He headed toward the door. "I wish you were cheating with some random guy." He spun around to face me. "That, I could handle. That was payback for my indiscretion years ago. I rationalized that. An eye for an eye. But this . . . Our friend? My child calls him *uncle*!" He shook his head. "I need to get out of here before I catch a case."

The disgusted look on his face broke my heart. The hurt expression tore at my insides, and the rage in his eyes told me I might have made the biggest mistake ever by coming clean.

45

Felise

I HAD WONDERED IF MAVIS HAD TOLD HER HUSBAND, Charles, about my situation. Judging from the look of disdain on his face, I realized she must have.

"Hello, Charles," I said anyway.

"Umph," he grunted as he stepped aside to let me in. "Mavis, it's your sister," he called out before disappearing back into the den.

Mavis came out of the kitchen, an apron wrapped around her waist. "Hey, lil sis. I was just cooking. What brings you by?"

"I just stopped by to see what you were up to." I felt so awful about everything with Greg yesterday. I hadn't slept at all. I'd called in sick to work, and I needed my sister to tell me that I had done the right thing. Not that it mattered now, but I needed to talk to her.

"Just cooking dinner. Phillip will be home for another two weeks before school starts," she said, referring to my nephew. "You know he doesn't eat worth anything up at that college, so I'm fixing all of his favorite things, fattening him up before he goes back."

I glanced back toward the door to make sure Charles was out of sight. "Why did you tell Charles?" I whispered.

She glanced over her shoulder, too, back toward the den, then motioned for me to follow her.

"Girl, I didn't tell Charles," she said once we were back in the kitchen. She lowered her voice. "Your husband did. He called Charles last night and told him everything. You didn't tell me you used Liz's college money to pay that girl off."

"I only used some of it. I was going to pay it back. How else did you think I was getting the money?" I asked when I saw the look of shock on her face.

She shook her head. "I don't know. I guess I didn't think about it. But your daughter's college fund?"

"I was desperate, Mavis." I didn't expect my sister to understand. Hell, I didn't even understand. I didn't know who this woman was that I had turned into.

She gave me a sympathetic look. "I know how hard this is for you, so I'm not going to beat you up anymore."

"Greg is pretty upset." I slid into a seat at the kitchen table.

"You do understand why, don't you?"

"I do. I just hope he forgives me." Even as I repeated the refrain that had been running through my head all night long, my heart told me it wasn't going to happen.

"Well, time heals all wounds, so we'll see. But don't you feel better about coming clean?"

I cut my eyes at her. This was one time I probably should have listened to Fran. "No."

"Well, right now you don't. But think about it. You don't have to spend the rest of your days wondering if Sabrina is going to pop up out of the woodwork, and you don't have to build one lie on top of the other."

I fidgeted with the salt and pepper shakers. "Almost. Paula still doesn't know." I knew that she was next on the list. She needed to hear it from me before Sabrina told her.

"I'm going to tell her. I have to. I just don't know when. You don't think Greg would tell her?" I asked, experiencing a sudden panic. "I didn't even think about that."

"I believe Greg really cares for Paula as well, so he wouldn't want to further hurt her like that," Mavis replied.

I nodded. "And he hasn't said he's leaving me for good. Greg is the type that if he stays, he wouldn't want anyone to know. That's why I'm a little shocked that he told Charles."

"Well, I'm praying it all works out," my sister said as she went back to stirring a huge pot on the stove. "I added you to the prayer circle at church. You might want to consider coming."

"Nah, I'm good. I don't think the Lord wants to hear from me right about now."

"He wants to hear from you all the time." She flashed a chastising look. "Not just when you're in trouble." She set the spoon down, wiped her hands again, and came over and sat across from me at the table.

"You know how I feel about what you did," she said. "But I also believe acceptance is a very important part to being able to move on. Acceptance will put an end to your internal struggle—the one where you keep wishing the affair had not happened the way it did or hurt as many people. Once you stop struggling with what happened, calmness will start to take its place and you can find the peace you need."

That was laughable. Even if Greg forgave me, I didn't see how I'd ever be at peace with what I'd done.

"I see your disbelief all over your face," she said. "God is capable of creating calm in the midst of a storm." Before I could respond, my sister took my hands, bowed her head, and began praying. At first, I was a little stunned, and then I began listening intently as she prayed for peace. Nothing else. Not for Greg or Paula to forgive me. Just peace.

"What was that for?" I asked when she was done.

"Because you need it," she said. "Now, learn to do that for yourself, and you might find your situation doing a huge turnaround." She stood and returned to the stove. Picking up the large spoon she was using to stir, she said, "You've got to try some of this chili. I think I finally make it better than Mama."

46

Paula

IF BURYING MY HUSBAND WAS THE HARDEST THING I ever had to do, this was the second hardest.

I put his Nike T-shirt up to my nose and inhaled. Even though it was clean, it still had his scent. I took a deep breath, folded it, and placed it in the box with the rest of his belongings.

I had been putting off this day since we put Steven in the ground. But sleeping in this room every night, surrounded by all things Steven, was making my healing harder.

I'd gone to a support group over the weekend. I wanted someone who was objective, who didn't know me or Steven. I needed someone to give me feedback on my grief. I had pushed aside all the things I didn't know—if he was with another woman, who she was, etc.—and just focused on my grief. I learned that everything I was feeling was natural. Each of the women, and men, in the group had felt the same at one time or another. And while they'd said every person's length of grieving was different, I sided with those who felt that in order to move on, they had to move out their loved ones' belongings.

I had to do it because every time I saw Steven's things, I wanted to cry. And while crying was healthy, it was keeping me locked in place. And for that reason, I knew that I needed to pack up his belongings.

My cell phone rang, and I answered when I saw Felise's name "Hey, Felise."

Silence filled the phone.

"Felise?"

"H-hey, Paula," she said. "Um, what are you doing?"

"Doing what I told you I would do—packing up Steven's things."

I had called Felise last night about my decision, and she thought it was a good idea as well. To my surprise, though, she had offered to come over to be here with me because she knew how difficult it would be. She had said she wanted to talk to me, but I wasn't in the mood for an it's-time-to-move-on pep talk. I was doing this, but on my own terms.

"Wow. So, you're really doing it?"

I had shifted his workout clothes out of the bottom drawer into a box. I hadn't decided what I was going to do with all his stuff. I wasn't ready to give it away just yet, so I was placing it in the attic for storage.

"Yeah, I know. I figured, why keep putting it off?"

"Are you sure you don't want me to help?" Felise asked. "I can come over there now. We can pack up, then, um, maybe we can sit down and, you know, just, um, talk."

"Thank you so much, but I'm sure." I glanced around

the room. I needed to be alone. "I'm not going to let Steven's memory die, but I have to remove this stuff so I can move on with living."

Felise was quiet. "I'm so sorry you're having to go through this," she softly said.

"Yeah, I don't understand why God does things the way he does. But I guess I have to live with it."

"We all do," she mumbled.

I shook off my melancholy thoughts. I was in a good place now, and I wanted to stay there. "So, what's on tap for you today?"

"I'm about to go to work. I'm going through some stuff over here myself," she confessed.

"I'm so sorry. I haven't even checked to see how things are going in your life." I didn't want to bring up her troubles with Greg. If she wanted to talk about it, she'd bring it up.

"You don't worry about me," Felise said. "I'm pulling myself together. Steven's mom called me, though. She's worried about you."

"I need to call her. This obsessive quest for some answers I was on had everybody concerned."

"Have you given that up?" Felise asked.

"Yep. It's time to let it go." I closed up one box and pulled another up on the bed. "I prayed for a sign and I got one, and now I'm trying to achieve some closure. My kids need me to pull it together. I've pawned them off on family for too long. It's time for me to get back to the mothering business."

"I am so happy to hear that," Felise said.

"Oh, yeah, and my new business," I added. Just the thought warmed my insides. *My* business.

"What business?" Felise asked, sounding surprised.

"Event planning. Party Wright Planning," I said. "Get the play on words? Paula Wright. Party Right."

She laughed. "I love it. In the midst of everything, you're branching out into your own business—that's so awesome. I'm so proud of you. I'll call you later."

I said good-bye, hung up, then resumed my packing. I stopped as I caught my reflection in the mirror. I was proud of me, too. I just wished that I'd discovered this when Steven was alive. It's like his death had given me new life. Maybe if I had . . . I caught myself. *I can't live in a world of maybes now*, I thought as I returned to packing up my husband's things.

47

Felise

I SAT ON THE SOFA AS MY HUSBAND STOOD TOWERING over me. I felt like a child being scolded, but I knew that I deserved any wrath that I might incur.

When he'd shown up this morning, I'd been hoping he would be bringing his belongings. He'd been gone a week since my confession, and Liz was starting to get suspicious. And each day he spent away made me less confident that he was coming back.

Greg took a deep breath. "I've thought long and hard about this. I don't understand how you could betray me, and betray your best friend like that. And I know you want to say that it *just happened*, but you carried that deception past that hotel room that night."

I wanted to speak out in my defense. Ask him, What was I supposed to do? How was I supposed to handle this? But I didn't know what else to say, and I knew nothing I said would be good enough. So I kept my mouth closed and prayed that my husband wasn't about to tell me that he was leaving me—leaving our family.

He swallowed hard like he was trying to keep his composure.

"I have played every minute over and over in my head. My emotions have ranged from devastated to downright distraught. You had sex with your best friend's husband on *our* anniversary. How do we heal from that? How do we move past that?"

I didn't realize until then that tears were dripping down my cheeks. I looked up at him and said, "I don't know, but we try. I'm willing to do whatever I have to do to get you to forgive me."

"At first, I was blaming myself," he continued, pacing the room, "saying that my neglect forced you into the arms of the man my child calls uncle. I kept asking myself, Where did I go wrong? How could I have kept her from cheating on me? And then over the last couple of days, the revelation came that you're a grown woman. Yes, we might've had our problems, but if you were that unhappy, then you should've left me. You don't seek solace in the arms of another man. You don't go to the other side, hoping the grass is greener. You water the lawn you have!" He took a deep breath, trying to calm himself down. I let him say what he needed to say.

"Over the years, you worked hard to assure me that you and Steven were strictly friends, that the vibes I had gotten in the beginning were all my imagination," he continued. "You make me feel like our whole marriage was built on a lie."

Now he was being extreme. No, I wasn't completely honest about my relationship with Steven. That was simply because I knew he wouldn't be able to handle it and it would end up affecting our relationship with Paula. At the time, though, I did believe it. I actually believed I didn't have feelings for Steven.

"How am I supposed to get over this?" he asked.

I couldn't help it. I said, "The same way I did."

He glared at me. "I knew that would come up. The two don't even compare. What I did with Miranda was wrong, but you didn't know her. I didn't bring her around, pretending that she was my friend. I didn't treat her like family."

I wasn't trying to get into a whose-affair-was-worse conversation. I just wanted my husband to forgive me.

"I'm sorry," I said. "I meant, I want you to find it in your heart to work through this."

"So you're saying you want me to just pretend none of this ever happened," he continued. "You want me to act like I don't know about your deception."

"No," I said softly. "I want you to forgive me, and I will spend every waking moment trying to make this up to you. But Liz and I need—"

"Don't!" he said, interrupting me. "Don't you dare bring our daughter into this! Because if you cared about our daughter at all, you would've picked up some random dude off the street before you picked up this man that we all loved and cared about. You betrayed us all!" He inhaled again. "I don't know how I'm going to get over this." He stood for a moment, then turned and looked at me. "But I'm willing to try."

I wanted to jump from my seat and throw my arms around his neck, but I stood slowly. "Thank you, that's all I can ask."

"Have you told Paula?" he asked.

"No." I prayed he didn't make telling her a condition of us staying together.

"Don't," he said. "She's in enough pain, and she is finally managing to move forward. Your betrayal would only set her back."

I wanted to dance a jig. I didn't know if that was really why he didn't want Paula to know, or if he didn't want people talking about him for staying with me. I didn't really care. I was just glad that he was staying.

"I promise, I'm going to spend my lifetime making this up to you." I stepped toward him to lean in for a kiss. He spun around and walked away.

"I'm staying, but I'll be sleeping in the guest room for now."

I watched him round the corner, and then any joy I felt vanished when I heard him say, "Oh, no, Liz!"

I jumped from my seat and hurried over to where he stood, towering over my baby. She was sitting on the floor, crouched against the wall, her knees pulled up to her chest. Judging from the way she was shaking and the tears streaming down her face, she'd heard everything.

"Liz, baby, I'm so sorry," I said, falling to the floor next to her.

I tried to take her in my arms, but she yanked herself away. "You had sex with Uncle Steven?"

I looked up at Greg, and any rage he'd managed to conquer had returned in full force. He charged out the door and left me to deal with our daughter alone.

48

Paula

"REMEMBER, I WANT THE PLAYLIST TO BE CLEAN AND a lot of old-school nineties music," I told the deejay. I'd spent the last hour tracking down DJ Xtreme, who I was told was one of the best deejays in Houston. I'd finally caught up with him and, after turning on the charm, convinced him to take this last-minute gig.

"Got it," he replied. "We are all set."

"Wonderful, so if you can be there about nine, that will be great," I told him.

"Who should I send this invoice to?" he asked.

"To Party Wright Planning at gmail dot com," I replied proudly.

"Cool, it's on the way."

I hung up the phone, feeling invigorated. In a matter of days, I'd confirmed a menu with the hotel, booked the deejay, secured decorations—shoot, planned a whole party. And I still had six days to spare.

"You sure are working hard," my mom said, walking into

the den, where I'd set up shop. Eventually, I would take over Steven's office, but I wasn't ready to do that yet. Even though I'd packed up most of his stuff in the bedroom, clearing out his office seemed so final.

"Yeah, Mom, I am so loving this. I can't believe I didn't get into this earlier."

"I can't either," my mom replied. "Now that I think about it, it's a natural fit. Remember, you and Felise were chair and co-chair of the junior and senior prom?"

"Oh, yeah." I laughed. "And I kept complaining because I was doing all the work while Felise was off somewhere goofing off."

"Well, you have definitely found your calling." My mom leaned in and looked at my computer screen. "Do you have a website already?"

"No, this is just the sample the web designer sent to me to approve." I leaned back so she could get a good look. "You like it?"

She shrugged. "You know I don't know anything about all that Internet stuff. But it looks nice to me."

I loved the bright, sleek design. I'd spent twenty minutes on the phone with the web designer, Jeremy, telling him my vision, and he'd come back with the perfect design. "Yeah, I think so, too." I handed her one of the invitations for Felise's party, which was lying next to my computer. "Aren't these cute?"

"Waste of paper if you ask me. Just call folks," my mother said.

I shook my head at her. "Are you coming to the party? Rodney said we can bring the boys back over there."

"Do I have to buy a gift?"

"No," I chuckled. "I'll write your name on my gift."

My mom grinned widely as she headed out the door. "Then I'm in like Flynn."

I shut my computer down and began cleaning up my desk. In addition to Felise's party, I'd already booked a baby shower for my next-door neighbor, so I'd begun planning that as well.

"Hey, anybody home?"

I smiled at the sound of my daughter bouncing up the stairs. She was riding back from cheer camp with one of her teammates and they were supposed to be back an hour ago, so I was glad to have her home.

"In my room, hon," I called out.

She eased into my room gingerly, as if she was trying to gauge my mood. I greeted her with a huge smile, which in turn made her smile.

"Hey, Mom," she said, coming over to hug me. It felt good to hug my daughter. We'd been so at odds since she'd turned thirteen.

"How was camp?"

"Super cool. Mrs. Vega said to tell you hi and that she's praying for you," Tahiry said, referring to her teammate's mother who had dropped her off. I made a mental note to call Mrs. Vega and thank her.

"So tell me all about camp," I said, turning and giving my daughter my undivided attention.

Tahiry plopped down on my bed and began running down all the things she'd done the past week.

"It was sooo much fun. I'm glad you made me go. My friend Shelby had these awesome twists. I want you to do my hair like that."

My mother had come in the room midway through Tahiry's camp rundown. She, too, had stood, listening intently. She finally interjected. "Sweetie, your mom is starting her own business, so her plate is full," my mom said. "But how about Granny twists them later on?"

Tahiry turned up her nose. "Granny, you don't know how to twist!"

"Well, I know how to plait. I can plait your hair." She reached for Tahiry's hair.

"Eww, as if!" Tahiry ducked out of her reach, and they both laughed.

"Go check on your brothers and I'll take you guys out for ice cream later on," my mother said.

"Ice cream? That is so elementary."

"I'll let you get sprinkles and nuts."

"All right, cool." She laughed before darting off.

Once again, I couldn't help but be grateful that Felise had stepped up and gotten everything Tahiry needed together to make sure she could go to camp. Judging by how she looked coming home, it had done her good. Maybe now both of us could get on the path to healing.

49

Felise

IT HAD TAKEN ME MORE THAN AN HOUR TO GET LIZ calmed down. Greg had locked himself in the guest room and hadn't come out. I know he was feeling a mixture of anger and sadness because although he was an absentee parent, he loved Liz with everything inside him. So I knew that it broke his heart to see her hurting. I hoped that Liz's finding out didn't change his decision to give our marriage another try. I would talk with him about it later that night, but right then I needed to focus on my daughter. She had literally cried herself to sleep, and now I was sitting in the corner of her bedroom, watching her.

I debated whether I should go talk to Greg, but I wanted to be here when she woke up. Besides, I needed to give him time to cool down.

Finally, she stirred, her eyes slowly fluttering open.

"Mom?" I could tell she was thinking as the memory of the last few hours came back to her.

"I'm here, sweetie."

Sadness blanketed her face as she pulled herself up against her headboard.

"Can we talk?"

She slowly nodded.

"I don't know how much you heard."

"Everything."

I got up and sat on her bed. "I'm really sorry, honey. There are so many things that I wish that I could do differently. I would die if you hated me."

She didn't respond at first, but once she'd considered what I said, she replied, "I don't hate you. I could never hate you."

I didn't know how much I should share with my daughter, but I knew she was inquisitive and she wouldn't be able to make sense of any of this until she had some answers.

"It's complicated," I began, "but long story short, your uncle Steven and I used to date back in college."

"What?"

"We were really good friends who crossed the line and started dating. We thought it was a mistake, and I ended up fixing him up with Paula."

"Ewww, I would never want Tahiry's sloppy seconds."

I managed a tight smile. "Well, we didn't see it as that, and we never told anyone how close we really were. In fact, I think we even convinced ourselves."

"I don't understand. What does that have to do with now?"

"The night before he died, well, we made a big mistake."

"And slept together?" she finished.

I nodded.

"Did you have anything to do with him dying?"

"No," I said. At least I hoped I didn't.

Liz didn't ask any more questions after that. I could tell that she was trying to put together such a grown-up complication in her own teenage terms. She wouldn't be able to figure it out right away. She'd need time to process how something like this could have happened. I was relieved, though, when she finally slumped against me, resting her head on my chest.

"You're in a lot more trouble than I've ever been."

50

Paula

"MOMMY! MASON WON'T LEAVE ME ALONE!"

"Tell him to stop looking at me."

I never thought I'd be happy to hear my kids fighting. But that meant that we were returning to some sense of normalcy. And that was a wonderful feeling.

"Mason, leave your brother alone. Marcus, stop looking at your brother. Stevie, can you take out the garbage?"

I was sitting at the bar, going over some details for Felise's party. I'd let Stevie move his PlayStation into the living room, an idea I'd adamantly opposed for the longest time, but I knew the last thing he needed was to be cooped up in his room.

"Aww, Ma. Why can't Marcus and Mason take it out?"

"You didn't start taking the garbage out until you were six, so they still have few more years. Come on, son."

He placed the controller on the couch cushion and stood up. I had to do a double take because usually I had to fight to get him to do anything. But I'd seen a change in my son since Steven's death.

"Uggh!" Tahiry screamed as she stomped into the kitchen.

"What in the world is wrong with you?" I asked.

"It's Chelsea." She plopped down in the barstool across from me. "She makes me sick. I hate her!"

"Chelsea as in your best friend Chelsea?" I asked.

"She's not my best friend anymore. I hate her." Tahiry had her bottom lip stuck out like she used to do when she was a little girl.

I set my paper down and gave her my undivided attention.

"Honey, hate is a wasted energy. But tell me what happened."

"She told Sonya Visor that I said Monica Jackson's brother would never go out with her because she was too fat, so then Sonya got on Kik and told everybody in the world that I wanted to go out with Andrew Cooper, but he wouldn't do it because he said my head was too big and I had a body odor."

I fought the urge to ridicule her ninth-grade problems. "Sweetie, you don't hate Chelsea, especially over some he-said, she-said stuff. What did Chelsea have to say about all of this?"

"I don't know." Tahiry poked her lips out. "I didn't talk to her. I'm never talking to her again."

"First of all, you have to talk to her. You have to get her side."

Tahiry raised an eyebrow. "Why do I have to do that?"

"Because what if this is all a misunderstanding? And not only do you have to get her side, but if she did do it, you have to find it in your heart to forgive her."

Tahiry rolled her eyes, like that was the craziest thing she'd ever heard of.

"She's supposed to be my friend. Why would she go talking about me?"

"You're supposed to be her friend, and you're not even giving her the benefit of the doubt," I replied. She saw some sense in that, and I continued, "You guys have been friends since the third grade. You have to find a way to forgive her."

"Forgive her? That's not going to happen. I do like Andrew. But he's never going to ask me out now after she put me on blast like that."

I let some sternness enter my voice. "First of all, he doesn't need to ask you out because you're too young to date."

"Uggh. Mom, you're missing the point," she protested.

"Second," I continued, "any guy that is interested in you is not going to let some stupid post change his mind."

She stopped short, like she was thinking about what I said.

I patted her hand. "Honey, people make mistakes, they do selfish things, and even intentionally try to hurt one another. It's going to happen. But you owe it to your friendship to try to work past the problems. Don't throw away years of friendship over a single mistake." I brushed my fingers along her cheek. "Talk to her."

She paused. "You really think I should?"

I nodded. "Nothing should come in the way of good friends."

Tahiry finally smiled. "I'm going to call her now." She stood. "Thanks, Mom. You're the best."

I smiled as she darted off. Then I went back to party planning for my own best friend. I couldn't wait for the day when Tahiry could know true friendship like that I shared with Felise.

51

Felise

GOD HAD TRULY TURNED OUR FAMILY AROUND. WHILE I knew I had a long road ahead with Greg, we were truly on the right track. I think seeing that Liz was okay helped the healing. Greg was still standoffish, and I could see the pain in his eyes every time we talked, but he was trying. He'd returned to our bedroom last night, and we'd made love. The sex was passionate, almost angry, but I knew he was feeling all kinds of mixed emotions, so I let him release his frustrations in the bedroom. I was just grateful to be with him again. I was grateful for his ability to forgive.

And this—my surprise birthday party—that he'd carefully planned hammered home how there *could* be healing after hurt.

Liz seemed like she understood. She was with Tahiry tonight. At first, I was nervous about that, but she'd assured me that she wouldn't tell Tahiry what had happened. Sabrina was still a potential problem and part of why I knew, despite what Greg said, I was going to have to come clean with Paula. And since Sabrina would be expecting another payment soon, I was going to have to do that sooner rather than later.

Tonight, though, I wanted to focus all my attention on my party—the first glimpse at happiness I'd had in a long time.

"If I may have everyone's attention, please?"

I smiled as my husband lightly tapped his fork against his wineglass. He looked magnificent in a tan blazer, a black Calvin Klein shirt, and my favorite jeans. When we'd arrived to the Hyatt, Greg had told me we were going to the Spindletop restaurant for an intimate dinner. We'd gotten a room so we didn't have to go home tonight.

Greg cleared his throat and continued as the room grew silent. "These past few weeks have been very trying for the people we love"—he looked at Paula and smiled—"and the people who love them." He looked at me.

I returned his smile. I was genuinely grateful. If you had asked me six weeks ago if I could ever love my husband more, I'd tell you no. Here we were, surrounded by family and friends. My sisters waved at me. I knew they were happy to see me happy. Some of my sorority sisters were here, as well as a couple of my colleagues. I didn't know how the night could get any more perfect.

Greg turned his attention back to Paula. "Paula, I want you to know that I have always admired your commitment to your family and your dedication to your friends. I want you to know no matter what, I will always be there for you."

That made me frown. "*I* will always be there"? Seems like it would have been more appropriate for Greg to say *we* will always be there. But I shook off that thought and continued listening.

He stared out at the audience. "I'm so glad you all are here to help me celebrate my wife's birthday. She has given so much to everyone. It's time that we gave her something back."

I found myself wishing Liz had come, but Greg had been adamant that he wanted our "dinner" to include just the two of us, so we'd done dinner with the three of us last night.

"To my wife, the birthday girl," Greg said, holding his glass as the others joined him. "The mother of my child, the love of my life, the woman who . . . broke my heart in a million pieces."

I froze as he lost his smile, and his eyes began filling with tears.

No, no, no, no, no. But it was too late. Greg turned back to the crowd. "I know this isn't the platform for this." He put his hand over his heart. "But when you're heartbroken, you sometimes do things you might not otherwise do. My first instinct was to take a pistol and put a bullet in my wife's head." Several gasps filled the room, and Greg managed a terse chuckle. "But don't worry, I'm not a violent man because if I were . . ." He shook his head as he let out a slow hiss.

"Greg, don't . . ." I managed to whisper.

He ignored me. His best friend stood and eased next to him. "Come on, man, don't do this," he whispered.

Greg jerked away from him. "No. No, everyone needs to know that the woman we're celebrating is the scum of the earth." He turned to Paula, who was looking mortified.

"Greg, what in the world are you doing?" she asked from the table directly in front of us. "I can't believe you're doing this to Felise!"

That made Greg crack up laughing. "Look at you, Paula.

Always coming to your friend's side." He wagged a finger at her. "What did you tell me on our wedding day? 'You'd better not hurt my girl.' Well, you should've told your girl that she'd better not hurt me."

"Greg, stop," Paula said. I wanted her to stop coming to my defense, but I was frozen in my seat. "Whatever is going on with you and Felise can be worked out," she sternly added.

That made Greg laugh again. "Can it, huh? Let me see if you feel the same way after I tell you what she did."

I finally managed to find my voice. "Greg, don't."

He ignored me and continued. "Do you know why she wasn't there when Steven died? In the beginning?"

"No, Greg. Please."

He continued to ignore me. All eyes in the room were planted on us like this was some reality show.

"She wasn't there because she felt guilty."

I saw the confused look on Paula's face. "About what?"

Greg continued. "I'm glad you asked."

"Greg," his friend said, tugging at his arm again. "Come on, man."

Greg turned to him. "Benny, have a seat, man. You're not going to stop me."

"This isn't the time or the place," Benny said.

"When is the time?" Greg shouted. "When is the time to let everyone know what my wife did?"

I saw a look of defeat cross Benny's face, and he looked at me apologetically as he sank back down in the chair.

Greg spun back toward Paula. "Felise wasn't there for you in the days after Steven's death because she's the reason your husband died."

"What?" Paula said, her brow creasing in confusion.

"Oh, she didn't kill him," Greg continued, "at least not outright, but somewhere in their passionate night of lovemaking, I'm sure he overexerted himself and that led to him dying."

Paula frowned, then looked at me like she was expecting me to jump up and call Greg a liar. Every eye in the room was planted on me.

"Felise, what is he talking about?" she said. Paula's mother was sitting next to her, just as horrified. In fact, everyone in the room was in shock.

I stared at my friend. The only thing that would come out of my mouth was, "I–I, ah . . ."

"Oh, she's speechless," Greg said, "so let me share the story for you. My wife, your best friend, and your husband met up for a secret rendezvous at the Four Seasons."

"We didn't meet up," I mumbled, my head lowered.

But Greg ignored me. He was on a roll. "Oh, I forgot the kicker. This was on our wedding anniversary!" He hit the podium and laughed like a madman. "Our wedding anniversary!"

Paula stood, holding onto the back of her chair like she was trying to steady herself. "This can't be true. Felise, tell me it's not true."

"I'm afraid it is," Greg said. "That's why she couldn't come by your side in the beginning. She felt guilty. Not enough to come clean, but guilty nonetheless. But she's such a liar that she stole some of our daughter's college tuition to pay off a blackmailer to keep her little secret safe."

Paula was shaking now. "Felise, what is he talking about?

You're my best friend. Tell me this isn't true." She came closer to the front table. "Tell me this isn't true," she slowly repeated when I didn't respond.

Greg glared at me. "Yeah, wifey. Tell her it isn't true."

I looked at Paula, then the sea of faces staring at me in shock, then back at Paula, and all I could say was "I'm so sorry."

"You bitch! How could you do this?" Paula screamed as she dove over the table. I saw my sisters move in to try to pull her off of me, but she was like a raging bull. All I could do was shield my face because Paula was out for blood. Just as I raised my arms I saw my husband, a mixture of hate and sadness across his face, exit out a side door.

The last thing I remembered was Paula's fist connecting with my face before everything went black.

52

Felise

"OOOOH," I MOANED. I FELT LIKE I'D BEEN IN A BOXING match with Laila Ali and hadn't landed a lick.

"Just take it easy. Sit up." Mavis was bent over by my side. She was trying to help me sit up.

"Are you sure we don't need to take her to the hospital?" I heard Fran ask.

My head was pounding and my vision was blurred, but I knew I had no desire to go to the hospital, especially because the nearest one was Memorial Hermann, where I worked.

"I'm okay," I mumbled, rubbing my forehead. Then I noticed the word *whore* spray-painted across the hotel room wall.

"What is that?" I asked.

Mavis and Fran frowned. "Yeah, we saw that when we brought you here," Mavis said. "At some point during the evening, Greg must've come up here and done that."

I shook my head. That must have been why he wanted to use my credit card for the room when we checked in. He wanted to make sure I'd be responsible for this mess.

"Why would he do this?" I said, adjusting the ice pack someone had placed on my jaw. "Go to this extreme?"

"It is low-down," Mavis replied. "But I told you, all consequences have actions."

"Not now, please," I said. I had a bad enough headache. Mavis's preaching would only make it worse.

"Oh, I'm not trying to preach because I feel horrible for you," Mavis said.

"Paula, how is she?" I asked.

"She's not too good. They had to sedate her," Mavis said.

I fell back against the headboard. "Oh, my God, she's never going to forgive me."

"Probably not," Mavis replied.

"This is all your punk-ass husband's fault," Fran said. "I should've known something was wrong. Greg is so anal, and he forgave you so easily."

Fran was right. Now that I thought back on his behavior, I should've seen this coming. But my need for redemption had blinded me. My husband never had been a forgiving man, so I don't know why in the world I thought he'd forgiven me for such a horrible betrayal, and so quickly. I was so blinded by my guilt that I didn't think about how vindictive my husband could be.

"So, what are you going to do?" Mavis asked.

"I don't know. I want to try and make it right. I don't know how that's possible, though," I replied. "But I need to talk to Paula."

"I agree."

"Girl, are you crazy?" Fran said. "You'd better stay far away from Paula right now."

"Unlike Fran, I do think you should go see Paula. Try to talk to her," Mavis said.

"She's not going to want to talk to me."

"But you have to try."

I couldn't believe I was in this predicament. "One weak moment has cost me everything."

"It sure did, and if you ask me, Steven got off easy," Fran said.

Mavis sighed heavily. "I understand the desires of the flesh. I understand temptation, but we can't get so far gone that we don't think about the consequences of our actions. We get so caught up in the minute that we don't worry about anything else."

My sister with all her preaching was right on the money. That night in the Four Seasons, Steven and I had thrown caution to the wind. We knew it was wrong, but we justified it because it felt right. We never thought about all the people we would hurt. We never thought our story would end like this.

"When bad things happen, most people don't see it coming. They think that they're going to be the one that can do this bad thing and everything will be all right. I'm not saying we won't get caught up in bad situations. But before you take that leap, we should always ask, is it worth it?" Mavis continued.

Even Fran looked like she was thinking about what my sister was saying. And it must have resonated with her because she didn't say a word.

"I made a mess of everything," I cried.

"Yeah, you did. But that's the reason Jesus died for our sins, so that we don't have to crucify ourselves for them."

"Preach, sis."

I side-eyed Fran.

"Don't worry," she replied, "I'm not about to turn into Joyce Meyer or anything, but Mavis is right. I may not be all super religious like her, but I know the Lord forgives. And if He can forgive, then so can you."

"And so can Greg. And so can Paula," Mavis added.

Fran shook her head. "Um, yeah, maybe not Paula."

"My point is, they *can*," Mavis continued. "So, give Paula time to cool down and in a couple of days, go see her. Talk to her. Tell her how you made a mistake and you're trying to make it right."

I let out a heavy sigh as I tried my best not to cry. Not that I had any tears left.

"Just remember, healing takes time and you got to have patience. Here," Mavis said, handing me a Bible out of her purse.

"What is this for?" I asked. "I have a Bible."

"But obviously you're not using it." She opened the book for me. "You see the pages with the yellow tabs? Read those passages. If you don't have strength, read Psalm 73:26. If you need help with forgiveness, try Acts 3:19. If you need to see a way out of no way, try First Corinthians 10:13."

"And if you want to feel empowered, try *The Book of Eli*."

Both Mavis and I stared at Fran.

"Isn't that a Denzel film?" I asked.

She shrugged. "Honey, if Denzel can't empower you, nothing can."

Mavis shook her head at Fran. "You're coming to Bible study with me next week. You need Jesus."

A part of me wanted to smile. But the way my heart hurt, I didn't have anything to smile about.

53

Paula

I HADN'T MOVED FROM MY SPOT ON THE SOFA. I HAD no plans on moving ever again. I'd lost my husband and my best friend in the ultimate act of betrayal. The pills—some prescription my mom had gotten for me—were helping me calm down. But they didn't quiet the raging pain in my heart.

"Mom, is it true?" Tahiry asked, standing over me. My precious daughter. So innocent, so oblivious. She'd been real subdued in the three days since I'd found out about Felise and Steven. At first I thought maybe she knew since Liz was with her the night of the party. But I had assumed Liz must not have known either because Tahiry hadn't said anything about it, and to be honest, I was just too blinded by my anger to focus anything else.

But now, judging by the look on my little girl's face, I knew without a doubt, she knew.

"So Nana slept with Daddy?"

"She's not your nana anymore. And yes, her and your daddy decided to get—"

"Paula!"

I stopped as my mom entered the room. She glared at me before turning to Tahiry. "Sweetheart, go to your room."

Tahiry looked at me, pain in her eyes, but she didn't argue as she walked out.

"Why did you stop me from telling her all the gory details?" I said, throwing my blanket back and sitting up on the sofa.

My mother's hands went to her hips like she was disappointed in me.

"That's grown folks' business. You don't need to be talking with your fourteen-year-old daughter about issues with your man."

I rolled my eyes and stared out the window.

"Baby, I know you're hurt," my mom said, sitting down next to me. "I'm hurting for you. I'm just as shocked as you are. But it doesn't surprise me."

That made me do a double take. "What? I thought you liked Felise."

"I do. Well, I did. But I told you, I've always been uneasy about that boyfriend-swapping thing y'all did."

"Boyfriend swapping? We didn't swap boyfriends."

"Did Steven or did he not used to date her?"

"Well, yes, but—"

"See, y'all and all this newfangled, new-age, peace-and-love crap is just too much. In my day, you didn't have no woman all up under your man like that, especially a woman that he had had relations with."

"I didn't have Felise up under him."

"Shoot, every time you turned around, you were driving to a double date, hanging out together. I guess you just wanted to pretend they'd never had a relationship." She patted my leg. "But everything happens for a reason. You wouldn't have had your beautiful family. I'm just trying to help you put things in perspective."

"They both told me they didn't have feelings for one another."

"Obviously, they lied," my mom replied. "I think they both may have really believed that, or tried to make themselves believe that. Maybe it was buried and they never acted on it out of respect, but something remained. But I'm sorry, I'm just from the school that friends don't date friends' men."

"Do you think I'm to blame?"

"Why would you think you're to blame?" my mom said.

"You told me I was going to drive my husband into the arms of another woman. Did I push and nag until he fell into my best friend's arms?"

She let out a long sigh. "Well, you know, if we're placing blame, then I'm as much to blame as you. I pushed you two into getting married. I worried so much about what folks would say about my daughter getting pregnant out of wedlock. But if I was being honest, you two didn't love each other. Not like a husband and wife should. And when you told me how close he was to Felise, my gut didn't feel right. But, that said, he was a good man and I wanted my granddaughter to come into this world in a proper fashion. I knew the day he proposed you didn't want to marry him, but I knew if I pushed the right guilt buttons, you'd do the right thing. And you did, but you haven't been truly happy. You tried, but you couldn't. Your children are a blessing from God, but the timing wasn't right, and if I could go back, I wouldn't force you to marry a man you didn't really love."

"But I did love Steven."

"*We* loved everything Steven represented—smart, successful, handsome, mannerable, from a good family. In the end, that blinded us both. Yes, you learned to love him. You did. You tried everything to be a good wife. But your heart wasn't really there. So if you want to blame anyone, it can go all the way around. Me, you, Steven, and Felise." She could tell I was getting outraged, and she continued on another track. "Still, the bulk of the blame lies on them. If the two of them had feelings back in the day, when they made the decision to bury their feelings, they should've kept them buried forever and always. If the Lord had meant for them to be together, they would've been together. And even if they couldn't walk away from their own lust, they should've respected you enough to walk away from each other." She lifted my chin and looked into my glistening eyes. "So you stop beating yourself up, because at the end of the day, the biggest blame goes to the two of them. The two of them were as wrong as Bobby and Whitney. You and Steven were together a long time. Felise and Steven are to blame for what they did. No one else. If they've been suppressing those feelings this long, they could've kept right on suppressing them."

Her down-to-earth logic made me half smile. "Mama, I love you."

"I love you, too, baby. And don't you dare beat yourself up. You loved that man as best you could, and when all is said and done, whatever decision he made is on him. I'm sure he's up there now explaining to God why he did what he did."

"Or Satan," I grumbled.

"Hush that talk," my mom said. "It's a good thing we serve a forgiving God. Don't you want to see him again?"

"Yeah, because I need to give him a piece of my mind."

"And ain't you going to Heaven?"

"Yes."

"Well, you'll see him there, and I'm sure God will give you a pass to smack Steven upside his head."

I forced a small smile, but it quickly faded. "I'm never going to forget what Felise did."

"And that's understandable. You don't have to forget. Just at some point, you gotta forgive. If for no other reason than hate doesn't need to reside in your heart."

I wiped the slow tear that was rolling its way down my cheek. "I can't believe they got together. I've been sitting here all night, tossing and turning, wondering how long they were having an affair, how did it happen. How could they both just keep smiling in my face while stabbing me in my back? I just can't believe this."

"Well, the only way you're going to get answers is to talk to her," my mom said matter-of-factly.

"Never! I'm never speaking to her again."

"Honey, you've been through a lot. Ask Felise what you want to know. Vent, yell, cuss her out, whatever you gotta do. Just don't keep it bottled up. If you're bent on holding grudges, you may become so wrapped up in past wrongs that you can't enjoy the present. If you don't get past some of the wounds of the past, you tend to bring them into everything else you pursue."

"That's easier said than done," I said with a scowl.

My mom didn't let my attitude dissuade her. "But it is doable. Nobody is saying forget. You've got to understand that forgiveness also doesn't justify or excuse what the other person did. It just helps you gain a sense of peace."

Peace? That was laughable. I didn't feel like I'd ever have peace again.

"Just think about what I'm saying," my mom said. "If not for you, for your family."

My bingo-playing, warped-Bible-verse-quoting mom had actually said something profound. Too bad I wasn't in the right frame of mind to fully receive her words.

54

Paula

I HAD MANAGED TO GET OFF THE SOFA, SHOWER, AND even fix me and the kids some breakfast when my front doorbell rang. My mom was in the back and the kids were upstairs, so I removed the last of the bacon from the pan, took the skillet off the stove, and headed to the door.

I looked out the peephole and suddenly wished I had that hot bacon grease in my hand.

"You have a lot of nerve showing your face here," I said, swinging the door open. I couldn't believe that Felise Mavins was standing on my doorstep.

"I know," she humbly responded. She looked tired and puffy-eyed, in a wrinkled maxi dress and some flip-flops.

I expected Felise to launch into a rationalization, trying to explain away what she'd done. Instead, she stood there waiting.

"So, can I come in?" she finally said.

"No," I replied. It was taking everything in my power not

to revert to my Southside DC ways and drop-kick this trick right here on my doorstep.

"Then, I'm just going to say what I have to say right here," she said, raising her head like she'd found some courage.

"You can say what you want to my front door because I'm about to slam it in your face." I took a step back and was surprised when I bumped right into my daughter. She was peering over my shoulder, looking out at Felise.

"Tahiry, go back to your room," I said

I expected Tahiry to protest, beg to stay, anything. But she just glared at Felise before turning and heading back down the hall.

"Please? Can I just have five minutes?" Felise said.

I wanted to tell her where she and her five minutes could go, but I needed to hear what she had to say. I finally stepped aside to let her in.

"Mind if I sit down?" Felise asked as I shut the front door.

"Yeah, I do," I replied. She didn't need to have a seat because she wasn't going to be here long. The only reason I had let her in was because I needed to hear how and why, not that anything she said could justify her betrayal, but I did need to make sense of it.

"Paula, you have every right to hate me," Felise began.

"Tell me something I don't know," I replied, folding my arms across my chest.

"I just . . . I just thought you might have questions, and I wanted to give you answers."

"Oh, there are answers to this? I mean, you really have an explanation as to why you screwed my husband?" I stood in front of her, my arms crossed. I never had any intention of sitting down because I needed to look this tramp straight in the eye.

Tears welled in Felise's eyes. I was not moved.

"No, I don't," she replied. "There is no rational reason to explain what I did. But I did want to—"

"How long?" I said, interrupting her.

"How long what?"

"How long were you having an affair?"

She looked surprised. "We weren't having an affair."

"You liar," I snapped.

She was upset that I would make such an accusation. "I'm not expecting you to believe anything I'm saying. I lost you. I lost my husband. I lost everything."

"Boo-hoo, cry me a freakin' river," I shot back.

"I'm not looking for sympathy."

"Good, because if you are, you rang the wrong damn doorbell."

"I'm just saying, you already hate me, justifiably so. So I have no reason not to be honest. So whatever you ask me, I'll tell you the absolute truth."

"Do you even know what that is?" I willed back the tears. No way was I going to shed a tear in front of her.

She nodded.

"How long?" I repeated.

She looked me dead in the eye. "We were *not* having an affair. It was just a one-time thing."

"Come on, Felise. You can do better than that," I said, rolling my eyes. "So all these years I had you in my home, up under my husband, y'all were secretly pining after each other?"

"No, absolutely not. Steven never did anything inappropriate. And we never crossed any lines. We loved and respected you too much," she said defensively.

"Don't say that!" I yelled, jabbing a finger in her face. She flinched. "Don't you ever say that again." My voice was cracking. "My husband didn't love me and you damn sure didn't because love would've stopped you from checking into a hotel room with my husband. Love would have stopped you before you did the butt-naked dance with the father of my children. And love wouldn't have let you stand by my side, pretending to be my friend, conv—" I paused as I remembered the last few weeks. Then I couldn't help but release a pained laugh. "Convincing me to drop my quest for answers. 'You're paranoid, Paula.' 'There is nobody else, Paula.' 'Let it go, Paula,'" I said, mocking her. "And it was just a game so I wouldn't find out you were the slut that was sleeping with my husband!"

"I'm sorry. It was a mistake."

I couldn't help it. I reached back and slapped her as hard as I could. She grabbed the side of her face but didn't respond.

My chest was heaving as I stepped up in her private space. She cowered but stood her ground. "You come in here, pretending like you're this lost little puppy who didn't know what was going on, oblivious to everything that was happening all around her, and then calling it a mistake? That's moronic stupidity, and a lame throw at redemption. You can call the encounter whatever you want, temporary amnesia or carnal mind block. It was selfish, and you didn't care about anyone but yourself."

"I made a mistake," she whispered, nursing her cheek.

"A horrible, horrible mistake. I'd been drinking, and we both just happened—"

"Don't give me that blame-it-on-the-alcohol mess," I hissed as my chest heaved up and down. "The fact that it's so easy to blame circumstances instead of yourself makes me sick to my stomach!"

"I'm not trying to make excuses." Tears were streaming down her face. "I just want you to know I'm so, so sorry. I just bumped into him at the hotel. I was sad. He was sad."

"And you gave him a shoulder to cry on. You comforted him right to the point of ecstasy." I hoped my words stung because each of them was meant to pierce what little soul she had left.

"It just happened."

I slammed my hand on the wall right behind her head. "That's not an excuse! You don't just happen to screw your best friend's husband. If you bump into him at a hotel and you're upset and he's upset, and you're drunk and he's drunk, worst case, you sit there all night and commiserate and then you take your ass home!"

"I know."

"No, obviously you don't." We stood in a face-off until finally I said, "I guess you want to say this is my fault for how I treated him. I guess you want to tell me how he never loved me anyway and only married me because I was pregnant with Tahiry."

Her eyes grew wide. "No, I would never say something like that."

"You think I don't know that? Neither one of us really loved each other at first. We just tried to do the right thing in the beginning and make it work. And I thought we had. But the two of you convinced me that that you were just friends. Yet you were sleeping with him all along."

"Mom?"

I turned to see my daughter in the doorway, her eyes filled with tears. "Oh, my God, Tahiry." I raced to her side. We'd never told her that I was pregnant when we got married.

But if that fazed her, she didn't let on. She stepped around me and toward Felise.

"Is it true?" she said. "What you told my mom? That it was only one time?"

"Tahiry, no," I said, grabbing her arm.

"No!" She snatched her arm away and stepped toward Felise. "I know you think I'm too young to know the truth, but I know you used to love my dad. That's what Liz said. Is that why you did it?"

Her words tore at my heart, and I hated Felise even more for what she was putting my baby through.

"Tahiry, I'm so sorry," Felise cried. "It was a horrible one-time mistake I will regret the rest of my life. Please don't hate me."

Tahiry stood shaking for a moment—before she bolted into Felise's arms. "I don't hate you, Nana. I don't! I know you're sorry."

My mouth dropped open in horror as Felise wrapped my daughter in the tightest of embraces as both of them released a river of tears.

55

Felise

I SET DOWN THE GROCERIES, DROPPED MY PURSE ON the floor, and made my way into the kitchen. Today had been the most draining day of my life. I wanted to slip into my tub, take a nice, long, hot bubble bath, and pretend that these last six weeks had never happened.

I glanced at my shoes and purse in the middle of the floor, and I found myself longing for my husband to chide me for leaving them. Never in a million years did I think I'd miss his quirky ways. I knew he was staying at the Hilton, but he wouldn't talk to me. The last thing he'd said was that his attorney would be in touch. I guess that meant he'd be filing for divorce, although I prayed it was just his anger talking.

I headed into the living room and flipped the light switch on. Liz was curled up on the couch, her cell phone in her hand.

"Hey, honey."

I could see her eyes were puffy and red.

"What's wrong?"

"That was Dad. He wants me to come live with him."

My heart sank. I'd lost Greg. I couldn't lose my daughter, too.

"Liz . . ." My voice trailed off. I wanted to ask her why she'd told Tahiry—at least I assumed that she had because I couldn't imagine Paula sharing that with her daughter. I decided against asking, though. It's not like any of it mattered at this point anyway.

"Tahiry told me what happened at the party," Liz said. "Did Dad really bust you out like that?"

I hesitated but then nodded.

"In front of all those people?" she asked, horrified.

"Honey, your dad is very upset with me—understandably so," I managed to add.

"Oh, my God. I'm so glad I didn't go. I would've died of embarrassment."

I patted her hand. "If you were there, I'm sure your dad wouldn't have done that. You know he loves you."

She hesitated. "I'm sorry I told Tahiry. But she kept asking me what was wrong. I was gonna lie, but I couldn't think of one."

My heart broke at the position I'd put my daughter in. Her whole life, I'd preached against lying and here she was trying to come up with a lie to cover for me.

"Liz, I'm so sorry for what I've done to this family," I told her. "I hope you know that I would never intentionally do anything to hurt you or your father."

She nodded, though she didn't seem so sure. Finally, she said, "Mom, you really messed up."

I slid next to her. "I know, honey. I wish I could do things differently. I swear I do. But I can't take that night back. All I can do is hope that the people I hurt can one day forgive me."

"Dad says he doesn't want me to be poisoned by your lack of morals."

I inhaled a sharp breath. "That's going too far. I'm not a bad person. I did a bad thing. But I'm not a bad person."

She studied me, trying to puzzle out what to think, before saying, "I know." She stood. "I'm gonna go to my room."

I wanted her to stay and talk some more so I could make sure she was okay, but I knew that I needed to give her space to deal with this on her own.

I went ahead and started cooking dinner. I was putting the finishing touches on my zuppa toscana soup when the doorbell rang. I didn't know if Liz was going to come downstairs and eat, as she hadn't been out her room since she'd gone up the stairs an hour and a half ago.

I set my bowl on the table, then made my way to the front door. I glanced through the peephole and didn't know whether to smile or cry.

I swung the door open. "Greg." I would've given anything for him to take me into his arms. As furious as I was about that stunt he pulled, I wanted everything to return to normal. The fact that he would so publicly humiliate me, and himself, told me just how deep this pain had run.

"Hi," I said, opening the door.

Greg barged past me. "Where's Liz?"

"Upstairs."

He spun around to face me. His tone was formal, his anger still frosty. "Did she tell you that I think she should come stay with me?"

Now, Greg was about to make me mad. It was one thing to have hatred for me. It was another to try and turn my daughter against me, especially when I'd been the primary caregiver all of these years.

"Don't do this, Greg. Our drama is between you and me. Don't drag our daughter into this."

He laughed. "Are you kidding me? You dragged our daughter in this when you decided to sleep with Steven."

I sighed and walked back into the kitchen. "Greg, I'm not going to fight with you."

"She's coming to stay with me," Greg said with finality as he followed me.

"You're at a hotel."

He drew himself up, like he was making an announcement. "Actually, only until the end of the week. My apartment will be ready then."

I slumped against the nearby wall. "Apartment? You can't be serious."

"What did you expect, Felise?" Greg said. "Did you expect to screw your best friend's husband, betray me and our marriage, try to cover it up, then think we would just go about life as usual?"

"I–I didn't think."

"You never do."

A wave of tears welled up. I don't know why. Why would I ever expect Greg to forgive me after what he'd done?

"But you said you forgave me," I found myself saying anyway.

"I lied," he said bitterly.

"So, this was all some elaborate revenge ploy?"

He shrugged. "Part of me wished that I could forget that you were a liar and a cheat. But I can't. And I wanted you to hurt like I was hurt. Should I have handled it a different way? I probably should have. But oh, well."

That birthday party speech was cold, calculated, and carefully planned out. My husband had turned into an assassin. But I knew that telling him that would ignite another outburst, so I lowered my head.

"Please, Greg?" I tried to grab his arm. "Don't leave me. Give me another chance."

I don't know why I was begging. I think I couldn't bear the thought that I had destroyed our family.

Greg pulled out of reach. "Even if I could forgive your betrayal, I could never forgive the elaborate lie you carried afterward. On top of your betrayal, you stole from your child's college fund to cover it up. I can never trust you again." He took a deep breath. "Can you go get Liz?"

"You're not taking my child," I firmly told him. He could leave the family, but it would be a cold day in hell before he took my child with him.

He stopped and glared at me. "The last thing you want to do is try to fight me over custody of our child. I promise you, you will lose."

"Dad?" We both turned to see Liz standing in the kitchen doorway. "I want to stay here," she announced.

He raced over to her and took her hands. "Liz, you're too young to know what you want."

"No, I'm not," she calmly replied. "Mom messed up, yes. But you don't turn your back on people you love just because they make a mistake."

Her words made me want to cry.

"You guys didn't turn your back on me when I broke your

iPad." She paused and looked him dead in the eye. "She didn't turn her back on you when you left her here crying alone all those nights."

"I didn't turn my back on you when you had an affair," I wanted to add, but I kept my mouth closed.

"This is different," Greg said, shaking his head. "You don't understand this."

"I understand that if you love someone, you give them a second chance. I understand that."

Thwarted in his plan, Greg glared at her for the longest time, then snapped, "Fine. You want to stay, stay." He headed toward the door before spinning around to face me. "Liz might be able to forgive your betrayal, but I never will."

I wanted to break into pieces, but my daughter moved in next to me and slowly intertwined her hand with mine.

"It's okay, Mom," she whispered as he stormed out. "Dad's just mad. He'll calm down and come around."

I knew that would never happen, but I was grateful that Liz had stood up for me. She had forgiven me. I still had my daughter by my side.

56

Paula

IN THE PAST, NO MATTER HOW DOWN I WAS FEELING, no matter how disgusted with my life I was, looking at my wedding pictures brought me joy. Despite the big wedding, despite the baby inside me, despite the mixed emotions, on that day I was in heaven. The day itself had been beautiful, and in the past the pictures had always reminded me of how happy I'd been.

Now they made me sick to my stomach.

Especially when I looked at the picture of Felise as my bridesmaid, standing up for me. I had asked her, over and over and over, whether she had feelings for Steven, and over and over she had told me no. She'd tried to act like they were strictly platonic but all along she'd had feelings for him. Now I felt like a fool.

"Ugh," I said, taking the picture out of the photo album and ripping it to shreds.

The next picture made me just as mad. It showed Steven, my sister, and Felise. Charlene was grinning from ear to ear. Both Steven and Felise looked uncomfortable. My mind started churning. Had they snuck off somewhere and got in a quickie? Had they cried because they could no longer be together? Is that when their affair began? Felise could say what she wanted. Even if I believed that her sleeping with Steven was a one-time thing, the fact that she would risk everything for that night of passion meant only one thing: she was in love with my husband.

Just the thought felt like a knife being plunged into my heart. I replayed the last six weeks and how she hadn't been my side. My mind churned as I tried to recall every word she'd said to me in the past six weeks, how she'd tried to get me to move on. How she'd tried to convince me how much Steven had loved me. The memories sent me on a screaming rampage. I cried. I cursed. I yelled as I snatched each photo out of the book and ripped them up.

When I finished, almost every picture in my wedding album was shredded and scattered all over my floor.

"Mom, what did you do?"

My daughter was standing in the doorway to my room, examining the wreckage.

I fought back tears as I fell back against my headboard.

"It's okay. Sometimes tearing stuff up makes me feel better, too," she said, coming into the room and sitting down next to me. She leaned over and picked up one of the torn photos. "And a lot of times I end up regretting destroying it." She gently set the mangled photo down on the coffee table.

I stared at my daughter. She was really becoming a beautiful young woman. "How did you get to be so smart?"

"I come from good stock." She smiled, and I took her hand as we sat in silence for long moments.

"Mama told me you said you didn't think I loved your dad," I finally said. My heart had plummeted when my mother told me that this morning. She was trying to get me to let my anger go and focus on my family. She said my kids needed me, but sitting here looking at my oldest, I was starting to think I needed them. "Is it true? Did you say that?"

She slowly nodded. "It is."

"I loved your father," I said firmly.

She hunched her shoulders. "Sometimes he—*we*—couldn't tell. You always seemed so mad at everybody. Like you wanted to be anywhere but here with us."

That made me cry. Yes, I vented and complained a lot, but I loved my family. I really did.

"That's not true," I said. "I just . . . I . . ." I had no excuse, so I said, "Is that why you were able to forgive Felise, because you think I didn't love your father anyway?"

She pursed her lips, thinking. "No. I forgave Nana because it was the right thing to do. You know Nana isn't a monster. Yes, what she did was wrong. What Dad did was wrong. But they aren't bad people. You just told me this the other day about Chelsea. We made up, and it was thanks to you."

"Sweetie, this is way different from you and Chelsea," I said defensively.

"Not really. Yes, it's a lot more painful, but it's still the same. You and Nana were best friends. Like you told me about Chelsea, friendships like that are worth forgiving."

I never thought my lectures to my daughter would come back to haunt me.

Tahiry continued, "Besides, you've taught me all my life that God wants us to be loving, forgiving people."

I gave her a half smile. "*Now* you want to start listening to me."

She smiled back. "I know this is harder on you than anybody. But you gotta know Nana isn't somewhere gloating. Uncle Greg moved out. Everybody knows."

I raised my eyebrow in an I-don't-care gesture, but Tahiry kept talking.

"And while Liz forgave her mother, it's still hard on her. And that means it's hard on Nana."

"Liz forgave her?" I asked.

"That's her mom. Wouldn't you want me to forgive you no matter what you did?"

I didn't know how to reply to that. Finally, I said, "Of course I would, but I'd never do anything like this."

"We should never say never," Tahiry replied. "Just think about it, Mom. Hate is a wasted energy. Isn't that what you said?"

Tears welled in my eyes as I stroked my daughter's cheek. I had wallowed in bitterness and self-pity for so long that I'd missed my daughter turning into a young woman.

"I'm so proud of you," I said. I didn't know if I could be as mature as my child in this whole forgiveness thing, but she'd definitely given me food for thought.

"I love you, Mom." She leaned down and started picking up all the destroyed photos. She reverted to her usual teenage voice as she said, "Now, can we tape these pictures back together? I need them to one day show my kids these ugly bridesmaid dresses."

For the first time in days, I laughed.

57

Felise

STEVEN JAMES WRIGHT
LOVING HUSBAND
DEVOTED FATHER
1977–2013

MY FINGERS GENTLY RAN OVER THE TOMBSTONE. I wasn't surprised that he had a headstone already. While most people had to wait six weeks, Ms. Lois was going to make certain her son went out in style.

"Nice headstone," I said as I laid the flowers down on his grave. The day was overcast and dreary, and matched my mood. Or at least the mood I'd come here with. I was hoping to leave cleansed and ready to move on.

"Your mother is always looking out for you," I said, as a memory came racing back. "You remember when your mom came up to campus when you got the presidential award and they put you at the back of the stadium?" I managed a laugh, which echoed in the silence all around me. "You were so embarrassed, and I calmed you down by reminding you how I would've given anything for my mother to come up."

I was talking to Steven like he could actually talk back. I'd give anything if he could.

I swallowed the lump in my throat and reminded myself that I came here today for closure. Not to reminisce.

My life was slowly but surely returning to normal. Things were a little uncomfortable when Tahiry came over, but I think that affected me more than her. Both of the girls had shown remarkable resilience.

I knew it was time to stop wallowing in my mistake. When we were in college and I'd get depressed about something, Steven used to always say, "I need you to be a victor, not a victim." I'd had a dream about him last night. He'd encouraged me to stop regretting and forgive myself. I'd woken up crying, but determined to heed his words.

I brushed my skirt down and continued saying what I had come to say. "Steven, I'm so sorry for the mess. I knew better. *We* knew better. I wish that I had never let you go, but I did and as much as I loved being with you that night, it should've never happened. Too many people were hurt behind our actions. Paula hates me. Greg is gone. For good, I'm thinking. And while I never wanted the marriage to turn out this way, it's probably best. I was really scared that I might have lost Liz, but you know she's my baby, so she's coming around." I inhaled, blew a ragged breath. This was getting harder as I went on. "Everyone misses you so much." I didn't realize I was crying until I saw the teardrops falling. "It's so hard," I said, kneeling down on his grave. "I don't know how I'm going to heal."

You're a victor, not a victim.

"But I'm going to be fine because I'm a victor. Not a victim," I repeated, raising my head. Even in his death, Steven had a way of giving me life. "So, I'm going to do like you said and stop regretting. Tomorrow will be a better day. I am going to live today, not yesterday. And I'm going to remember what you told me that semester I failed English Lit: 'It doesn't matter what you did, its what you will do.'" I smiled at that memory. Steven was talking about my grades then, but it definitely applied to my situation now.

I stood in silence for a minute, inhaling the brisk air, and feeling Steven's presence surround me.

Finally, I said, "I just wanted to come see you. And say good-bye. I'm going to go. The girls will be home soon." I placed my palm on his headstone. "Good-bye, Steven. I'll love you forever and always."

I thought about the last few months and what I could have done differently. I didn't know how someone could stop beating herself up when she'd done something bad, but I knew I needed to figure it out. I needed to leave my guilt here with Steven.

I made my way back to my car and felt an odd sense of peace on the ride home. I turned on the gospel station and let Yolanda Adams fill my spirit. I felt freer than I had in a long time. But my new attitude was short-lived. When I turned on my street, I saw Paula parked in my driveway. I knew my good day had just come to an end.

58

Paula

I DEFINITELY HAD GROWN AS A PERSON. MENTALLY, spiritually, and emotionally. Because for the first time since I'd found out about my best friend's betrayal, I didn't have the urge to body-slam her.

"Hi, Paula," she said tentatively, approaching me.

I was leaned up against my car in her driveway. Tahiry had told me she and Liz were at the mall and they'd left Felise here alone. I was surprised when I arrived and she was gone, but I forced myself to wait because I had no idea when I'd get up the nerve to come back.

I'd been waiting twenty minutes when Felise's car turned onto her street. I know she was shocked to see me because she'd slowed down as she approached her driveway, as if she didn't know whether to speed off or pull in.

"What's up?" I replied.

I could tell she didn't know what my reaction was going to be because she kept her distance.

She stood there awkwardly. "I don't think Tahiry is here," she informed me.

"I know where my child is," I said. "I didn't come to see her. I came to see you."

She shifted uncomfortably. "Um, well, do you want to come in?"

I debated whether I should go inside. She was looking like she hoped that I would say no. I decided to do the opposite. "Yes, I want to talk to you."

I took a deep breath and followed her inside. I had practiced this speech all the way over here. This wasn't about Felise. This was about me. This was about remembering the good part of my life with Steven, then closing this chapter and moving on.

"I just want to know how you could do it," I said once we were in her living room.

She didn't hesitate. "I don't have an excuse."

"That's not good enough," I replied.

I could see pain in her eyes. The old me would've known this was hurting her, but after all we'd been through, I'd concluded that I didn't know my friend at all.

"We go way back," I went on, my voice not carrying as much anger as I had anticipated. "And out of everyone on this earth, you are the last person I would've ever expected to do something like this."

"I know—" she began.

I held up my hand to stop her. "Then I thought about it. If I had been thinking clearly, I would've realized you were the *most* likely to do this."

She looked shocked. "What does that mean?"

"It means, I've always known that you loved Steven, even when you wouldn't admit it. But you kept denying it until I convinced myself that you really didn't have feelings for him. I knew better, and I was crazy to think that love had somehow disappeared."

"No, don't blame yourself—"

"Oh, don't get it twisted," I said, wagging a finger at her. "Trust and believe, I'm not blaming myself. What you and Steven did was only on you and Steven."

She retreated to her former cautious, wary stance.

"All I'm saying is that I recognize that this is something that was festering for a long time," I continued. "I get that. It doesn't make it right. It definitely doesn't excuse what you did. But I get it."

She appeared relieved, but I wasn't done.

"But I came here for the truth. Was that the first time?"

She held up her hand like she was being sworn in at a trial. "As God as my witness, it was."

I hated that I believed her. But I did. "You know, it's not that your word means anything to me anymore, but either you're a helluva an actress or you're telling the truth."

"I'm telling the truth. I've never said anything different."

I began pacing back and forth in her living room. "I've replayed this over and over. How you weren't there for me after Steven died. You were there for Tahiry and I'm grateful for that, but I couldn't understand why you weren't there for me. Now I do."

Felise didn't say anything. She just let me rant.

"Had you all ever talked about getting together? Googly-eyed each other, anything?" I demanded to know.

"No. Nothing," she said, her voice reeking of desperation. But not like she was desperate to cover up a lie. Like she was desperate for me to believe she was telling the truth. "We buried our feelings a long time ago. And from the day I fixed him up with you, I have never, ever crossed the line."

I narrowed my eyes at her.

"I mean, except, you know . . . that one time."

I wanted to ask her some intimate details, but I had come so far and I didn't need my memory of my husband tainted any more than it already was.

"I asked him for a divorce that night. Is that why you did it?" I said.

She vehemently shook her head. "No, absolutely not. Honestly, we both just fell to temptation, and after it was over, we swore it would never happen again."

I glared at her, then said, "I would like to believe that you're not that low-down. I just can't imagine that you have been my friend all these years—my best friend—and you were secretly harboring feelings for my husband."

She took a step toward me. "You've got to believe me."

I didn't have to do any such thing, but I said, "Fine."

We stood in silence, former friends facing off. Then I said, "I came to let you know I forgive you." I waited to feel like this great weight was being lifted from my shoulders. It didn't happen.

She smiled, greatly relieved. "Thank you, Paula. I just want us to get back to where we were."

I looked at her like she had lost her mind. "Girl, please. I'm forgiving you for me. Not because you deserve it. I just want to close this chapter of my life."

She sadly nodded in understanding. "What about Liz and Tahiry?" she asked.

"They are innocent in all of this. I'm not going to interfere in their friendship."

Her shoulders slumped in relief. I don't know what kind of monster she thought I was. Just because I complained about my kids a lot didn't mean that I didn't have their best interests at heart. And Tahiry and Liz loved each other. I wasn't going to take that away from them.

"I'm sorry." She stepped toward me again.

The look on my face stopped her, and she lowered her gaze.

"Yes, you are," I said. I turned and walked away.

Inside my car, I finally let my river of tears escape. Yes, I was crying for a friendship lost, but forgiving—or trying to forgive—had cleansed my soul. Never in a million years did I think I'd be capable of forgiving such a betrayal, and while I still had a long road to complete healing, I was definitely on my way.

I'd cried enough. I wiped my face, tossed my curls over my shoulder, started my car, and drove toward my future.

59

Felise

THESE HAD BEEN THE ABSOLUTE LONGEST THREE months of my life. I felt empty without Paula in my life, but I was grateful that she'd found it in her heart to forgive me. Or at least taken steps toward forgiveness. And I was really grateful that Paula remained loving and cordial to Liz. For them, nothing had changed.

I truly was sorry for how I'd hurt Paula. I was especially sorry for my deception afterward, but my pity party was shut down. I was no longer going to wallow in the mess I'd made.

I knew that our friendship would never be the same, but forgiveness was a powerful drug. Having Paula's forgiveness set me free. Forgiving myself allowed me to pick up the pieces and move forward.

"Hey, Felise, thanks so much for giving me the name of your friend. She had some great ideas for my parents' fiftieth wedding anniversary."

I smiled at my coworker April. I'd heard through the

grapevine that Paula's event-planning business was doing really well, so when April mentioned that she was looking for someone, I'd immediately given her Paula's name.

"I'm so glad to hear that," I said. "I'm sure the party will be wonderful."

April smiled as she darted off to answer a call button from one of the patient rooms.

Her parents had made it to fifty years. That's a goal I would never attain. As he had promised, Greg officially filed for divorce right after my birthday, and our divorce was finalized last week.

I tried not to think about the past—and only focus on the future—as I made my way out to my car. I hummed along to Mary Mary on the radio as I made my way home. It was getting late, so I decided to pick up something to eat. I called and placed an order at Kim Son, which was one of my favorite Chinese restaurants. It had been one of the places where Greg and I loved to eat, so I almost didn't go, but I was starving and not in the mood to cook.

I had just given the hostess my name when I glanced toward the front door and saw Greg walk in—with a date!

"Oh, wow. Hi, Felise," he said.

"Hi," I replied. Outside of issues with Liz, we never talked any more.

His date squeezed him tighter as if signaling that she wanted to be introduced.

"Um, Gina, this is my ex-wife, Felise. Felise, this is my girlfriend, Gina."

I felt like someone had taken a sledgehammer and slammed it into my abdomen. But I managed a "Nice to meet you."

"Nice to finally meet you, too," she said. "I see where Liz gets her beauty from." She smiled. I didn't.

"Oh, you've met Liz?" I asked.

"Met her?" she giggled. "I adore her. She kept me in stitches last week at the lake house."

The ink was barely dry on our divorce papers and he'd already moved on—and had this woman spending weekends with my daughter? And I didn't know how to feel about the fact that my daughter hadn't shared this bit of information with me.

Greg could see that I was stewing about his news, so I was grateful when he said, "I'm still picking Liz up from Tahiry's tomorrow, right?"

I nodded, keeping a lid on what I wanted to say.

Mercifully, the clerk appeared and handed me a plastic bag. "Ms. Mavins, your to-go order is ready." He read the receipt. "Shrimp fried rice and spring roll for one, right?"

I heard Gina chuckle, but I refused to look her way. I just said, "Right." I fumbled for my credit card as the hostess walked up and said, "All right, Mr. Mavins, table for you and your lovely wife, right this way."

Greg looked uncomfortable, but Gina simply said, "Oh, I'm not his wife—yet," as she took his hand and led him away without looking back at me.

While seeing Greg with this woman had caught me off guard, I felt a sense of resolution sweep over me. I loved Greg, but I'd never truly been *in love* with Greg. Not like a wife should be in love with her husband. Maybe that's why we never managed to make things work. Plus, as I thought back over the past fifteen years, I decided that Gina could have him. Maybe she liked a clean house.

"That which does not break us makes us stronger," I mumbled as I signed the credit card receipt.

"Excuse me?" the clerk said.

"Nothing. I was just talking to myself."

He smiled at me like I was another crazy American. I took my food and headed home to my empty house.

I had to accept that what was done was done. I had to accept that I'd had an affair and I had caused a lot of suffering. I personally had to change what I thought of myself. Once I had done this, I knew I would choose a different course next time—if there ever was a next time.

I eased into my car, setting the food on my passenger seat. Yes, moving on had been difficult, but I had to do it. With Liz becoming a young woman the road ahead was about to get really bumpy. I had to pull myself together and get my life on track. My child needed me. My *children* needed me.

I reached in my purse and pulled out a photo. I'd been carrying that photo for the last four weeks. I'd shed many tears over that picture, but it had given me a new resolve. I didn't know what the future held, but this picture gave me the strength to face it.

I slowly fingered the sonogram. "I love you, sweetie. Just like I loved your daddy, may he rest in peace." I kissed the picture, dropped it back in my purse, and drove back home as I softly rubbed my stomach.

A NOTE FROM THE AUTHOR

After you've written thirty-plus books, some would say that it makes no sense to pen an acknowledgments or Note from the Author. But for me, each book is made possible by the grace of God and a network of people who allow me to live my dream as a full-time author.

My friend, the talented Eric Jerome Dickey, calls us Imagination Engineers. I think this is a wonderful title for what we do.

The great thing about what I do is that, while fictional, my stories mirror the lives of so many people. I can't tell you the number of readers who say they've learned to forgive, to love, to heal, to be open and honest; who renewed their relationship with God; who gave their marriage a second chance, etc., etc.—all because they were moved by one of my books.

That's some powerful stuff, and it makes everything I do worthwhile.

But I wouldn't be able to do what I do if not for some important people who make my writing career possible. First and foremost, thank you, God, for blessing me with a talent to write.

Much thanks to the man who has been there from the very beginning, who nurtured and encouraged my dream when it was still a concept, Dr. Miron Billingsley. Thank you to my three lovely children, who bear with me when I'm writing and traveling.

And to my absolutely incredible support system, there are not enough words to show my gratitude for helping my writing career flourish by making my personal life flow as smoothly as possible. My mother, Nancy Blacknell, I am what I am because of you. This has been the most trying time of our lives, but your resilience shines and you'll be back to your old self in no time. Thank you to my sister Tanisha Tate, who in our most trying time has picked up the ball and carried it alone so I could keep doing my book thing. For that, I am eternally grateful.

As always, many, many thanks to my agent, Sara Camilli; my editor, Brigitte Smith; publicist, Melissa Gramstad; Louise Burke; the wonderful people who design my covers (I've never met you, but you are the best!); the most awesomest copy editor, Mary Beth Constant (let's see if she'll let awesomest slide); and everyone else at Gallery Books. I've been so lucky to have found a publishing home I've loved from the beginning. Thanks for all your hard work! And of course, I can't forget editor extraordinaire, John Paine, who helps take my books from good to great!

Thank you also to my extended support system: Jaimi Canady, Raquelle Lewis, Kim Wright, and Clemelia Richardson. You know that core group of people you should always keep in your life, the ones who will be there whether you're up or down, hot or not—you guys are my core. Thank you for always having my back.

To Pat Tucker Wilson, my sister in spirit, who has been an unbelievable support and a write-or-die friend, thank you for always being there. You know how much your friendship means.

To my writing twin and now business partner, Victoria

Christopher Murray, thanks for the inspiration, the friendship, and the never-ending support. We are truly about to change the game! To my Brown Girls family (Jason, Lissa, Raine, JL, and Jessica), thanks for all you do.

To Yolanda Gore, Sheretta Edwards, and Gina Johnson, thank you. That's all I can say. A hundred times, thank you. Much love to my wonderful sister-writers from the Motherhood Diaries—Crystal, Kimyatta, Deborah, Jamesina, Edna, Marcena, Makasha, Roishina, Lichell, Norlita, Sadeqa, Felicia, Shelby, Keileigh, Gail, Tia, Gina, and C. Mikki.

Lots of love to my literary colleagues who always offer words of advice, encouragement, and are just trying to run this race with me . . . Nina Foxx, Tiffany L. Warren, Naleighna Kai, J. L. Woodson, Dwayne Joseph, La Jill Hunt, Angel Hunter, Renee Flagler, JL King, and Rhonda McKnight.

Once again, I have to say thanks to Reina and Regina King, Crystal Garrett, Roger Bobb, Shelby Stone, Queen Latifah, Charlie, Loretha, Tamara, and all the fabulous folks at BET. Thank you soooooo much for making my movie dreams come true! It's been a long journey, but I'm so confident in the final product!

I know it may seem odd to some folks that I want to thank my social media family, but these folks have been there for me—even though many of them I've never personally met. They have reached through cyberspace to encourage, motivate, empower, inspire, and celebrate me. They have prayed for me, encouraged me, enlightened me, and oftentimes put a huge smile on my face. Thank you so much to JE, Carla, Tashmir, Bettie, Yasmin, Jetola, Julie, Sheryl, Noelle, Sheretta, Crystal, Sammi, Cindy, Kimberlee, Alicia, Marsha, Jonathan, Judy, Olivia, Juanita, Angela, Ashara, Nicole, Gwen,

Denise, Tanisha, Deborah, Romenia, Sonia, Kim, Beverly, Shannon, Antoinette, Gina, Carmen, Christina, Princess, Maurice, Lisa, Nedra, Donna, Nicki, Gee Gee, Dorothy, Jackie, Gloria, Nikki, Tracey, Christina, Paula, Tonia, Chevonne, Rochelle, Mia, Demetria, Sheila, Raquel, Loretta, Allyson, Stacy, Jakki, Chenoa, Gwen, Karen, Tameka, Cebrina, Margueritte, Tiffany, Tawni, Bernice, Errie, Miracle, Dawn, Charlene, Pam, Donnie, Seven, Dee, and Cecelia. (I know there are many more, but I need to wrap up at some point!)

I'm not going to start naming book clubs because I always leave someone out. But major love to the book clubs who show me so much love, including those who have me back time and time again.

As always, much love goes to my wonderful, illustrious sorors, especially the Houston Metropolitan Chapters (including my own, Mu Kappa Omega), our wonderful Regional Director Chelle Wilson, and my sister moms in the Missouri City/Sugar Land Chapter of Jack and Jill.

And finally, thank *you*. Yeah, you holding this book. If it weren't for your support, I wouldn't be where I am today. If you're a new reader, thanks for checking me out. I hope you'll get hooked. If you're a previous reader, thanks for coming back. If you enjoy this story, I just ask one more thing . . . pass the word, not the book!

I know I said I wasn't going to get caught up doing acknowledgments again, but when you have such wonderful people in your life, that's a promise that's just hard to keep.

Until the next book . . . thanks for the love.

ReShonda

G

READING GROUP GUIDE

What's Done in the Dark

ReShonda Tate
BILLINGSLEY

INTRODUCTION

When is a mistake meant to be? When Felise introduces her old flame Steven to her childhood best friend, she doesn't expect them to date, let alone get married and have kids. More than ten years later, their two families remain as close as ever, but Felise feels miserable and unappreciated in her marriage. When her obsessive-compulsive workaholic husband finally pushes her too far, she flees to a nearby hotel bar hoping to find some clarity—but instead finds Steven, her best friend's husband.

One too many drinks later, they discover their mutual attraction to each other never quite faded, and fueled by the discontent in their respective marriages, they share a night of forbidden passion. In a dark, devastating twist of fate, Felise wakes up to a dead Steven and a choice. Does she confess her sins to her friends and family and risk losing everything, or leave the love of her life dead in a hotel room and her dearest friend with a million questions?

DISCUSSION QUESTIONS

1. In *What's Done in the Dark*, we're introduced to Felise and Paula, two best friends unhappy in their respective lives. In what ways are they similar and different? Who do you think has more reason to be unsatisfied?
2. Felise says her husband, Greg, doesn't "see" her. What does she mean by this? Why do think she's unable to

make him "see" her, even after she tries to plan a romantic evening?

3. Greg only begins to pay attention to Felise and show affection when he's afraid she wants to leave him. Do you think this would have lasted if the situation with Steven hadn't interfered?
4. After Felise and Steven's fateful night in the hotel room, Felise decides to call her sister Fran. Why do you think, of all people, she chose to call Fran?
5. Greg says to Felise, "You water the lawn you have" (p. 192). Do you agree with this sentiment?
6. Do you think Paula's unhappiness was rooted in her perspective? What aspects of her life did she have control over, and which did she not?
7. Why do you think Felise stopped seeing Steven in college? Why do you think she wasn't honest with Paula about having feelings for him? If you had been in Paula's position, would you have trusted Felise when she reassured her she didn't have feelings for Steven?
8. Fear drives all of the main characters in distinct ways in *What's Done in the Dark*. How does fear function as a positive and negative motivation? Do you think fear ultimately drove Felise to settle for someone unfit for her?
9. Is there ever any excuse for a spouse to cheat? In what scenarios would you consider it "acceptable"? What about in Felise's and Steven's situations?
10. How would you characterize Greg's reaction to Felise's confession? What about his actions at her birthday dinner? Do you think his behavior was understandable given the circumstances? What would you have done in Paula's position?

11. What kind of role does religion and faith play in *What's Done in the Dark*? How does it drive (or not drive) Felise and Paula? What are the major moral takeaways from the book?
12. Felise's sister Mavis firmly believes God forgives all of our mistakes. Do you think Felise believes this? What do you believe?
13. What choices could Felise and Paula have made early on in their lives that may have led to happier marriages and families? What kind of things do you wish you could redo in your past?
14. How do you feel about Felise's secret that the author finally reveals on the last page? How do you think Paula will react to the news?

ENHANCE YOUR BOOK CLUB

1. ReShonda Tate Bilingsley has a knack for exposing her characters' deepest flaws—but shows that there's always a path to redemption. Select another title from her collection to read with your book club. Compare and contrast the flaws of the characters with *What's Done in the Dark* and analyze through what devices the author communicates these traits.
2. Was there a time in your life when you needed to forgive someone? What about forgiving yourself? During your next book club meeting, ask everyone to share an expe-

rience with forgiveness and how it helped bring them peace (or regret).

3. Steven's heart condition, which ultimately led to tragedy, set off the majority of events in *What's Done in the Dark*. Support heart health awareness by scheduling a physical with your doctor or collecting donations from your book club to give to the American Heart Association.
4. It's book club happy hour! Serve virgin margaritas and piña coladas at your next meet-up for a fun, festive treat—sans booze and bad decision-making.

Check out these teen titles by
ReShonda Tate Billingsley!
THE GOOD GIRLZ
#1 Essence bestselling author of Caught Up in the Drama
DRAMA QUEENS
ReShonda Tate Billingsley
THE GOOD GIRLZ
#1 Essence bestselling author of Fair-Weather Friends
FRIENDS 'TIL THE END
When life gets tough, these friends just get stronger!
ReShonda Tate Billingsley
THE GOOD GIRLZ
#1 Essence bestselling author of Friends 'Til the End
CAUGHT UP IN THE DRAMA
Fame might come and go, but good friends are forever!
ReShonda Tate Billingsley
#1 Essence bestselling author of With Friends Like These
THE GOOD GIRLZ
GETTING EVEN
One sweet-talking guy is playing with their hearts. Can four girlfriends forgive and forget?
ReShonda Tate Billingsley
THE GOOD GIRLZ
#1 Essence bestselling author of Getting Even
FAIR-WEATHER FRIENDS
Can sorority sisters come between four girlfriends who are sisters at heart?
ReShonda Tate Billingsley
#1 Essence bestselling author of Nothing But Drama
WITH FRIENDS LIKE THESE
When the truth comes out, four girlfriends must decide which they value more: their ambitions or each other.
ReShonda Tate Billingsley
BLESSINGS IN DISGUISE
ReShonda Tate Billingsley
NOTHING BUT DRAMA
Four girlfriends discover that honoring their parents is a commandment worth keeping.
ReShonda Tate Billingsley
Available wherever books are sold or at www.simonandschuster.com.
GALLERY BOOKS
A Division of Simon & Schuster
A CBS COMPANY
25564